PRAISE FOR
MUST LOVE BOOKS

"*Must Love Books* is a heartfelt and exciting debut. With a relatable protagonist in Nora, frank discussions of the millennial experience, and pitch-perfect sweetness, Shauna Robinson puts forth a wise and honest story of how it feels to be a young woman in search of yourself."

—Taylor Jenkins Reid, *New York Times* bestselling author of *The Seven Husbands of Evelyn Hugo* and *Malibu Rising*

"A book for book lovers that takes a hard look at the predatory approach of the corporate world with a heroine who's easy to love and root for. I enjoyed all of the inside look at the publishing industry from the perspective of a young woman scraping together all of her wits just to get by. It's impossible not to root for Nora!"

—Jesse Q. Sutanto, bestselling author of *Dial A for Aunties*

"Honest, relatable, and real, *Must Love Books* is a tender reflection on finding your person while you're still desperately searching for yourself rolled up in a thoughtful novel about the changing work world."

—KJ Dell'Antonia, *New York Times* bestselling author of *The Chicken Sisters*

D1021471

"A compelling love story, dishy publishing goss, and a chic urban setting? Yes, yes, yes! But like the works she shepherds through publication, Shauna Robinson's true-to-life story of a struggling editorial assistant is much more than the sum of its parts. Within the pages of *Must Love Books*, the lucky reader will find themselves on an poignant journey of a young book lover with too little support and too many dreams—a place we've all been at one point or another. With emotional honesty and a surprising wit that I found addictive, Robinson's debut is everything a book-about-books fan wants in a novel."

—Kelly Harms, *Washington Post* bestselling author of *The Overdue Life of Amy Byler*

"Readers will be rooting for Nora from the first page and experiencing her grand highs and heartbreaking lows with their entire heart. Get comfy because you won't be able to put this book down!"

—Sajni Patel, award-winning author of *The Trouble with Hating You*

Must Love Books

a novel

SHAUNA ROBINSON

Published by Sourcebooks Landmark, an imprint of Sourcebooks
P.O. Box 4410, Naperville, Illinois 60567-4410
(630) 961-3900
sourcebooks.com

Library of Congress Cataloging-in-Publication Data

Names: Robinson, Shauna, author.
Title: Must love books / Shauna Robinson.
Description: Naperville, Illinois : Sourcebooks Landmark, [2021]
Identifiers: LCCN 2021003882 (print) | LCCN 2021003883
(ebook) | (trade paperback) | (epub)
Subjects: LCSH: Publishers and publishing--Fiction. | Book
    editors--Fiction. | GSAFD: Love stories.
Classification: LCC PS3618.O333723 M87 2021 (print) | LCC PS3618.O333723
    (ebook) | DDC 813/.6--dc23
LC record available at https://lccn.loc.gov/2021003882
LC ebook record available at https://lccn.loc.gov/2021003883

Printed and bound in the United States of America.
SB 10 9 8 7 6 5 4 3

CHAPTER ONE

Would you recommend this job to a friend?

The question echoed in Nora's mind as the silence ticked by. She glanced from the twenty-two-year-old girl across from her to the résumé on the table. Large, bold letters spelled out *Kelly Brown* at the top of the page. Nora folded and unfolded a corner of the paper as she tried to think of a response.

Recommend was a strong word. There were a lot of people Nora would recommend the job to. She thought about the man on her commute that morning, dozing with his legs spread wide enough to occupy two seats while Nora clutched a pole and practiced her resentful stare. She'd recommend the job to him any day. She'd recommend it like a curse.

But *friend*, that was the kicker. Nora lifted her eyes. Kelly's lips were curved in a trusting smile. She held her pen over her legal pad, ready to write down whatever tumbled out of Nora's mouth.

It was nonsense, frankly, that Nora was interviewing someone. This girl was interviewing for the same job title as Nora: Editorial Assistant of MBB. Meaningless Business Bullshit. Not the official title, but at this point Nora couldn't be bothered to remember the exact jargon. Either way, as a mere publishing peasant, Nora had no standing to interview a potential peer.

Nora did have seniority, she supposed, looking down at the résumé and seeing that Kelly graduated from college just this month, five years after Nora. That made five years of wisdom Nora had over Kelly, in theory—except Nora spent all five of those years here, as an editorial assistant, with no promotion in sight. There was nothing wise about that. Nothing to recommend there. Not without lying—and she wasn't sure she was okay with that.

Nora darted another glance Kelly's way. Kelly, by this point, was now politely looking around the room, taking interest in the blank walls, as if there was a greater chance of the beige paint answering her question before Nora did.

"Yes," Nora said slowly, stretching out the word as though it would precede a speech full of encouragement and experience. But now she'd kept her waiting, and it would be weird to end on her very long *yes*, so speech time it was.

"As long as you know what you're getting yourself into," Nora continued. "I mean, I've been here almost five years and I love it"—huh, so she *was* okay with lying, apparently—"but you have to be willing to adapt. Your responsibilities might change, or your title, or your boss. If you're okay with things changing on you, you should be fine. People are so friendly here," she added, wanting to end on a positive note.

Kelly nodded and wrote something down. Nora peered at the paper, imagining what the notes might say. *Took five minutes to answer one question. Shady as hell.*

When Kelly had no further questions to fluster Nora with,

Nora escorted her to the next interviewer to continue the charade. On the walk to her desk, she replayed the interview in her head. Whenever Nora mentioned anything to do with publishing—manuscripts, books, working with authors—there was a faraway look in Kelly's eyes, like she was on the verge of swooning.

And Nora didn't blame her. With an English degree and a love of books, she was just like Nora had been—just like everyone who came to work at Parsons Press. Even in Nora's interview five years ago, she remembered only half-listening to her interviewer as her mind played a montage of what it would be like to get paid to publish books.

It was a dream come true, wasn't it? Her childhood spent smuggling books and cracking covers everywhere she went—at the dinner table, in the lunch line, occasionally in the shower—felt like practice for a career in books. And when she spotted the listing for a publishing internship during her sophomore year of college, it was like a beacon pointing the way to her future. She'd clicked on it immediately, hope rising in her chest as she read the job responsibilities referencing authors and manuscripts. And the final line under the desired skills and qualifications section sealed her fate, three little words that curled around Nora's heart and told her she belonged in publishing: *Must love books*.

Three words was all it took for Nora to start spinning fantasies of her life in publishing. She imagined talking to the authors she'd admired as a kid, shyly asking Judy Blume to sign her tattered copy of *Just as Long as We're Together*. Talking through the changes Judy needed to make to her latest manuscript. Shaping books readers might cling to, the same way Nora clutched her own books like a lifeline. When it sometimes felt, growing up, that books were her only friends, the thought of being an editor and connecting books to those lonely and quiet readers like herself made Nora feel like she could be part of something magnificent.

Magnificent was another strong word. She didn't realize, then, how misguided her fantasies were. Not only was Nora laughably far from being an editor, but all her division published were business books that made her eyes glaze over.

Nora tried making it clear in the interview that Kelly could expect to work on only business books, but Kelly was too dazzled by the publishing fantasy to let the words sink in. And Nora, tired and drained and utterly dazzle-free against Kelly's faraway eyes, was once again reminded of two certainties: One, Parsons Press was no dream job. Two, she needed to get out.

Nora checked the time. Five minutes until Beth's goodbye party, and she hadn't even started setting up yet. She hurried to the office kitchenette and got to work, opening the cabinet, grabbing wine bottles by their necks, and hauling them to the board room. She noticed, rummaging through the cabinets, that they were out of plastic cups. Nora opened the first cabinet again, looked behind the stacks of shrink-wrapped paper plates and napkins. No cups.

Well, they could drink from the bottle.

She kept an eye on the boardroom's glass walls while wrestling the lid off the cheese platter. She spotted Beth—or, specifically, Beth's forehead and a hint of ruffled brown hair as someone leaned down to hug her. Beth was five feet tall, and Nora knew she hated hugs from tall people. Beth smoothed down her hair and got swept into another hug a few seconds later. It was no surprise she was so surrounded. People had been surrounding Beth for the last two weeks. Offering congratulations. Sharing memories. Wishing her well.

Nora swallowed her jealousy and carried the platter to the boardroom. She edged closer to the conversation Beth was having with their IT administrator.

"Oh, I don't know anyone there," Beth said. "I haven't started yet."

"Well, if you run into a Bill Davis, tell him I said hi."

"Will do!"

Maybe that was why Beth got out and Nora didn't. Beth was so kind. And happy. People liked happy people. More importantly, people hired happy people. But Nora couldn't stop herself from thinking how silly it sounded, that Beth would run into Bill Davis at her new job one day and take the time to deliver a meaningless message on behalf of someone she'd likely never see again. She'd probably do it, too. Nora would have deleted the mental message immediately.

By this time, Joe and Beth had finished talking, giving Nora a chance to sidle up to her before anyone else could treat her like a carrier pigeon.

"I thought he hated me," Beth murmured once he was out of earshot.

Nora watched him cross the room to the wine table. "Maybe he forgot."

"That I got a computer virus from torrenting *Seinfeld* at work?"

Nora laughed. Beth grinned back at her, but Nora remembered when Beth came to her desk, wide-eyed and frantic. She remembered how they stood in Beth's cubicle, watching the pop-ups flash on her screen. It was almost cute how they'd worried, then, that she might get in trouble. They spent two hours deliberating the pros and cons of telling IT, but in the end, Joe just sighed and told Beth to drop off her laptop and pick up a loaner. That was their first inkling that maybe no one gave a shit.

That feeling only grew when executives at the Parsons Press headquarters in New York started dropping ominous hints about a restructuring plan "coming down the pipeline." During that hazy six-month period before the plan was revealed, everyone let loose a little. Nora took a later train to work, coming in at 9:15 instead of 8:55. Beth moved on to torrenting *Arrested Development*. They both started job hunting.

"You'll have to top that one," Beth said, evoking the future tense with impossible ease.

"Who will I tell?"

Beth blinked. "Me."

"Will I?"

She gave Nora a gentle, patient stare. "We'll still see each other. We'll still text. You're not getting rid of me."

"You're right," Nora said, knowing they could debate this forever, Beth with her optimism and Nora with her everything. She shoved a grape in her mouth to keep from casting any more gloom on the occasion.

It wasn't a big deal that Beth was leaving, she told herself. It wasn't even the first time Beth had set her sights on something new. Nora and Beth may have started out as editorial assistants together, but two years in, Beth ditched the editorial dream and forged a new path for herself.

Like Nora, Beth grew tired of the administrative work that came with editorial. Being an editorial assistant wasn't reading manuscripts and being captivated by prose like Nora had imagined. It was repeatedly reminding authors of deadlines, wrestling with Microsoft Word to format manuscripts, and forwarding those formatted manuscripts to her bosses. The actual interesting parts—reading projects, making suggestions for improvement, working alongside authors—Nora and Beth never had a hand in.

While Nora gritted her teeth and continued on, willing to pay any price to become an editor, Beth applied for a marketing coordinator job on their team. It gave Beth a new challenge, something else to explore and master. And now Beth and her roving eye had landed a sales job at an app development start-up.

Nora poured some of—whatever this was, from the bottle beside her—into her Parsons Press mug as Beth looked on.

"My mug is in my cubicle," Beth said, a touch of longing in her voice.

"Oh, you thought there would be cups?" Nora handed Beth her mug. "At a party?" She frowned a little to sell it.

Beth laughed and brought the mug to her lips. "Stupid, I know. I don't know what I was thinking."

Nora cracked a smile. "This way's probably better. Gives us more opportunities to *innovate*."

Beth made gagging noises at the buzzword and Nora laughed. Her smile faded as she surveyed the room. People stood in clusters holding plates and mugs, talking and laughing. All clusters she'd never been part of. Beth was her cluster.

"It'll be weird being here without you," Nora said.

"And with our anniversary coming up, too."

Nora nodded, staring into the mug Beth handed back to her. She and Beth had started on the same day, sharing embarrassed smiles about feeling overdressed that first morning, all blazers and dress pants in a sea of slouchy tops and jeans. Then Beth rolled her chair to Nora's desk ten minutes after their debrief with HR, navy blazer flung over her chair like an afterthought, asking how many allowances to claim on her W-4.

On the anniversary of their first year at Parsons, they each got a generic card from HR. Beth had peeked her head over the wall of Nora's cube and wished her a happy work friendiversary. The tradition had continued each year. Nora tried not to think about her five-year anniversary a few months away. There would be no one to celebrate with this time around.

"You okay?" Beth asked, peering closer at Nora.

Nora blinked her thoughts away. "Yeah." She forced a smile. "I'm excited for you."

"I'm excited for *you*," Beth insisted, making Nora's heart swell with appreciation. Only Beth could spend her own goodbye party hyping up someone else. "You've got that BookTap interview next week, right?"

"Yeah." Nora tried to mirror Beth's hopeful tone. She'd been thrilled to see the marketing specialist job listing for BookTap a few weeks ago. Parsons Press may have jaded her view of publishing, but she couldn't find it in herself to completely give up the chance to work with books. BookTap was another opportunity—a good one. Nora actually enjoyed using BookTap's app to rate and review books and see what others were reading. Beth, for instance, gave *Red Velvet Revenge* five stars yesterday (but Beth gave everything five stars).

Nora had made it through the phone screen and past the assessment assignment, which she still thought of with pride. In it, she'd managed to make steampunk sound interesting, which made her both brilliant and generous. Now all she had to do was make a good impression at the in-person interview next week.

But with Beth leaving, everything felt more urgent. Parsons

was only bearable because of Beth. If she left—and if Nora didn't get the job at BookTap—Nora didn't want to think about where that would leave her.

Beth seemed to pick up on Nora's uncertainty, maybe from the way Nora plunked her head on Beth's shoulder. "It'll go great," she said.

Nora nodded, deciding not to disagree. Then someone else came to steal Beth, and Nora was left alone. She nibbled on a piece of not-sharp-enough cheddar and watched Beth laugh with someone from accounting.

Nora had known from her first day that Parsons Press wasn't what it used to be. This whale of a company had been around since the 1800s, since Dickens and Brontë and Poe—not that Parsons ever published anything that interesting. Parsons did publish Mark Twain's first novel, *The Gilded Age*, though no one Nora knew had ever read or heard of it. They hadn't published his other works, certainly nothing as beloved as *Adventures of Huckleberry Finn*. Which seemed like a bit of an oversight on the part of that particular acquisitions editor, Nora thought.

But still, Parsons was around during that time. She hadn't cared, at first, that Parsons only published nonfiction now, or that her division published business books teeming with snappy buzzwords: *synergy*, *leverage*, *disruptor*. Nora planned to use the position as a stepping-stone to the San Francisco office's more compelling divisions, like cooking, travel, or current events.

But the New York execs saw fit to cut these divisions before Nora could defect. The restructuring plan followed, aptly named the Disrupt, Innovate, and Change plan, or DIC for short. While Nora and Beth cheerfully referred to this as the DIC(k) plan, joking that it was Parsons's dickish alternative to a 401(k), the changes it wrought took a toll. Some employees were promoted into new roles, but others, like Nora's bosses, lost their jobs. What remained of Nora's team merged with another under-staffed division, and they were expected to publish the same number of business books with half the employees to maximize profits. Meanwhile, going-away parties like Beth's had become near-constant attractions in the Parsons boardroom.

After the party came to a close, Nora watched Beth empty her drawers in the eerie, quiet office and wondered when it would be her turn to leave Parsons behind. She accepted the cardboard box Beth handed her, and they each carried a box of Beth's belong-ings on their way to the elevator. As she walked, Nora peered into the box in her arms. She recognized the first Parsons book that mentioned Beth in the acknowledgments and birthday cards Nora remembered signing, but it was the pink hedgehog pencil holder that brought a rush of nostalgic joy. Beth threw away a lot of office tchotchkes tonight, but this present Nora gave her two years ago, now dotted with ink from Beth and her careless pens, had made the cut.

They sat side by side on BART, discussing books as the train hummed along. She listened to Beth rant about how Shirley Jackson's books didn't get the attention they deserved. When Beth asked Nora what she was reading, she pulled *Kindred* out of her purse, as if that answered the question. As Nora tucked the book into her bag, she caught the way Beth nodded a beat too long, knew Beth was too polite to ask why Nora had been stuck on the same book for over a month when she was used to Nora reading a book a week.

The dreaded moment came. The train sped away from 12th Street, giving them only seconds until Beth's stop at 19th. Beth stood and Nora followed suit, her head still buzzy with wine from the party as she tried to think of the perfect parting words. The well-wishes she wrote in others' goodbye cards sounded so superficial now.

Mind spinning, Nora gave a small half smile and said, "I love you."

She felt exposed, saying it. There was an implied distance in work friendships. But it was so plainly true that Nora couldn't *not* say it.

Beth didn't show any surprise, just said, "I love you too." Like it was fact. As the train slowed, Beth set her box down on her seat, Nora did the same, and Beth pulled her in for a hug.

Nora let her chin rest on Beth's shoulder. They stepped back when the doors opened. Beth picked up the two stacked boxes, grinned at Nora, and stepped off the train.

Passengers elbowed their way past Nora on their way in. She moved aside. The seats she and Beth had sat in less than a minute ago were already taken.

Nora braced herself against a pole, thinking of what tomorrow would bring. It was bad enough that an important author was coming to the office the next day. Worse that Nora would have to plaster a smile on her face to serve sandwiches at a meeting she wasn't invited to. But getting through it alone, without a friend to commiserate with, might be the worst part. The train sped onward as Nora stared mindlessly ahead, already dreading work tomorrow.

CHAPTER TWO

Nora's stomach gave a growly whine in the elevator, twine handles of twin paper bags digging into her hands. As she turned the corner, the voices in the conference room softened to murmurs, then fell silent altogether. The skin on the back of her neck prickled. She didn't have to look up to know her coworkers had spotted her—or, more accurately, they'd spotted lunch. She suspected this was the real reason the conference room had glass walls. No one liked guessing, not when food was on the line. Her boss, Rita, closest to the door, swiveled in her chair for a better look.

Nora knew by their eager glances that they wanted her to burst through the doors and make it rain sandwiches, but just to spite them, she knocked on the glass—even added a timid, "Can I come in?"

"Yes, yes." Rita opened the door before Nora could reach for the handle. "You can start setting up back there. Let me help you." Rita's long black hair, usually thrown into a loose ponytail, was straightened smooth today. She wore a navy blouse and pencil skirt—a far cry from Rita's usual faded jeans and knit sweaters. Everyone was more put together today, putting their best foot forward to impress the author they'd invited over. There he was at the table, dressed the part in a blue button-down and tie. He leaned back and twirled a pen between his fingers as he, too, rested his curious gaze on Nora.

Nora felt a dart of self-consciousness before reminding herself that her own outfit—a hastily thrown-on flannel shirt and leggings with a small hole in the knee—was also acceptable under Parsons's lax dress code. She would have dressed up, too, if she'd been invited.

Author meetings were typically rare at Parsons, often the result of an author saying they were in town for some conference or other. Editors grumbled at having to look presentable for a day, but they'd be accommodating, show authors around the office, and take them out to lunch.

But this was another kind of author meeting. The kind where editors tried not to reek of desperation in their efforts to woo a big author into signing with them.

The object of today's mating ritual was Andrew Santos, still riding the wave of his runaway bestseller. The success of his book, a new edition of a beloved Parsons-published guide on effective communication, was a staggering surprise. The author of the first edition, a long-retired professor, only brought on Santos as a coauthor to help him meet his deadlines. Nora had noticed, spotting his birthday on the new author paperwork, that Santos was just six years older than she was, making him decades younger than most of their authors.

The manuscript came in ahead of schedule, as hoped. But to the surprise of Nora and the rest of the Parsons staff, reviewers and readers alike were soon commenting on the fresh perspective and new insights this unknown doctoral student had offered. The book became Parsons's first in years to hit the *New York Times* monthly business bestseller list, a rare feat for a new edition that was only ever expected to bring steady sales. When the lead author died a few months after the book published, Santos took on the brunt of the marketing. As he advanced in his career, publishing research, writing articles, and giving interviews, book sales advanced right along with him.

And now came the dog and pony show to keep Santos and sign his next title. If Parsons secured his next book, Nora's team would get more money, possibly hire more staff. It might even signal a new era for Parsons, one in which their books were actually interesting, relevant, and widely read.

After several shameless nudges from Rita asking Santos what he might like to write next, he'd submitted a proposal for a book on communication styles. For any other author, this would mean looking it over, drawing up sales projections, calling a meeting, and deciding whether to offer a contract. For Santos, it meant fawning over him and all but pressing a pen into his hand, in case he wanted to sign on the spot.

Nora kept her eyes straight ahead as she walked through the meeting room. She wouldn't give them the satisfaction of curiosity. No matter that she was the one who put together the slides on the screen about Parsons's marketing reach and their promotion plan for his second book. All they wanted from her now was lunch.

She hefted the bags onto the table. It wouldn't be the usual bloodbath this time around—no one-size-fits-all sandwich platters, no reason to crowd around a tray. It was Nora's first time as the provider of the food, the first big meeting since the last round of layoffs that took, among others, their administrative assistant, who usually ordered the food for these meetings. It seemed to Nora that the best option would be ordering individual lunch boxes. If they were going to have an author over and act like they had money, she was going to act like it too. Not that she wanted anyone to think she was thriving under the two-jobs-one-salary thing, but she'd grown tired of the sandwich platter—tired, specifically, of the good sandwiches being gone by the time she came back with extra napkins.

Plus, the lunch boxes had cookies.

She worked quickly to take the boxes out of the paper bags, setting them on the table where everyone could read the writing. She grabbed her *Trky Crnbry* box—no one said she could order a sandwich for herself, but she dared them to take it from her—and walked toward the door to the tune of distracted *thank-you*s.

"Which one's yours?" she heard someone say.

"Whatever's no avocado," a deep voice said. "Though I don't see it here."

Even with her back turned, she knew it was Andrew Santos speaking. And, lucrative author or not, he'd gotten his own order wrong.

Nora turned and, sure enough, it was him standing over the boxes, looking for his order while the others tried to help. But he didn't seem as concerned as everyone else. Rita's eyes darted from box to box while he surveyed them casually—lazily, even. The sleeves of his button-down were rolled up to his forearms, giving off an *I'm here to work, but it's whatever* vibe.

She thought back to the last author who visited, one Keith White last year: pale, wrinkled, and squat. She eyed Santos, his tall figure and angular, clean-shaven face dipping into a square jaw. The hint of amusement flickering in his dark-brown eyes, as though anything about a lunch order mix-up was funny.

Nora glanced from his amused expression to Rita's panicked face and felt an urgent need to correct the situation. And him.

"Uh, it was no tomato," Nora said.

He looked around, took a few moments to identify her as the source of the unfamiliar voice. Nora wasn't deemed important enough to meet him before the meeting. Or during. Or now. It shouldn't have been hard for him to spot her, considering she was the only nonwhite person in the room besides him. It didn't mean anything, really, that he was Filipino and she was half Black, but publishing was so white that Nora couldn't help but feel a sense of camaraderie any time a nonwhite person was in the office. Although he was very much testing her attempts at camaraderie right now.

"Is there avocado on it?" he asked.

Not that it was her job to know about these sandwiches—or even order them, for that matter—but she remembered what she ordered.

"Yes," she said. She paused when she saw him nod and look back at the boxes. She didn't want to ask, but she felt compelled to. "Is that a problem?"

"No." He said it too quickly to be believable. Nora waited for the other shoe to drop. "I just have this avocado allergy."

A chorus of concerned murmurs went through the room. Nora's face burned. Every pair of eyes in the room zeroed in on either Nora, the reason for this awkward moment, or Santos, the victim of her alleged mistake.

"Sorry, Andrew, mine has avocado or I'd switch," their publisher, Candace, said. It was strange to hear him called by his first name. Around the office, everyone referred to authors' projects by their last names. The fact that authors had first names always took Nora some getting used to.

Faces looked from Santos—*Andrew*—to Nora, standing in the doorway holding a box with a perfectly avocado-free sandwich.

Nora swallowed past her dry throat and tried to keep her voice upbeat as she said, "I thought you said no tomato."

What he'd emailed exactly was *As long as it doesn't have tomato, I'm happy!!* Nora remembered because it was impossible to forget those two exclamation points. Most of Parsons's authors were older, grumpier, and wouldn't use an exclamation point if it were the only punctuation mark on the keyboard. Then came Andrew Santos, throwing them around like confetti.

"I'm sure I mistyped," he said, again so quickly that Nora was now doubting herself. "Sorry about that."

"No, I'm sorry," she heard herself say. Even worse, she said, "Mine's turkey cranberry and it doesn't have avocado, if you want to switch." She refrained from adding how difficult turkey cranberry sandwiches were to come by in May.

He shook his head. "No, it's fine."

"Go on, I love avocado!!" She wasn't quite sure if she'd added two exclamation points' worth of enthusiasm, but she was trying. Whatever it took to avoid the ultimate shame of Andrew graciously foregoing his lunch and making everyone feel like assholes for eating.

Andrew took several long seconds to eye the box in her outstretched hand, then Nora's pleading (she hoped) expression, then the box again. He broke into an easy grin, dimples showing. "Sure, if you don't mind."

"Not at all." She handed him her lunch and took his boring box. "Sorry again," she added for good measure.

"No problem. Thanks, um…what was your name?"

It was only natural that he had to ask. When his last book was published, most of her communication had been with the lead author. And now, well. Her name wasn't something he would find on the agenda for today's meeting.

"Nora."

"Thank you, Nora." He actually sounded sincere, which annoyed her a little. Sincerity didn't change that everyone now doubted her sandwich-ordering skills.

She nodded and closed the door behind her. Once out of sight from the glass walls, Nora rushed to her cubicle. She dropped the box onto her desk and shook the mouse to wake her computer. She typed *Santos* into her inbox's search bar, and there it was, the only email they'd exchanged for at least a year. Nora opened the email.

As long as it doesn't have avocado, I'm happy!!

She stared at the words, resignation flooding her as she chewed her lip. She tried to think back to that day, how she could have missed this, but nothing stood out. She always prided herself on her attention to detail, but with so many new responsibilities, it was harder to do her job as well as she used to. Especially when her job kept expanding beyond what any person could do in an eight-hour period.

The day continued, over the course of which Nora begrudgingly ate her bland sandwich, picked at her onion pretzels, and took bites of her oatmeal cookie. She wondered if Andrew was enjoying her turkey cranberry sandwich on brioche. If he even ate the chili-lime cashews she'd ordered specifically for her box, or if he was allergic to nuts too. He probably didn't even appreciate molasses cookies—their spiced warmth, the crunch of coarse sugar sprinkled on top. Nora eyed her plain oatmeal cookie and took another reluctant bite.

She thought about how Andrew—and everyone in that room—could afford to order lunch out any day they wanted. Nora, whose lunches were an endless stretch of peanut butter sandwiches and the occasional, carefully budgeted meal out with Beth, had been dreaming of her custom lunch box all week. But it was fine. If Andrew Santos required a sacrificial sandwich, who was she to stand in his way?

While scheduling chipper tweets for the business division's Twitter account, Nora heard muted chatter coming from the conference room. If she rolled her chair three feet to the left and eight feet forward, she'd be able to see what was happening in the Santos meeting. She'd read in one of the career books Parsons published that the only thing stopping you from getting a seat at the table was yourself. It may have been true for the author, a middle-aged businessman, and Parsons's target audience, other middle-aged businessmen. But it couldn't be true for Nora, perpetual editorial assistant that she was.

She could have tried, she supposed. Asking to attend the meeting. Making a case for why she belonged there. But the possibility of rejection felt more crushing, somehow. Like it would be confirmation of her place here, the editorial assistant who couldn't even order a sandwich right.

Eventually the door opened, and the chatter grew louder. She saw Andrew walk past, followed by the four or so women from the meeting, like a groomsman with far too many bridesmaids. Or a herd of hyenas stalking their prey.

Once Andrew was gone, post-meeting follow-up would come next. They'd discuss revenue projections and marketing plans and whatever other high hopes they had for Andrew Santos. Nora wouldn't be invited to that meeting, either—even though she was the only person left from her old team who'd worked on Andrew's first book. She could discuss the marketing strategy they had for his first book, pinpoint the ways they'd underestimated his reach the first time around, and list the outlets he got attention from last time that weren't on their radar now. But again—inviting herself would be presumptuous.

And then Candace stepped in front of Nora's cubicle. Instinctively, Nora smoothed down her shirt. As the only publisher left standing after the layoffs, Candace was now the highest-ranking person in the San Francisco office. Nora's eyes fell over Candace's delicate silver bracelet, her pearl-buttoned black cardigan, her red hair tied back in a neat bun. Not even a hint of gray roots, though she had to be past sixty. Nora took a breath, wondering if this might be the invitation she was too afraid to ask for.

"Can we talk?" Candace asked.

Just the question had Nora's heart racing. She searched Candace's face for clues, but her polite smile betrayed nothing. Considering the unfortunate fact that Candace's most recent memory of Nora was watching her screw up Andrew Santos's sandwich order, she couldn't see a world in which this talk wasn't about her mistake.

Nora followed Candace to a meeting room, preparing herself for well-meaning advice on the importance of attention to detail. She took a seat and waited for the spiel.

"I had to wait until after the meeting to talk to you, but... there have been some discussions with the New York office," Candace said.

This did little to quell Nora's anxiety. Nothing good came from Parsons's headquarters in New York. All communication from them was news no one wanted, whether delivered in an unintelligible, company-wide email or trickled down the chain in whispered mandates. Nora, seeing the way Candace was looking down, steeled herself.

"What about?" she asked.

Candace lifted her head. "It's about the restructuring," she said.

Nora relaxed slightly. The DIC(k) wasn't a threat to her. So far, Parsons's Disrupt, Innovate, and Change plan mostly impacted higher-ups. It was this very streamlining that had laid off her former bosses, Tom and Lynn, lead editors of the business line, and merged the remnants of Nora's business team with Candace's leadership team. While Tom and Lynn's more lucrative authors had been reassigned to Rita (see Exhibit Santos), Nora had been left to manage the rest. A year later, these forgotten authors still didn't have an editor assigned—only Nora to shepherd their books along. Whatever this next phase brought, Nora knew her job was safe. Someone had to do the work the layoffs left behind.

"As part of the restructuring, our VP of operations has been working with a consultant to maximize profitability and secure the company's future," Candace said, sounding like she was reading from a script. "They did a review of salary bands across the board, and..." Candace sighed. "They've decided some departments currently have salaries that are not sustainable.

Editorial is one of those departments." Candace set her jaw and stared ahead, like she couldn't believe the words she'd just said aloud.

"Editorial?" Nora repeated. It was such an absurd concept that she wondered, for a moment, if she'd heard wrong. "Including editorial assistants?"

Candace nodded slowly. "They said this method of…future-proofing…is the best way for us to invest in ourselves."

"Maybe no one's told them what investing means," Nora remarked. She glanced at Candace. No reaction. Beth would have laughed.

"I hope you know this is no reflection on you," Candace said, settling her gaze on Nora. "You've been so helpful, and I'm grateful that—" Candace paused. *That you still haven't gotten any job offers* was what Nora would have gone with; maybe Candace was too tactful to mention it.

Nora nodded and tried to make her face as blank as possible. "Okay." She felt Candace looking at her, curious how Nora would respond. Nora was also curious how Nora would respond. Her mind reeled with questions, rants, and every spiteful thought she'd ever had toward Parsons execs. But she knew, combing through these thoughts, that there was nothing she could do. She sighed and met Candace's eyes. "How much?"

Candace opened a folder and shuffled through papers. Nora counted one for everyone on the team. "It's 15 percent." Candace flipped the paper over and there it was, her name, her employee ID. Her old income. Her new income. Everything carefully thought out and typed up by someone in New York with no regard for what it actually meant for Nora Beatrice Hughes, employee number 775036, to depreciate so drastically.

"I understand," Candace said, watching Nora study the numbers on the paper, "if this is a deal breaker for you."

She wanted to laugh, but she couldn't. She was realizing then, as she stared at the numbers she was and was not worth, that she didn't *have* any deal breakers. No matter what happened, no matter who left or how much work they left her, she would still be here. Unless she found somewhere else to go.

CHAPTER THREE

Nora spent her cramped BART ride home running numbers in her head.

Eleven hundred dollars twice a month was already a stretch when one paycheck barely covered rent. Much of the second paycheck went to student loans, leaving Nora to divide the remainder between utilities, credit card debt, and groceries. It was a careful balance as it was, checking the calendar, checking the calculator, knowing what was paid and what still remained. It left her muzzled, bound, reluctant to admit out loud how many of her choices revolved around her bank account. Lunches out with Beth restricted to once a month. Haircuts self-administered with a pair of scissors and a belief that if she messed up the back, she'd never know anyway.

She stared at the book in her hands—*Kindred*, one of her favorites—but the words blurred together as her mind pulsed with the thought that eleven hundred minus 15 percent might knock her paychecks from four digits to three.

Nora trudged up the steps to her third-floor apartment and shoved her key into the door, listening for sounds of her roommate,

Allie. But the living room was empty. No *The Handmaid's Tale* on the TV, no true-crime podcasts blaring over the rhythmic *thunk* of chopping vegetables. It was a toss-up as to who got home first on Fridays. Sometimes Allie showed up early to work from home for the afternoon. Sometimes Nora left work early because she was sick of it.

Nora waited for her frozen meal to finish microwaving, glancing toward the door every time she thought she heard footsteps. She wondered, watching the numbers count down on the microwave, what had Allie renewing their lease every year. For Nora, the choice was easy: here in Oakland, in a place where she could hear the rumbling highway from her bedroom, rent was cheaper than what she could manage anywhere else.

But Allie had options. She didn't five years ago, when her previous roommate left for grad school, and Allie posted an ad on Craigslist to fill the vacancy before the next month's rent was due. Of course she'd take a chance on Nora, who had everything she needed: a check that cleared and an assurance that she wasn't a murderer. But now, because Allie had made more friends over the years and landed a job as a UX designer for a digital marketplace start-up, she could afford to pull the plug on their arrangement and find a place with air-conditioning and a roommate she didn't meet off the internet.

It was probably the neighborhood that did it—walking distance from a restaurant that sold fifteen different kinds of mac and cheese, her pick of Korean restaurants in any direction, proximity to the hipster coffee shop from which Allie had bought the overpriced coffee maker sitting on the kitchen counter.

Nora eyed it, sleek and silver with an air of money. She'd gaped at first, watching Allie purchase the two-hundred-dollar coffee maker one Sunday morning with the same sense of indulgence it gave Nora to spend six dollars on an occasional mocha latte. But now, thinking of her pay cut, she felt a shred of relief that at least she could be sure of her housing. Allie had already broached the topic last month, asked if Nora was fine staying another year. Nora replied as she did every year: a measured pause, a shrug of the shoulder, and a firm *Yes* that implied she had options.

The microwave beeped just as the front door scraped open. Footsteps approached the kitchen while Nora pulled out her dinner and wished she'd been faster.

"Hey," Allie said. "I was gonna ask if you wanted to go in on pizza. Too late, I guess."

Ordering delivery with Allie was another once-monthly extravagance. Nora peeled the plastic off her tray and forced a laugh. "Yeah, sorry."

Nora took a fork from the silverware drawer and perched it on the rim of her plastic microwave tray. She lifted her eyes to Allie, saw her engrossed in her phone. That was as good a cue to leave as any.

"Oh," Allie said, "there's a new season of *Baking Show* on Netflix, but I just realized we never finished the last one. If you're free tonight, we could pick up where we left off." She raked a hand through her short, dark hair, exposing the neat line of an undercut before her hair fluttered back into place.

Nora buried a pang of dismay. Over the years, *The Great British Baking Show* had evolved from a shared interest into a tradition. A year in, high from the relief of their first lease renewal conversation and tipsy from the martinis Allie made to break in her new cocktail shaker, Nora had started imitating the judges' voices.

Watching Paul Hollywood examine a baker's elaborate creation—a four-layer cake topped with an assortment of cream puffs and a red caramel windmill that actually spun—Nora had lowered her voice and said, in her best Liverpudlian accent, "It's rather basic."

The payoff was immediate, a surprised laugh from the other end of the couch that sent ripples of pride through Nora. In addition to being, as Allie later said, the moment she finally saw Nora come out of her shell, it cemented their *Great British Baking Show* tradition as something watched with giggles and bad accents.

"I wish I could," Nora said. "I've got some stuff to do tonight. Next time." As if she hadn't been dodging Allie's invitations for a few months now.

"Sure." Allie's tone was chipper, but Nora caught the slight droop in her shoulder.

Nora crossed the kitchen with her now-lukewarm dinner and hesitated on her way out. It wasn't too late to accept the invitation, plunk down on the couch, and try to get into the spirit of things. But just the thought exhausted her. Since the layoffs last year, something dark and poisonous had started seeping into the cracks of Nora's mind, the ones she always pretended not to notice.

It was subtle at first, wispy and mostly transparent. But as Parsons stretched Nora thin and the job rejections piled up, it all got darker, stickier, harder to avoid. And now, with Beth gone and a pay cut to contend with, a cold fear ran through Nora at the idea of trying to cope with this when she was already so bad at coping before.

It all put a damper on socializing. And existing.

Nora left the kitchen without a word and crept into her room. She eyed her paperback copy of *Kindred* again, splayed out on her bed like she'd tuckered it out from the whole four pages she'd managed to read during the number-crunching BART ride home.

She longed to pick up the book and start reading. She could finish it by tomorrow night, post some musings on BookTap about wishing *Kindred* could be made into a movie already, and start another before the weekend was over. That used to be her favorite kind of weekend. Lying on her stomach, turning pages well into the night, getting swept into a book she couldn't put down. The freedom of checking the clock, seeing it was past 1:00 a.m., and knowing she could read for as long as she wanted, because she didn't have anywhere to be tomorrow.

And then the next day, waking up at noon with the hazy remnants of a book-induced dream, remembering that she fell asleep too soon, feeling the urgent need to finish the rest before breakfast. Then she might pick an entirely different genre for her next book—if she finished a thriller, then maybe a YA rom-com. If it was a memoir, maybe the silliness of P. G. Wodehouse. The possibilities were infinite.

But somehow, books weren't enough anymore. Staring at ink on a page and trying to get swept away was harder lately. It left her spending five minutes on a single paragraph, blinking at nothing while her mind swirled darkly. Then she would move on to the next chunk of text, sure that the words would stick this time. Again she would come away blank. It was the worst possible kind of meditation.

She'd recently picked up a new hobby, though: watching the ceiling fan spin. Sometimes she picked a blade and focused on it, watching it twirl around and around, until she blinked and lost track. Then she'd stare at the blur of blades, too apathetic to find another to concentrate on, letting them float around and past and through her. It didn't help her forget about her worries, exactly, but they all hung suspended, unable to sink in for as long as she stared at the fan.

But she couldn't do that now. Nora scrolled through her recent contacts, pausing at Beth's name. She could tell Beth about the pay cut but not its full impact. Nora would need to frame it as *What an inconvenience* rather than *How do I survive*. Talking to someone who didn't get it, who didn't have student loans, and whose parents paid part of her rent, would just bring pity.

She paused again at *Mom*. Her mother would remind her, as she did every few months, that if Nora moved back to her rural Oregon hometown, she could get a two-bedroom for the same price she was paying for a room here. And Nora would cycle through the arguments again that there was no point moving back to a town she couldn't wait to leave. A childhood of feeling out of place, from the color of her skin to the Obama sticker on her father's truck, had compelled her to get out and find where she belonged. Even if she'd chosen a very white industry to work in, San Francisco had a freedom she craved. She wasn't ready to give up on it yet.

Nora scrolled through her contacts again. When she reached Lynn, her former boss, she stopped. Just seeing the name was like being wrapped in a hug, instantly transporting her to Parsons before the layoffs, when everything was normal and full of possibility. Lynn might know what to do. Even if she didn't have any job openings at the new publishing company she worked for—which Nora knew they didn't, persistent as she was in her job site hauntings—just sitting across from her, hearing kind words delivered in a Southern rasp, would bring solace.

Nora typed out a text to Lynn, asking if she wanted to have lunch next week. Lynn would know what to say. And it didn't hurt that she always paid for lunch.

Text sent, Nora heaved a sigh and plopped her head down on her pillow. No point keeping the ceiling fan waiting.

CHAPTER FOUR

Having lunch with Lynn always made Nora feel like an outlaw.

It felt like cheating on Rita, to see the boss she had before her. Or like cheating on Parsons by meeting with the new executive editor of their competitor, Weber Book Group. Both of these disloyal feelings made Nora feel powerful. It was her own tiny form of revenge.

Nora entered the restaurant, a place she and Lynn used to take authors to. It was too upscale for Nora to ever visit alone. She breathed in the smell of oysters and fresh pasta as she scanned the tables for a mass of wavy blond hair. There she was at a booth against the window, hair frizzy and untamed, red-framed glasses from an era past. Lynn lifted her hand in a wave and Nora nearly bumped into a waiter in her rush to join her.

Lynn opened her arms for a hug. "How're you doing, sweetheart?" she asked in her gravelly voice. Her tone always sounded comforting and warm, which Nora suspected had something to do with her Southern accent. But there was something else to it this time. Something like pity.

"Did you hear?" Nora asked as they settled into their seats.

"Hear what?"

So Lynn didn't even need a reason to pity her. Nora just elicited that reaction in people now. But she'd take it. She pitied herself.

Nora recapped the quiet conversation, the pay cut. She left out what she did after getting the news, frantically running numbers to figure out what she could and couldn't afford. It was an impossible equation—she technically couldn't afford her current situation. When she entered her salary and monthly debts into an online calculator that was supposed to tell her how much to spend on rent, it spit out a number less than what she was currently paying. And when she moved the slider to the amount she was actually paying, it changed from green to red, like she'd offended its reason with her reality.

So if she couldn't really afford what she was paying now, what did it matter that she couldn't afford it on her new, lower salary? If she was making it work now, she should be able to make it work on 15 percent less, maybe. That was what she was trying to convince herself, but she wasn't sure how long she could keep the charade going.

"Awful. Just awful." Lynn shook her head. "On the peanuts they pay you as it is." She opened the menu, then closed it and leaned forward. Nora leaned in too. "If they're capable of this, it makes you wonder if they've got something else planned," Lynn said.

"This is almost the end of it, actually," Nora said. "The last all-staff email from the execs said we're on our way to 'total innovation.'" Nora couldn't be certain how total innovation differed from regular innovation, but the answer was probably in one of their books.

"That's good," Lynn said.

"Yeah." Nora didn't want to dwell on her secure future as Parsons's perpetual EA. "How are things at Weber?"

"Different." Lynn opened the menu again, closed it again, and looked back up at Nora. "It's more fast paced than I'm used to."

"I'll bet," Nora said, forcing a laugh. Weber hadn't even existed a decade ago, and now it was one of Parsons's strongest competitors. Unlike Parsons, publishing the same types of titles for the same boring businessmen year after year, Weber cast a wider net, publishing everything from financial management guides by young upstarts to adult coloring books. Even their business books seemed interesting. The last time Nora was on their website, checking for openings they may have failed to post on job sites, their business page featured a vibrant cover for a book about navigating microaggressions in the workplace.

"But it's been good," Lynn said. "Did you know they see Parsons as their main competition for their business line? I didn't know we were on their radar that much."

Nora loved how normal that sounded. *We.* They were still a *we*. It was easy to pretend they still worked together when Lynn came by to take Nora out to lunch sometimes. Her other former boss, Tom, had gone in a different direction after the layoffs. His Facebook posts were now a sea of gardening anecdotes and dog photos, all the joys of retiring early and moving to Santa Rosa. Tom may have left the working world, but at least she still had Lynn and their occasional lunches. It was one of the few scraps of normalcy Nora had left.

Later, as Nora speared the last of the sweet potato gnocchi on her plate, Lynn brought the conversation back to Weber.

"Would you be interested in working at Weber if a job came up?"

Nora's eyes flicked up from her water glass. Her breath hitched at the thought of being handed an out, working with Lynn again. She waited a beat to compose herself. "Yeah, that could be interesting. Why do you ask?"

"Just so I know to keep an ear out for you. We've been expanding a lot recently. I'm sure a position is bound to open up."

"Really?" Nora asked. "Expanding how?"

"We're actually starting to acquire fiction."

"Fiction?" she echoed. She had to have misheard. Nora had long ago cast aside her fantasy of working on important novels with her favorite authors. She'd crumpled it up and buried it deep inside her where no one could see how naïve she'd been. She eyed Lynn, waiting for the catch.

Lynn nodded so vigorously, her head was almost bobbing. "Can you believe it? They hired me for their business line, but they're starting to move into fiction. They said I could start building a fiction list too."

"Wow," she breathed. Was it possible Nora wasn't the only one with that fantasy? That Lynn had those dreams too? Slowly, hesitantly, Nora found the crumpled-up fantasy and let it unfurl. She smoothed out the wrinkles and added Lynn to the mix. She imagined sitting side by side with Lynn in the Weber office, making notes on manuscripts and discussing plotlines with the same fervor they used to talk about their favorite novels.

"I'll keep an ear out for you, okay?"

"I would love that," Nora said, letting herself break into a smile. It felt so alien to admit, to accept that this was something that could happen.

The bill arrived, and as usual, Lynn reached for it before Nora could. "In the meantime, we *are* looking for a couple of remote freelance acquisitions editors. It's only part-time, but if—god forbid—Parsons lays you off, it could be an option for making a little extra money in the interim." Lynn tucked her credit card into the bill holder and set it on the edge of the table.

"They'd consider *me* for an editor position?"

Lynn looked Nora up and down, feigning shock. "Why wouldn't they? You've got the experience, and you're more than capable. I'd put in a good word for you. They're not too picky about the freelancers," she confided. "They need some help getting authors to meet their deadlines so editors can focus on expanding into other areas."

"I'll think about it," Nora said. Though she knew she wouldn't. She had to follow the money, and a full-time salary—even a recently reduced full-time salary—was better than anything part-time.

The conversation turned to books, as it always did. Lynn asked Nora if she'd ever read Dorothy Dunnett and slid a book across the table like she already knew the answer—another unsolicited but welcome loan from the library of Lynn. Nora studied the back cover wistfully and tucked it into her purse. Maybe this would be the book that got her back into reading.

After lunch, while Nora sat at her desk crossing items off her to-do list, her mind wandered to what it would be like to jump ship from Parsons and freelance for Weber. Working with Lynn again. And, if a full-time job opened up, working on fiction. She wouldn't have to wake up every morning feeling like nothing she did that day would matter. She could free herself of Parsons and its black hole of buzzwords. She could be the person she'd always imagined being, working on books—novels—that could actually help someone. Not help them leverage synergy to maximize productivity, but help them the way books had helped Nora. Help someone feel connected to something. Help someone feel less alone.

She let the thought drift away. It was no use daydreaming when there were tangible opportunities before her. BookTap was still an option—she just needed to think about it positively. One of Parsons's books had said something like that, about visualizing your goals to achieve transformation, which had made Nora roll her eyes and wonder why anyone would buy into this nonsense. (It turned out to be one of their top sellers that quarter.) But now she would try it. Her BookTap interview tomorrow would go well. They would hire her. They would pay her enough to live on. The BookTap job would fulfill her. She would spend the rest of her life feeling passionate about marketing coordination, and she would be happy. She repeated these thoughts, determined, if not actually positive. It had to happen. There was no alternative.

CHAPTER FIVE

There was something unsettling about BookTap.

Nora looked around as she sat in the lobby. Everything was so open. She could see past the reception area to the entire BookTap office, filled with row after row of people sitting at desks.

She knew many start-ups had open floor plans, but for some reason she thought BookTap was different, cozier. Less techies in hoodies, more bookshelves and reading nooks. They were an app, yes, but it was an app for booklovers, for reviewing and recommending books. She couldn't help but imagine its office as a reader's paradise.

But BookTap was definitely a start-up. There were even beanbag chairs in a corner and a cereal bar by the kitchen. It was unclear why an office of adults needed all-day access to cereal.

As Nora waited, she brought a hand to her hairline, checking for any rogue hairs. Her short curls were still neatly coaxed back with a too-tight headband. She tugged on her blazer. All morning, it had been settling too high on her shoulders in a way that made her wiggle to correct it, like she was doing a shimmy.

She reminded herself not to focus on these discomforts. She

was committed to exuding positivity, visualizing her goals, every-thing one of Parsons's stupid books preached. She'd try anything at this point.

Nora turned her attention to the bookshelf across the room. The books weren't organized by color, which was a good sign. Organizing books by aesthetics was a sin as far as Nora was concerned. She was trying to work out how they were shelved when a man her age strolled up to her.

"Hi, Nora?"

He introduced himself as Chad, and they shook hands. Chad took her on a tour of the office, pointing out the cereal bar, the foosball table, the rows of people sitting at desks on identical MacBooks.

He led her to a small room with a stark white table. There was a water bottle at each place. She wondered whose job it was to put them there.

Nora settled into a chair across from Chad, studying him more closely. He didn't look like a Chad. Weren't all Chads supposed to be blond? How did this brown-eyed brunette slip through?

He was white; at least he met the minimum Chad requirements.

"You didn't have any issues with the schedule today, did you?" Chad asked, hunching over to peer at something on his laptop.

Only in the sense that she thought three hours was an offen-sively long time for an interview. But she'd been too polite to say that.

"No," Nora said. "This is perfect." As perfect as it could be to wager a half-day of PTO on a job she might not get. *Will get*, she reminded herself. Positivity and such.

"Oh, never mind." Chad shook his head. "It was someone

else who had the conflict. Sorry about that. My coffee hasn't kicked in yet, if you couldn't tell," he said with a sheepish grin.

She returned a weak smile, feeling a little more at ease. What followed was an exercise in anecdotes. A time she had to manage multiple deadlines? Well, with Tom and Lynn gone, she was responsible for twenty books, each with a dozen deadlines, and it was on her to make sure every deadline was met. She had her own system, in fact, for keeping these deadlines straight and checking in with suspiciously silent authors whose deadlines were drawing near. She felt her confidence growing when Chad enthused about a color-coded spreadsheet he'd made to keep track of his projects.

When Chad's forty-five minutes were up, next came Josh, whose jaw was dotted with patchy stubble. Nora played *Connect the Stubble* in her mind as she answered his questions. Josh's reactions were muted, nods and notes rather than the conversational interview with Chad. Ah, Chad. She almost missed him.

When Josh left she repositioned in her seat, keeping an eye on the door. A hand automatically went to her headband, wanting to loosen the pressure it was putting on her scalp, but she fought the urge and forced her hands to her lap. Another glance at the door. She felt like a child without a babysitter.

At last, voices drew near and the door swung open. A woman introduced herself as Zoe, and Nora complimented her earrings, little black quotation marks that seemed to bracket every word she spoke. As they shook hands, in slunk a man named Shawn, who looked like the type of person who spent a lot of time wondering if he could pull off a fedora.

Nora settled into her seat and eyed the pair in front of her. One more interview to go. Back to the well of anecdotal questions they went.

A time she had to pay attention to detail? Besides being a top-notch sandwich orderer (the Santos Incident remained a prickling anomaly), Nora rattled off all the moments when her job involved managing small details others tended to miss. As she finished an anecdote about spotting an incorrect ISBN on a final cover layout—something she was particularly proud of because it was so minute—she could see Shawn's eyes glazing over.

Registering his blank face, she was aware that there was a lot of explaining involved when she talked about her job. Somehow, in her efforts to apply her publishing experience to questions like these, she ended up making her skills sound utterly nontransferable.

"That's great," Zoe said. She looked down at the paper in front of her. "Can you tell me about why you're interested in marketing?"

She wasn't sure, really. Why she was interested in it or whether she was interested at all. She just knew she wanted to *do* something. To prove she was capable of having ideas, of doing something that wasn't routing a contract or requesting an ISBN.

Her favorite part of her job was emailing authors their book cover. She had to write with enough finality that authors thought the decision was already made, while leaving a tiny bit of room for the author to respond and disagree. The author *could* disagree, of course. Parsons Press just didn't like for them to know that.

But she never minded if they did, because it gave her a chance to really try to persuade them. She got to bust out the bullshitting skills all English majors carefully honed through years of writing lit papers. She would use phrases like *We feel the abstract design really captures the ambiguous nature of organizational change*, or *We like how the flower represents a new beginning, much like onboarding.* Sometimes authors fought back hard enough that Nora had to admit defeat and get a new cover designed. But in the moments Nora was proudest of, she found the words to make authors see what she saw in their cover. It was one of the few times she got to share her own ideas. When her daily routine revolved around administrative tasks, Nora cherished these little victories.

And maybe marketing was something like that, more creative than administrative. She hoped so, anyway.

She took a breath and smiled at Zoe. "I've worked closely with our marketing department on all our projects, and I like that it's more of a creative role. I enjoy looking for opportunities to assist our marketing team, whether I'm helping them write copy, brainstorm book titles, or find different ways to increase our reach. Just last week, we launched a new social media campaign for an upcoming book, and it's so much fun to check the engagement stats to see how it's going."

So much fun was a stretch, but Zoe was nodding at this. Shawn jotted something down and then looked up like he'd caught her in a lie.

"I noticed you're saying 'we,'" he said. "You didn't launch the campaign yourself?"

"No," Nora said, squinting at him. "That's our marketing manager's responsibility. But I assisted."

His head tilt suggested a vague sort of interest. The loose strands of dark hair that didn't fit into his man bun tilted along with him. He glanced down at her résumé. "You've been an assistant for five years now?"

"My title has remained the same, but my responsibilities have increased the longer I've been in the position." She didn't add that layoffs were the primary reason Parsons saw fit to increase her responsibilities.

He did that head tilt again. Shawn seemed to have mastered the art of listening disinterestedly. If he wasn't tilting his head, he was looking off to the side or typing something on his MacBook.

Parsons didn't have a cereal bar, but they did have eye contact.

"I think that says a lot about the quality of work you do," Zoe said. Nora tore her eyes from Shawn and his tilt-a-whirl head and rested her stare on Zoe. "I started here as a receptionist, but people gave me more to do because I kept asking for extra work, and then my job just kind of morphed into social media management."

A glimmer of hope stirred in Nora. Shawn may not have been impressed with Nora and her assistantly existence, but Zoe seemed to understand.

"That's so inspiring," Nora said. "I love when jobs have that kind of upward mobility."

"Can you tell me your salary requirements?" Shawn asked.

Classic Shawn, whipping out the cruelest question to ask someone in publishing. No matter how much Nora researched typical salary ranges for positions, the range always seemed wildly out of reach. She felt like a fraud saying a number twenty-five thousand dollars higher than her current salary, even though the difference was solely a reflection on the low salaries in publishing, not astronomical salaries elsewhere.

Nora tried it out, saying *sixty thousand dollars* with a straight face, pretending she was thinking *What a normal salary* when the only thing running through her head was *Don't be suspicious*. Shawn made a note on his laptop. She exhaled quietly.

"Do you have any questions for us?" he asked.

Nora had exhausted her supply of questions by now. She'd improvised new ones even as she was losing steam, but for Shawn, she decided, she would ask the question she'd struggled to answer herself. And she hoped it made him suffer.

"Would you recommend this position to a friend?"

Shawn smirked. "Of course. We have catered lunches; we go on group outings. People can set their own schedules or bring their pets to work. I don't know who wouldn't want to work here."

Of course. Of course.

"Actually," he continued, "I did recommend the position to a friend. I thought she'd be a good fit for it. She went through a few stages of the interview process, but it didn't work out in the end."

Well, shit.

"So you literally did recommend the position to a friend," Nora said, trying to sound amused through her defeat as he expertly relayed his answer. No stumble or pause in sight.

He laughed. "Yeah, pretty much. She's great, but she just didn't have the marketing experience we were looking for."

There was an awkward pause as Nora considered her own lack of marketing experience. Her gaze fell to her lap.

"But everyone brings a different mix of things to the table," Zoe said. "That's why we're interviewing people with all sorts of backgrounds. Your publishing experience would bring a valuable perspective."

That was true, Nora realized, squaring her shoulders a little. She *did* have a valuable perspective. Why should she let Shawn get to her? That wasn't the attitude she was striving for. She needed to get back to channeling that. Posi-fucking-tivity.

"We're also looking for a strong culture fit," Shawn added. He looked through the glass walls at the rows of people working at their desks. "We like people who find new ways to innovate, and who are willing to put in the work to see things through. The reason our benefits are popular is because we're so passionate about what we do that we don't want to leave. We don't do the strictly nine-to-five thing because that's not how people operate, you know?"

Nora did not know. She absolutely operated on the strictly nine-to-five thing.

"Yeah, that's great," she said. "It kind of blurs the lines between work and home. I love that."

"Exactly." Shawn smiled proudly, like he invented start-up culture.

Next came the ruse of thanking each other for the interview. Shawn disappeared like he had more important things to do, but Zoe walked her to the elevators, telling her she could expect to hear back by next week.

In the elevator, Nora took off her headband and rubbed her aching scalp. The only upside of interviews was the relief she felt afterwards, but this was a muddled sort of relief. Shawn's words about culture fit—code for accepting catered lunches as a fair trade-off for never going home—gnawed at her. She pushed it out of her mind and thought about Chad and his color-coded spreadsheets, Zoe and her receptionist beginnings. Having a creative role at a book app she loved. There was a lot of good here, too.

And this job was her ticket out of Parsons. She needed it to be.

CHAPTER SIX

"Can you send Santos the contract?"

Nora removed her earbuds. Rita stood at her cubicle, looking at her expectantly, like perhaps this wasn't the first time she'd said these words to Nora.

"The contract?" Nora repeated. Dark eyes and avocados flashed in her mind. She blinked away the thought. "Sure. Can you send it to me?"

"I sent it to you yesterday, but it must not have gone through. I'll resend it." Rita waved it off like she wasn't inconvenienced at all. Rita was too polite and unassuming to place blame on others, even when, in Nora's case, they deserved it. Nora's half-day absence for yesterday's BookTap interview had turned her inbox into chaos. She'd stayed late and crept in early this morning to try to make a dent in it, but for every email she replied to, it seemed six more kept coming.

Ever dependable, Rita emailed the contract within a minute. Nora opened a new email, pasted Andrew's email address into it, and attached the contract. She stared at the blank window, unsure whether to acknowledge their meeting last week.

Actually, no, it wasn't a meeting. Andrew had had a meeting with the team, and Nora hadn't been invited. So really it was nothing more than an accident, and why shed light on an accident?

She typed out the same basic contract email she'd send any author whose sandwich order she didn't mess up and sent it without another thought.

A few minutes later, however, as she was cleaning up a manuscript from a particularly lazy author, she got a reply.

Hi Nora,

Thanks! I'll review it and let you know if I have any questions. Gotta make sure it's free of avocado and all that :)

Best,
Andrew

The wound was too fresh for Nora to joke about. She still mourned the loss of her turkey cranberry sandwich, and it still made her cringe to think her bosses knew she'd messed up the order for one of their biggest authors.

Nora hit Reply and typed:

Don't worry, I stopped them from adding the avocado clause just in time.

No greetings, no "best," no name. She felt there was a certain point during email exchanges when continuing the charade of "Hi ____," and "Best, ____" started to feel awkward.

She went back to the manuscript. While scrolling slowly

down each page to check for excerpts they would need to seek permission for, she couldn't even follow along. Sometimes she learned interesting tidbits when transmitting some of the titles they published, but this book's jargon about employment law, compliance, and record-keeping flew over her head.

A notification interrupted her scrolling. She clicked back to her inbox.

Hi Nora (apparently they had not reached the point of disregarding salutations),

Thanks for saving me from that deadly clause! I have a question, but not about the contract. I think I was supposed to get a royalty check last month, but I didn't receive anything. Can you confirm whether you have my new address on file? It's the same address that's in the contract.

Thanks!
Andrew

He was so *nice*.

It could go either way with big authors. After years of dealing with Parsons Press, these authors knew how things were supposed to go, and they knew when they could push. But a few were more down to earth—didn't want to make a fuss, understood that theirs was not the only book at hand.

She hadn't known what kind of author Andrew was because she'd only ever communicated with the lead author of his last book. But because of its wild success, and because people around the office dropped his name so much lately, she'd mentally added him to the list of persnickety lucrative authors.

Nora opened Parsons's payment record system, so ancient it could only be navigated via keyboard commands. She arrived at the record for Andrew Santos and breathed a sigh of relief when she saw the correct address listed. She wasn't sure she could handle another mistake.

She pressed a few more keys to confirm that his royalty check had been cut. Slowly, horizontal bar by horizontal bar, the royalty history loaded on the screen.

Nora stared.

His last royalty check had been for nearly $40,000.

Twice a year, he received a check for more than her entire annual salary. And he had a day job as an assistant professor. This was just his extra income. An extra $80,000 a year.

Usually when their business authors asked her to check on their royalties, the figure tended to be smaller. Much smaller. A few hundred for authors who hadn't published in a while, but whose old books quietly sold a little every year. One or two thousand for an author whose book was doing moderately well—a figure that would drop off until it quietly settled into the low hundreds.

Certainly not, however, a steady stream of five figures.

Nora ran a fingernail up and down the pad of her thumb as she continued to stare. Taking his day job into account, this man had to make a full six figures more than her per year. And he got to eat her turkey cranberry sandwich.

Deciding Andrew could wait a little longer to hear back about his forty large, Nora checked her personal email. There, in the bold type of her inbox, was an unread email from the recruiter at BookTap.

Heart beating in a mixture of excitement and dread, she clicked on the email. Her eyes scrolled past the words, landing squarely on *We have unfortunately decided not to move forward with your application*. The rest of it became a blur. She swallowed past the bitter taste in her mouth and took a shuddery sigh.

Flashes of the interview—Chad's warmth, Zoe's understanding, the *valuable perspective* Nora could bring to the table—reeled through her. All reminders of how naïve she'd been to let herself believe she could get this rare, book-adjacent job so teasingly within her reach. For all of Shawn's doubt, for everything she hated about start-up culture, she still, somehow, had let herself get swept away in the idea that she could fit in at BookTap.

The bridge of her nose tingled unpleasantly as she wondered how she was going to pay rent now. A salary from BookTap would have given her room to breathe. Not just breathe, but *live*. Pay more than the minimum on her loans. Order dinner on a whim like Allie, instead of planning and plotting and saving and calculating. Nora rubbed her nose and blinked back tears, willing the feeling away.

She meant to return to her Parsons inbox and reply to Andrew's email about his royalties, but she couldn't stomach the idea—the fate of his forty-thousand-dollar check sitting in her outbox when she had less than a hundred dollars in her bank account and an email from BookTap telling her it was going to stay that way.

Instead, she clicked over to the Weber website. Its crisp layout with bright, poppy covers was a stark contrast to Parsons's site, an ode to stock images of smiling people sitting at blank computers and speaking in empty meetings. She thought about her lunch with Lynn, the freelance opening. The excitement in

Lynn's eyes when she revealed she was expanding into fiction. Like a childhood dream come true.

The freelance job alone wouldn't be enough to cover Nora's expenses. But if it got her foot in the door, if she could freelance until something permanent opened up, she'd have her career back on track and a higher, full-time salary from Weber. But she'd need another job to keep her afloat in the meantime.

Or...a thought hung dangerously close. Or she could do both jobs—her Parsons position and the Weber freelance gig at the same time. If she was already doing the work of several people now, what was one more job? The Weber position would more than make up for her salary cut. And, once she got in good standing, she could apply for a job and cut ties with Parsons for good.

It was absurd. And definitely not company sanctioned. In fact, if things went south, this could ruin her reputation and her career in one fell swoop—and yet. Glancing back at the email from BookTap, tears weren't brimming anymore. She read the email over and over, relishing how it didn't sting now that she had a new out in mind. Nora thought it all through at rapid speed—what could go wrong, what could go right. Her heart was still racing, but her breaths were steady. It felt doable.

She sat very still at her desk, only breathing and blinking, until she realized her decision was already made. She felt herself standing. Nora glanced at her phone on her desk, then reached a hand out to pick it up. And then she was stalking into a phone room, closing the door with a certainty she didn't know she possessed. Her thumb hovered over the Call button for just a moment before she pressed it. She tapped her nails on the table as the phone rang. And rang.

When Lynn's voicemail came on, Nora thought about hanging

up. She could hang up now, and that would be the end of it. If Lynn asked her about it, she could chalk it up to a butt dial. But she stayed on, took a breath, and waited for the beep.

"Hi, this is Nora. I've decided to—I'm thinking I might just quit and look for another job that pays better, so I'll be open for the freelance job after all. How can I apply?"

CHAPTER SEVEN

As Nora sat at her desk on Monday morning, she was still replaying the whirlwind Weber interview that had followed her rash voicemail to Lynn—if it could even be called an interview. It was mostly listening to Lynn compliment her to Weber's publisher, a woman named Violet with silver hair in a short bob. Violet's occasional questions were easy, about how she managed authors who weren't meeting deadlines, how she researched potential new authors. With every answer Nora gave, Lynn chimed in with an example of Nora's capabilities. From the way Lynn told it, Nora did everything from schmoozing authors to signing them while Lynn sat in a corner and drooled in a cup.

The work sounded manageable. As a freelance acquisitions editor for the business division, her primary duties would be handling miscellaneous tasks full-time editors might be too busy for, like prodding authors into meeting their deadlines, researching possible new contacts, and reaching out to experts to gauge their interest in publishing with Weber. Any authors she brought on would be passed off to an editor at Weber.

There would be one meeting a week she had to join by phone,

in addition to any calls she scheduled with authors. About twenty hours a week on average. All work she could do from home—or, if she was feeling bold, Nora thought, from the Parsons office. She could do this.

When Nora asked about the possibility of full-time work—feeling like she was putting all her fragile hopes in a basket and handing them to Violet—the response made her feel like there was a light at the end of the tunnel. Dimmer than she hoped for, but light nonetheless.

"If all goes well—if you can bring on authors with promise—we probably would be interested in extending an offer for full-time work after a reasonable period of time," Violet had said. "Usually six months or so. But if you were to join us full-time, it would be under a different title that matched your experience. Acquisitions editor is just a blanket term we use for our editorial freelancers. With your experience..." Violet looked down at Nora's résumé. "Editorial coordinator would be your next step here. There's some of that administrative work still, but we'd work with you on starting to take ownership of a couple of books to get you going down that editor path."

Even now, replaying the interview in her mind, Nora felt a wrinkle of injustice at that. She had ownership in spades after taking on the brunt of Tom and Lynn's forgotten titles, but no matter how she tried to convey that on her résumé, her title said more than the bullet points underneath it ever could.

But it was what Violet said next, in response to Nora's question about what books she could expect to work on in this hypothetical full-time position, that sent hope fluttering in her chest.

"Whatever interests you, really," Violet had said with a shrug. "You'd be working with Lynn primarily. If you wanted to continue on with business, like what you're currently working on, that's fine." (Nora had nearly shuddered at this.) "If you wanted to branch out into something else, like politics, food, fiction, that would be fine too."

Editorial coordinator was just a toe away from editorial assistant, but the chance to work on fiction—with Lynn—tapped at that dormant desire she'd long abandoned.

The rest of the interview was standard, if Nora ignored her shaking hands and the slimy feeling it gave her to lie about no longer working for Parsons. A few days later, Nora got a text from Lynn. They're talking about sending you an offer on Monday. Act surprised...

After a weekend spent stalking the Weber website and practicing her surprised voice, the day was here at last. All they had to do was hold up their end of the bargain and call. Nora stared intently at her phone, as if she could will it to obey her wishes. Moments later, it buzzed. Heart leaping, she picked it up to see a notification to download an update. She sighed and dismissed it. If her phone didn't give her what she wanted, she certainly wasn't going to do what it asked.

She knew, on some level, that bargaining with phones was not how people got jobs. But it couldn't hurt.

Hours into the silent standoff between Nora and her phone, she got a visit from Candace.

Nora's first thought was that Candace knew what she'd done—which would explain why her phone wasn't ringing. Lynn had figured out Nora's lie, called Candace to inform her, and Nora was going to lose this job, her shot at working on fiction, and her ability to pay rent all in an instant.

And then Candace smiled at her gingerly. Relief and wariness flooded through Nora. This had to be about something else. Apologetic smiles from publishers were always accompanied by unreasonable requests.

"I got an email from Henry Brook. In marketing?"

"Marketing?" Nora repeated. There was one marketing manager left on their team, and her name wasn't Henry Brook.

Candace tried again. "In New York?"

"Oh." It was Candace's fault for assuming anyone below the level of publisher was on even a first-and-last name basis with anyone in the New York office. But Nora tried to look contrite anyway, for Candace's sake. "Yes," Nora said. "New York."

"Since Greg Miller retired, Henry's been assigned to our line," Candace explained in a way that explained nothing.

"Right."

Candace brightened, pleased that Nora remembered the impossible. "Henry needs some information to help him get up to speed on our team. He has a spreadsheet of titles he needs the tip sheets for. Would you mind getting those for him?"

Henry Brook existed for one minute, and already he was sinking in Nora's estimation. He couldn't press a few buttons to download some tip sheets? He was so important that he needed someone to download them for him?

As she thought about this, her gaze settled on Candace, standing there, patiently awaiting Nora's response. Nora supposed the same line of thought could apply to Candace, who was also capable of downloading tip sheets. Everyone at Parsons had access to their database that housed tip sheets for every book they published, containing basic information like description copy, author bios, competing titles, and sales potential. But Candace was busy trying to keep their team afloat, and anyway, Candace brought everyone biscotti and Linzer cookies from the Italian bakery whenever she had an appointment on Columbus Avenue. Candace got a pass. Henry did nothing to earn her favors.

But Candace was asking, and it was Nora's job as the lowest-ranking (and lowest-paid, mustn't forget lowest-paid) person on the team to do what no one else wanted to.

"Sure," Nora said, giving a friendly grimace in surrender. Candace darted off to forward the email to Nora. Left alone again, Nora wondered if she had the fortitude to take on the Weber job. The work was one thing, but the sustained lie was quite another. She was jumpy already, and she didn't even have the job yet. What would happen if she got it? She couldn't spend six months jumping out of her seat every time Candace or Rita wanted to talk to her.

The email Candace forwarded popped into her inbox a few moments later.

Candice,

Can someone on your team get me tip sheets for the attached titles. thx, H

The lack of a greeting. The misspelled name. The period where a question mark should be. The uncapitalized, abbreviated thanks. The initial in lieu of a name. Nora hated him.

Then, opening the spreadsheet and scrolling down to the seventy-eight titles he wanted her to download individual tip sheets for: she wanted him dead.

Suddenly six months of jumpiness didn't seem so bad. Nora checked her phone again, just in case she'd missed a call while Candace was talking (she hadn't).

Nora began downloading the tip sheets, eyes flicking back to her phone every few minutes. She was less than ten tip sheets in when, suddenly, miraculously, her phone lit up.

Nora ducked into a phone room to take the call. She pretended to be surprised when Violet offered her the freelance acquisitions editor position. Nora promised to send her the completed paperwork by the next day.

She felt different when she emerged from the phone room, head held high. Confident. For nearly five years, she'd been Nora Hughes, Editorial Assistant, and now, finally, she was something else. And there was potential for so much more. All she had to do was balance her Weber and Parsons jobs for six months. Show the Weber team she could do what they asked of her, help writers meet deadlines and bring on new authors. Make sure no one at Parsons found out about her second job. Hang on long enough for Weber to offer her the editorial coordinator position, and then she'd be free. Free of buzzwords. Free to work on fiction. Free to believe there was a dream job for her after all.

And if she had to lie to get it, that hardly seemed relevant.

CHAPTER EIGHT

It was strange to think that, as Nora clicked her way through Parsons's finicky payment system, it was her first day of work somewhere else. Her lie had officially begun.

Ordinarily, she hated processing invoices, another task inherited after the layoffs. But everything was different now. She wasn't even annoyed when the system identified a nonexistent error in the invoice she uploaded. She re-uploaded it without a sigh. Knowing she had a purpose beyond dull admin work was doing wonders for her self-esteem.

She sipped her coffee and kept an eye on the time, feeling more jittery the closer it got to eleven o'clock, when she'd have to call in to Weber's weekly editorial meeting. She made it as far as half past ten before she picked up her laptop and disappeared into a phone room around the corner.

Even in the quiet of the small room, her knee jiggled under the table. Was it first-day nerves, even though it wasn't a real first day? The morning of her first day at Parsons, she couldn't even finish her toast, nervous as she was to make a good impression. She supposed it was the same this time—wanting to prove herself as an acquisitions editor, impress Lynn and Violet, secure the coordinator position.

It couldn't be the lie. Parsons more than deserved it. Last week, she got her first paycheck since the pay cut, and seeing the smaller number in her bank account only made her more confident in her decision. Parsons did what it had to do to stay afloat. So did she.

At a minute to eleven, she picked up the phone and typed in the number for the conference call. A small beep ushered her into silence.

"Hello?" she tried.

"Hi, who do we have?" asked a high-pitched voice. Nora scanned through her mental list of Weber employees, curated via a lengthy LinkedIn stalking session, to try to match a prospective face with the voice in her ear.

"This is Nora."

"Hi, Nora!" the voice chirped. "We're still settling in. We've got Violet, Lynn, and Jeremy here so far, and we're waiting on the others before we get started."

After a few minutes of murmured greetings and small talk Nora didn't fully pick up on, the mystery voice called the meeting to start.

"First I want to welcome our new acquisitions editor, Nora Hughes," said a voice Nora assumed was Violet. Then, at Violet(?)'s request, everyone went around the room, introducing themselves. The mystery voice turned out to be Emily, Violet's assistant, but Nora lost track of everyone else as the disembodied introductions piled up.

A male voice, meaning it had to be either Jeremy or Steven, said he was in talks with an author who was submitting a proposal for next week's pitch meeting. Lynn gave an update on an author whose marketing plan was far more robust than Weber's, making Violet-Stacy-Donna-or-Janine chuckle and say she wished all authors were as proactive about marketing their books. Finally, someone who was probably Violet spoke Nora's name into the phone.

"Yes?" Nora said.

"The first project we're sending you is a bit of a beast," probably-Violet said, laughing. "The author is—how late is she?"

"Two years," Lynn chimed in.

"Two years," echoed probably-Violet. "She finally sent her manuscript last week, and it's not what she told us it would be. We'd love if you could look at it and work with her on revisions."

Nora hesitated, just to make double sure that Violet wasn't talking to someone else. It would make sense for a task this important and editorly to go to an actual editor—someone who wasn't Nora. But the silence wore on, confirming, once and for all, that Nora was an editor.

"Sure," she said, chest ballooning. "Just send me what you've got, and I'll take a look. When were you planning on this one going to production?"

Emily sent her the publication schedule less than a minute later. The rest of the meeting continued on, unidentifiable voices talking about the status of upcoming books.

As the call drew to a close, probably-Violet said, "Don't forget about next fall." She had to speak up to be heard over the end-meeting chatter.

Nora listened intently, waiting for the news about next fall, but the only sounds were the rustles of paper and mumbled side conversations. She hesitated, debating whether to ask. Then her resolve kicked in—an editorial assistant might stay quiet, but an editor would ask. And she was an editor, damn it.

"What was that about next fall?" Nora asked.

"The business line is a few books short of its target for next year," probably-Violet said. "It'll be on the agenda for every meeting until we can fill the gap. If you have any ideas, just reach out."

"Okay." It would take some getting used to, this concept of people asking for her ideas. "I'll let you know."

When the call ended, Nora scrolled through Weber's publication schedule, spotting several of Lynn's authors who had published with Parsons. Evidently, Lynn had used her connections with these authors to bring them on to Weber. It was smart. They'd probably jump at the opportunity to publish with a growing upstart like Weber, a company more amenable to publishing books that didn't rehash the same ten topics Parsons published over and over again.

And if Violet needed more business authors to fill their list… and if Nora had connections with Parsons authors Lynn hadn't worked with…

Nora pulled out Parsons's latest publication schedule and looked for the authors with Tom's name in the editor column. Tom, with no plans to return to the working world, too busy waiting for his asparagus to grow, wouldn't be calling these authors any time soon.

Parsons cycled through their authors repetitively. If an author published a book with Parsons and it sold moderately well (and sometimes not even that), their future projects were nearly always green-lit. A known author with a book to their name was far less of a risk than one without. And here was a list of known authors—authors with promise, Violet would call them. And then Lynn and Violet would lavish praise on Nora for finding projects so quickly, authors with an established track record who could help Weber fill out their business line. She'd be sure to get the coordinator job then.

Her gaze fell on Andrew Santos's name. He was an author with promise, alright. But he was already destined for Parsons, contract drawn up and awaiting his signature.

But suppose the other authors were up for grabs? She counted at least five of Tom's authors whose books were due to publish in the next few months and didn't have anything else planned. *They* might be interested in Weber.

Nora uncapped her pen, hovered it over their names to—what, exactly? Make note of authors to steal from a company she was still working at? At least Lynn was out of Parsons when she worked her connections. If Nora managed to convince some of Parsons's authors to sign with Weber, she alone would have to deal with the repercussions. Rita and Candace, confused. Asking questions. Uncovering her lies.

She gnawed on the cap of her pen, mentally chastising herself. She'd already broken a major boundary by taking on the Weber job. Anything more was reckless. And Nora wasn't desperate enough to stoop to recklessness. She hoped she wasn't, anyway.

———

Nora was surprised at how little her new job impacted her daily life at Parsons. Sitting in her weekly check-in with Rita, nothing felt unusual. She spent every meeting pretending to care about Parsons's books anyway. Now she would just also pretend she didn't have a secret second job.

"You're all set for CEF next week, right?" Rita asked. "It's the same time I'll be at LSS."

Nora took a moment to parse through the alphabet soup. She would be going to the Capital Excellence Forum, a management conference in Maryland. Rita would be going to the Leadership and Strategy Summit. They'd discussed this a while back, she remembered.

"Yes," Nora said. She'd booked the flight months ago without a second thought, aside from the usual conference dread of manning the Parsons booth alone. Now, though, panic swirled in her stomach as she considered what could happen if Weber attended the conference. She didn't think they would, but she felt an urgent need to confirm this. A few innocent questions about why she was behind the Parsons booth, a stumbled word or a misremembered lie, and it could all unravel.

"Santos will be there," Rita said. "He hasn't signed the contract yet, has he?"

No, he hadn't. Which was strange. Nora sent him a follow-up email the week before, and he replied that he was *still thinking it over*, something that made her sit back in her seat and frown suspiciously. Authors were usually eager to sign contracts. Some might have a lawyer review it first, but they usually said so. Santos's silence had to mean something else was going on.

He might be looking to move to another publisher. Perhaps a publisher with a wider reach, whose books were marketed to a demographic outside of aging businessmen. It occurred to Nora that, if he was looking, Weber might be a good fit for him. Their authors skewed younger, their books more relevant to people who weren't in the C-suite. Not to mention how overjoyed Lynn and Violet would be if Nora signed him to Weber. It would go a long way toward earning her that coordinator job.

Rita closed her laptop with an air of finality. "There's one last thing I want to discuss."

How quickly Nora's mind jumped to conclusions about Rita somehow knowing about Weber. Heart thundering in her ears, she assumed an inquisitive expression and met Rita's gaze.

"I've been working on a promotion for you for a while," Rita said. "I put in for one at the end of this last fiscal year, and New York said no."

Nora blinked. "Oh." Maybe Rita had worked at Parsons for too long—read one too many DIC(k) announcements—and could no longer judge what qualified as newsworthy. "I appreciate that you tried."

"But," Rita said, lifting a finger, "I got them to agree that if we sign Santos, you get promoted to assistant editor. It would come with a pay bump too. Even after the salary cut, you should come out ahead of where you were before."

Nora's gaze drifted around the room as the news sank in. She settled her stare, still blinking, on Rita. "Really?" More surprising than a possible promotion was the notion that even after her old team was gone, someone was still looking out for her.

"Of course. You deserve it," Rita said. "I'm sorry it's conditional like this. It was the only way I could get them to agree."

"I understand." Nora had read enough DIC(k) propaganda to know Parsons's practices going forward were steeped in caution. "Thank you," she said, surprise still touching her voice.

Rita squeezed her shoulder on her way out. Nora stayed where she was. A month ago, this would have been a godsend—the answer to her problems handed to her on a platter. But now it just complicated things, had her tracing a box around Andrew's name in lines so thick it smeared ink on her hand and filled her nostrils with a chemical smell.

The practical side of her said this was all she needed. She could hold onto the Weber job to keep the money coming until she signed Andrew to Parsons, and then she could drop the second job, enjoy her new title and pay bump, and stay at Parsons. No more secrecy. No more jumping out of her seat every time a superior wanted to have a word with her.

But did she want to stay at Parsons? Was the promotion enough to justify working on books she despised? It might have been, a few weeks ago. But with a job in fiction within reach, the thought of killing that dream felt like a mistake.

If she were really serious about following that dream, she could go all in. Sign Andrew to Weber. Turn a blind eye to any fuss Parsons raised over it. Stick it out until the coordinator job was available, and then she'd be free to work at Weber full-time. If she could handle six months of jumpiness.

Nora wrote a question mark next to Andrew's name. She would need an answer for it by the time she saw him at the conference.

CHAPTER NINE

One day, Nora hoped, she would associate Baltimore with something other than this hotel ballroom. She was sure Baltimore had plenty to offer the world, but all she knew of it for four years running now was the same Hilton on the same dreary square mile of land.

She yawned and started toward the shipping center at the end of the room, where a mountain of boxes awaited her. As she lugged the boxes one by one to the Parsons booth, her mind went back to the question she'd been asking herself for the last few days.

Nora had thought about it on the plane, in the Uber, while counting cracks in the ceiling in her hotel room. Santos was her ticket to a promotion. At Parsons, the promotion was a certainty. It would happen while the ink on his signature was still wet. With it came a title she deserved, retroactive credit for all the work she'd done.

At Weber, it was murkier. A full-time position could happen if all went well after six months or longer, and the position would be administrative. But its appeal was stronger: working with Lynn. Working on fiction.

That old saying came to her, about a bird in the hand worth two in the bush. But that presumed she could get the bird to agree to anything. Santos was still radio silent on his contract. If he was a bird, he was soaring with abandon, definitely not in her hand, certainly not in her—well, he was hard to pin down, was the point.

Thankfully, no one from Weber was here. She'd checked as soon as she could, scouring the conference website for a mention of them. But the website confirmed what Nora knew: Weber attended only large industry events. At this small conference that Parsons insisted on attending every year, Nora was safe.

Once she carried all twenty-one boxes of books to the Parsons booth, Nora began setting up. She pulled out copy after copy of Andrew's book, sighing at the extra work he was causing her. Keynote speakers' books were always in high demand.

If Beth were here, she would have made a big deal over this. Beth got silly if left at the booth for too long. She liked to print bookmarks on card stock for conferences, and when she got bored, she'd write notes on them and place them in the books. Simple facts directly related to the conference, like *Session Speaker* or *Award Winner,* all the way up to statements that made no sense, like *Two Thumbs Up!* When Nora asked her once whose thumbs, exactly, were up in this scenario, Beth just shrugged and said, "I've got thumbs."

Nora examined the stack of bookmarks she'd brought, Beth's handiwork from a couple of years ago. *Buy Now for 25% Off!* was printed in bold black letters at the top of each one.

She may as well make Andrew Santos's book easier to find. She grabbed a Sharpie and flipped the bookmark over. On its blank side she wrote *Keynote Speaker!!* She asked herself what

Beth would do and added an exclamation point. Then she considered the author in question and added another. She plunked the bookmark in the middle of Andrew's book.

Nora took a picture of it and texted it to Beth. Proud? she wrote.

She knew Beth wouldn't reply for a while, as it was still the crack of dawn in California, but here in Baltimore the keynote was due to end in a few minutes. Nora settled into place behind the Parsons booth.

A door hinge groaned. Nora looked up to see a middle-aged woman in a red scarf leaving the keynote session and heading toward her.

"Do you have that book by—" The woman stopped when she saw it. Nora had put the book front and center, the most obvious place she could think of, with the *Keynote Speaker!!* bookmark sticking straight out of it.

While Nora scanned the book, the door opened long enough for Andrew's voice to waft through. He was thanking the crowd for coming. The end was near.

A Black man with graying hair and a Black woman with tortoiseshell glasses came to the booth. They picked up the Santos book and murmured about shipping.

"We offer free shipping," Nora volunteered in a cheery voice. This was her conference personality. And, as it was like spending the day with a very extroverted friend, it was exhausting.

The pair perked up at that and bought a few copies. While Nora confirmed their shipping address, the door hinge sounded again, one long creak followed by a slam. Soon the room filled with overlapping voices, all speaking at a murmur that grew louder as more people filed out. They milled at separate booths at first, but they soon came to a simultaneous unspoken under-standing that Nora's booth was the one they needed.

"I'm looking for a book about communication skills," said a man in a pink cardigan.

"Was it Andrew Santos's book?" she asked. "We have it right here."

As he picked it up, a woman piped up behind him. "Can I buy my book now and wait for the signing?"

Nora peered around the man. "What signing?" she asked the unseen space behind him.

A small woman with curly brown hair stepped toward Nora with the easy confidence of someone who knows they are right. "Andrew Santos said he'd stop by the booth after the keynote to sign a few copies."

Nora stared back at her. "There isn't a signing scheduled."

"Oh, it shouldn't be too much fuss."

Thank goodness for this woman's clairvoyance.

It seemed everyone had the same idea. After Nora processed their orders, they lingered around the booth, waiting for Andrew. As the awkward minutes ticked past, Nora considered the ethics of forging signatures at unplanned book signings. She wasn't above ducking under the booth with a pen and "finding" signed copies if it meant the crowd would disperse and leave her alone.

"Sorry I'm late! I got held up after the speech. Hey, it's the avocado killer!"

Nora looked up to find him standing next to her. In his navy suit, white button-down, and striped tie, he certainly looked the part of a keynote speaker. But his boyish grin never left him. Nora smiled back, or she tried to. She had to get into conference friendly-with-authors mode, but she wasn't sure how to transition to that from why-the-impromptu-book-signing mode.

"Hi," she said. It was a sort of compromise between the two. "It's good to see you."

"Great keynote," the curly-haired woman said, beaming up at him.

Andrew turned, a polite smile coming over him. "Thank you. Can I sign your book?"

"Please!"

They looked at Nora, as if she had anything to do with this. She blinked.

Andrew's expectant stare fell into realization. "I'm so sorry," he said, shaking his head. Turning to the woman, he explained, "This wasn't a planned signing. She had no idea. It was just something that came out of my mouth when I was onstage."

The woman laughed, pleased to have been let in on the secret. Andrew turned back to Nora. "A few minutes and we'll be on our way," he said. "Is that okay?" His pleading eyes wore her down.

"You'll need a chair, because there's only one back here." *And I am not standing up for you* was the unspoken rest of that sentence, but he was polite enough not to acknowledge that.

"A chair! I can get a chair." As the booth-millers watched in amusement, Andrew strode to the booth next to hers and exchanged a few words with the man there. "I have a chair!" He set down the newly acquired chair next to Nora. "Now what?"

"I…" She shrugged, knowing it was futile to point out that she'd never done a signing before either. "Pen or Sharpie?"

"Pen or Sharpie?" Andrew asked the booth-millers.

"Sharpie!" the woman exclaimed.

"Sharpie!" he said. "You're bold. I like it."

Nora handed him the Sharpie and the others formed a line. While Andrew made casual conversation as he signed, Nora dealt with a second wave of people who'd noticed the commotion and thought now might be a nice time to add to the chaos.

While processing an order for a man who wasn't part of the keynote flock, Nora noticed him peering at the Santos book in everyone else's hands.

"Is your book any good?" the man asked.

"She seems to think so," Andrew said. "They're the ones who published it." He nudged Nora's arm with his own, an unexpected touch she didn't mind.

"Oh, I definitely didn't read it," she said.

Andrew and the man both laughed. "Really?" Andrew asked. The start of a smile crossed his face, but his eyes lingered on her, like he couldn't fully react until he knew whether she was joking. She shrugged and returned to processing the order.

"First the avocado, and now this," he said.

"Oh, you're fine."

The rest of the booth-millers got their signatures, and the exhibit hall began to quiet down. The first round of sessions would be starting, giving Nora a temporary break from the crowds. She watched the last person in line—a man who bought five copies to give his employees, prompting Andrew to ask for their names so he could personalize each signature—amble off with the stack of books cradled in his arms. Nora became very aware that she was alone with an author. This was new. Very new.

Andrew rolled the marker to her side of the table. "Your Sharpie."

Nora hesitated, not sure what mode to respond with. She decided on no mode. "I was starting to worry you wouldn't come," she confided. She cast a glance at him while picking up the Sharpie. "I was five minutes away from forging your signature."

Andrew's expression was unreadable when he eyed her and said, "I'm not sure you should be telling me that."

She froze, self-consciousness swarming her as she thought of a way to backtrack. Ten minutes behind the booth didn't make them friends. "I didn't really—"

"Everyone knows the first rule of forgery is secrecy," he said, amusement flickering in his eyes.

A small smile overtook her. "My forgery textbook failed to mention that. Then again, it might be a fake."

Andrew laughed. "Well, I'm glad you didn't have to resort to forgery. Thanks for doing this, and I'm sorry for springing it on you. I was hoping they'd forget I said it. I hope it wasn't too much trouble."

Back into conference mode she went. "That's okay," she chirped. "You obviously compelled them to buy copies of the book. We like that." Her *we* didn't include herself, but that wasn't important.

His gaze remained on her, as if trying to decipher something. "Any time," he said. "Well, I've got to run." He stood and gripped the back of his borrowed chair. "Are you attending any sessions?"

His innocent question left a tiny sting. It was generous of him to imply she had a choice.

"No, I thought I'd watch the books and make sure no one steals them."

He gave a surprised laugh. "You are the rudest Parsons representative I have ever met."

Nora paused, uncertain. This was far from conference mode. Something about Andrew had her slipping into her natural sarcasm, but maybe she actually had misjudged this time and gotten too comfortable. He was still an author.

But, casting a glance and meeting his stare, noting his eyes were curious but animated, she realized he was enjoying it. "Too much?" she asked.

He shrugged. "I didn't say that."

Nora, feeling her cheeks grow warm, fought back a smile.

He was first to look away, glancing down at the books displayed on the table and then at her. "So you can't leave the booth?"

"I can for a quick break, but the whole reason I'm here is to sell books, so." She gestured an arm out to the unsold books displayed before them.

"Wow, okay." His tone was almost reverent. "I appreciate your commitment to the cause." He saluted her and walked off with the chair.

Commitment was the last thing Nora would have called it, but as she watched him return the chair and walk away, she had to admit that if she truly didn't care, she wouldn't have set up the booth in time for the keynote, and she certainly wouldn't have allowed the improvised signing. It was annoying to still care.

The morning dragged on, as it usually did at conferences. Nora got a brief diversion mid-morning when her phone buzzed with Beth's reply.

The proudest!

Another text followed:

Kinda jealous you get to see daddy Santos.

Nora's mouth twisted in mortification as the memory ambushed her. At a conference in Phoenix, passing time at the Parsons booth and counting down the minutes until dinner, she and Beth played Fuck, Marry, Kill: Author Edition. Nora remembered Santos's name coming up, back when he was just a name on a book and a headshot on Parsons's website. While other authors blended together in Nora's mind, often some combination of pallid, wrinkled, smug, or all of the above, Santos was different. It wasn't just his youth. He looked at the camera with playful eyes, like he'd either just told a joke or was about to regale his unsuspecting audience with one. With his slightly tousled hair and dark-brown eyes, it was an easy decision. They'd both filed him under *fuck*.

She had completely buried the memory in her brain. Now, she'd never be able to look him in the eye again. Worse, she realized that—if she were truly being honest—her answer was still the same. Even after the hassle of the impromptu signing, all she could think of was his confidence, the spark in his eye, how easy he made it for her to shed the conference persona and become herself.

Maybe he was a hypnotist.

During a lull, as someone stood at Nora's booth contemplating a book, Nora watched the Friedman Books booth. A young Black woman about Nora's age was rearranging books. Nora had seen her at several conferences before. She had company at other conferences but, like Nora, she was always alone at this one. Nora watched the way the woman's hair—long, chunky braids that reached her waist—swayed when she leaned forward to position a book stand.

Was this the fourth year running that Nora sat here at the booth across from Friedman Books Woman without saying a word to her? They'd never spoken to one another. Never even waved across the hall. The closest they'd come was once, last year, when a man came to Nora's booth while holding a Friedman

Books paperback he hadn't paid for. The woman came running to the Parsons booth and politely explained to the man that he had her book. Nora had smiled tentatively at her then, wanting to give some kind of signal that she, too, understood the struggles of babysitting books. But the woman was too distracted to notice.

Always, as Nora sat alone at her booth, watching the woman sit alone at hers, she thought about talking to her, befriending her. They could form some kind of partnership where Nora kept an eye on their booths when the woman went to the bathroom and vice versa. And once they got to talking, as they inevitably did in Nora's fantasies, they could talk about the obvious fact that they were both Black women in publishing, and wasn't that interesting? Wasn't publishing so incredibly white? Did she also find it strange when publishers took pains to depict people of all races on their book covers, even though the authors who wrote these books were almost always white? Had she ever managed to call anyone out on it, or did she also feel too low-ranking and awkward to bring it up?

And then maybe the woman could give her tips on how to do her hair, because neither Nora nor her white mother could fully understand Black hair.

Nora watched her straighten a corner of the tablecloth under the books with such care that it put Nora's slapdash booth setup to shame. If she could just make herself talk to this person, this Other Nora, maybe she would learn the secret to being happy in a job. In life.

The day passed slowly, and the end of the last session brought on the evening's grand finale: a long line at the Parsons booth. While scanning a book, Nora checked her phone for the time: thirty-five minutes until exhibit hours were over.

Wiggling subtly in her chair as she took orders and chatted with customers, she reminded herself there were just thirty-five minutes to go. Her bladder could last thirty-five minutes.

At the twenty-five-minute mark, Nora wasn't sure. There were still too many people hanging around the booth, thumbing through books. Lingering had never been so offensive.

It was then, as she was wiggling more frantically than before, willing someone to buy a book just to give her something to do, that she heard the voice she was quickly learning to recognize. She remembered Beth's text and fought the temptation to dive under the booth.

"It's at the Parsons booth, actually." Andrew walked toward her with a tall, blond man following closely behind. "Nora, this is Carl from Lund University. He wants to take a suitcase of books back with him to Sweden. Especially my book."

Carl laughed, and Nora thought she saw his cheeks redden. People needed to stop being charmed by Andrew. It just resulted in inconveniences for her.

Andrew turned toward her, looking sheepish. "He's also heard something about signed copies floating around…"

"Right," Nora said, nodding quickly. "Sure. The only thing is just—"

"Oh, are you closing down?"

"Not for another twenty minutes, but I was just gonna…" She couldn't bring herself to say *piss like a racehorse*, nor the more acceptable *use the restroom*, so she just trailed off and let the sentence die quietly.

Thankfully, Andrew could manage social situations with ease. "If you need to step away for a minute, I can watch the booth."

She fought the urge to accept it and run. "But you don't know how to use the system."

He shrugged, a playful look in his eye. "I'll just stall them. Go ahead."

That was all the encouragement she needed. When she returned a few minutes later, more grateful to Andrew than she'd ever admit, she could have laughed at the sight of him hunched over in her chair, frowning at the sales computer. He stroked his bottom lip with the knuckle of his thumb as he stared.

"Thanks for keeping things in order," she said.

He looked up, then returned to the computer. "The good news is Carl bought four hundred dollars' worth of books."

Nora laughed. "You said you were just gonna stall."

"Yeah, but the system seemed intuitive enough. I thought I'd give it a try."

"All right."

"But I don't think his credit card went through," he admitted, giving her a worried glance. "I wanted to pull up the order, but I don't know how."

Nora pressed her lips together to keep from smiling. "Not so intuitive now, huh?"

"I'm so sorry," he said. "I can cover the cost."

"I don't think I need you dipping into your royalties to bail us out. Let me see."

He chuckled but looked down at the mention of royalties, a modesty Nora couldn't fathom. However much money he made off his books, Parsons made far more. The difference was none of Parsons's share ever trickled its way down to her.

Andrew stood behind her as she pulled up the record of past

orders, Carl Samuelsson at the top of the list. As she was about to click on it, Andrew's finger poked the name.

"There's the order."

"Yeah, I got that," she said.

"Just making sure."

She clicked on the order and reviewed the screen. "Okay, so—bad news." She turned to Andrew, who awaited her response with alarm in his eyes. "The payment information did not go through."

His face fell. "I'm so sorry."

"Good news," Nora continued, enjoying the way he perked up at this, "our customer care team will call him after the conference to get his payment information. It's totally fine."

He gave a sigh of relief. "Thank god. You're sure?"

She couldn't stop herself from smiling at this image of him, eyes concerned, lips slightly parted as he awaited her answer. "I'm sure. Thanks again for taking over."

"Are you still open?"

Nora turned, meeting the inquisitive brown eyes of a woman holding a stack of books. "We are for a few more minutes. Did you want to buy those, or are you still browsing?"

"I think I'm ready to buy now."

Maybe it was the extreme relief of not peeing herself, or maybe Andrew amused her, but Nora turned and asked him, "Do you want to redeem yourself?"

He brightened. She let him take the chair and stood next to him.

"Okay. First, I'm going to take your information," he said in a questioning tone. Next to him, Nora nodded. She watched him type out the woman's name and address. He was a hunt-and-peck typist. She could have pushed him aside and typed it out in half the time with her eyes closed, but then she wouldn't get to watch his finger hover over the keyboard, alternating between hesitation and decisiveness as he searched for and plunked down on each letter he wanted. Well, at least there wasn't a line at the booth.

"Did you want to take these books with you, or have them shipped for free?" Nora asked the woman. When she chose to have them shipped, Nora bent over the computer. Hovering over him as she showed him where to mark the box for shipping, she caught a whiff of his shampoo, something clean and musky that made her straighten right back up because editorial assistants did not smell authors' hair.

"I would have gotten to that if I'd known there was shipping," he said.

"I have no proof of that."

He shot Nora a reproachful look and she hid a smile.

"Okay," Andrew said once he reached the next screen, "that'll be…$56.73. Really, for two books?" He turned back to Nora.

The woman also looked at Nora, like she wasn't sure if she should be suspicious.

"Yeah, that includes the conference discount. You saved twelve dollars," she told her. "Nineteen if you count shipping."

Reassured, the woman nodded and handed over her credit card. Andrew hesitated, then took it. He glanced back at Nora, who kept her face expressionless. He took a breath before running the card through the card reader. It beeped once and the payment information materialized on the screen.

"Oh, *now* it works," he said.

"It tends to work when you do it right."

"All I'm hearing is I did it right."

Nora laughed. She stepped back to let him finish processing the order on his own. He was almost beaming as he bid the woman a good evening.

"I'd call that a success," he said as they watched her walk away.

Nora leaned against the wall behind her, crossing her arms. "A little constructive criticism?" she offered.

He reluctantly turned to face her. "If you must."

"Next time, try not to act surprised by our prices."

"They seemed steep!"

"They have to be." Nora leaned toward him and added quietly, "I don't know if you know this, but some of our authors make bank because of these prices." At this, Andrew gave her a stern look. She lifted an eyebrow in return.

He stood and surveyed the room. Some attendees remained, mingling around the refreshment table, but their interest in books seemed to have died down.

"What happens now?" he asked.

She checked the time—five minutes to closing—and reached for a book stand. "I think I'm within bounds to start shutting down."

"Let me help."

Nora paused and looked up. "You want to help?"

Andrew nodded. When she didn't respond, he asked, "Is that okay?"

"Um." Nora scratched the nape of her neck, running her eyes over Andrew's expectant face as it sank in that an author was offering to help her. "Yeah," she said slowly. She shook herself out of her daze. "Yes, that's fine. It's harder to screw it up, at any rate." She smiled just enough to mask any remaining surprise.

He chuckled, but she couldn't tell if it was in response to her joke or her attempt at being aloof. "I appreciate the vote of confidence," he said.

Nora looked down and picked up a book, but she could still feel his eyes on her. She cleared her throat and moved on to showing him how to flatten the book stands and lay the books flat. They each took a side of the table and got to work. Nora glanced up just once to take in the image of Andrew flattening a book stand while simultaneously reading the back of the book next to it.

Eventually, they came to meet in the middle. Andrew picked up his book, propped in the center of the table, and pointed to the *Keynote Speaker!!* bookmark.

"Did you write that?" There was such pride and pleasure in his voice that Nora didn't want to burst his bubble and tell him she'd only done it because of Beth.

She shrugged and flattened a book stand. "Maybe."

When she reached for the next book, her arm brushed against his. She hesitated, apology at the ready, but he picked up another book like nothing happened. Nora relaxed and let the silent spark run through her. They finished flattening the books, neither acknowledging that their arms were still touching.

Next came covering the books. They each took two corners of a tablecloth and shook it out over the booth like they were making a bed. After he lowered his side, he gestured to it with a look of satisfaction.

"Not bad, huh?" he asked.

Nora pretended to survey his handiwork before glancing back at him with a serious expression. "You are definitely better at lowering tablecloths than you are at selling books."

He laughed. "Fair enough." His gaze shifted to the escalators, packed with people heading to the main floor. The exhibit area was emptying out as other booths closed down. "Is the restaurant here any good?"

It took her a moment to switch to that line of thought. "What, the hotel restaurant?" she asked. "For dinner?"

"Yeah."

Nora squinted at him, trying to understand.

"What?" he asked.

"I thought you'd have dinner plans or something."

He scratched his head and sighed. "I thought I might?"

"Why?"

"When I read that Parsons was coming, I thought it meant Rita would be here. I figured she'd take me to dinner and try to get me to sign the contract or something."

"And then you got me," Nora said, shaking her head in mock seriousness. "Bummer, huh?"

His eyes widened. "No, it's not like that. I'm glad no one's trying to convince me to sign."

"Right." She avoided his eyes and tried not to think about how she'd spent the last few days debating which publisher to convince him to sign with. "We could still do that, if you want," she said. "I mean, it's a free meal. On Parsons."

There it was, hanging in the air. She'd asked an author to dinner. If he accepted the invitation, she'd commend herself on her boldness, and if he rejected it, she'd tell him—and herself— that she'd been joking. She pretended to be interested in the escalators while she awaited his response.

"You won't try to make me sign the contract?"

Nora glanced at him, then returned her gaze to the escalators.

"I don't care what you do." She said it so coolly that she almost believed herself.

"I'm touched."

"I try."

She looked back at him. He was watching her with curious consideration, eyes slightly narrowed. "All right," he said. "Let's have dinner."

They rode the escalator in silence. Nora spent the ride staring straight ahead, trying to make sense of everything mingling together in her mind: Violet discussing the possibility of a full-time position if she brought on authors with promise. Rita's excitement when sharing the news about Nora's promotion if they signed Santos. And, swirling around these considerations, unprovoked and uninvited: the smell of Andrew's hair.

The question mark loomed larger as she followed him to the restaurant.

CHAPTER TEN

Sitting across from the author she'd invited to dinner, Nora hid behind the drink menu and thought about the author lunches she'd attended with Tom and Lynn. They ordered wine, appetizers, dessert—whatever authors wanted—and said it was all on Parsons. She knew they did this to make them feel pampered. Sitting there pretending to study the drink menu, though, she wasn't sure how to extend the same courtesy to Andrew.

"All right," she said, setting the drink menu down. "Your presence means this is an author meal, so we can order whatever we want. What do you want?"

He was still immersed in his menu. "These prices are ridiculous."

Nora almost laughed. "Oh, come on."

"What?" he asked.

"Well, so far I've learned our books are too expensive for you. Dinners in mediocre hotel restaurants are too expensive for you. What *is* in the price range of a bestselling author?"

His eyes gleamed over his menu. "There's a place near my apartment where I can get four tacos for ten dollars."

Nora cocked her head to the side, trying to make sense of this. "Not what I would have expected."

"I guess I never really let go of that grad school mindset. Trying to make a nine-month stipend last a year will do that to you." He gave an ironic smile. While he returned to his menu, Nora was left watching him, wanting more.

"How did you manage?" she asked.

Andrew shrugged. "Any way I could. I waited tables pretty much year-round, and during the school year, I'd tutor and grade papers for extra money. One summer, I tried secretly renting out my roommate's bedroom on Airbnb, since he spent most weekends at his girlfriend's anyway." He gave Nora a rueful grin, leaning in like he was telling a secret. "Not one of my better ideas."

Nora laughed, mostly out of surprise. It would take some time to adjust to the knowledge that Andrew Santos, king of royalties, once struggled with money too.

She was still thinking about it after they placed their orders. With no menu to hide behind, she voiced the question on her tongue.

"How did you know you wanted to go to grad school?"

His expression turned thoughtful. She got the sense this was something he hadn't been asked in a while. "I guess I knew it would help me in my career."

"You always knew what you wanted to do?"

Andrew shrugged and took a drink of water. "I think it became clear in my first job out of college. I realized interpersonal relationships between colleagues, or managers and employees, or executives and managers, are a crucial part of the workplace. People weren't communicating in the ways they needed to. I wanted to do something about that."

It sounded like an elevator pitch. Like something he might have said in that meeting at Parsons a few weeks back. He probably had, many times, maybe even during his keynote that morning. But there was a sincerity behind it. A certainty.

"But how do you know?"

His brow wrinkled. "What do you mean?"

"I don't know. I guess I don't know how people just...know... what they want to do with their lives."

He nodded, considering. "I take it you don't?" he asked.

Nora played with the cloth napkin in her lap and tried to think of the right way to phrase it. "I thought I did." Before Parsons promised her a world of books and then shut her behind a door labeled *Assistant*. Even after Rita's promotion news, it was hard to reconcile one glittery promise with the last five years of her life. It left her doubting the existence of dream jobs, wondering if even Weber and its allure of fiction wasn't what it seemed.

Now he looked the way she imagined she did anytime she brought up his royalties. Like he was about to raise a dangerous topic. "What changed?"

Thoughts of Tom, Lynn, and the rest of her old team swirled around her mind. Goodbye parties, email announcements, Parsons's DIC(k) that made sure the only person left standing was Nora, alone. Working on books she didn't understand or give a damn about, with authors who rearranged the same words on different pages year after year to make another royalty check. She met his eyes and he shot her a knowing look, like he was proving a point.

"And that's why I don't want to talk contracts," he said. "I think we both know what's going on over there."

She paused her fidgeting fingers. "What's that?"

"People talk," he said.

Nora eyed him, gauging what he knew. *How* he knew. "People?"

"Authors."

"Authors don't know," she said. But even as the words left her mouth, she couldn't help wondering what authors discussed when they talked about Parsons Press. She'd gotten a taste of it, the disgruntled emails they'd sent her after learning their editor was gone. She knew they were getting impatient, one year later and still more than half of her old team's authors without an editor. She just hadn't expected Andrew to be part of that group. Rita had taken over as his editor the day Tom and Lynn left, he had that rigamarole of a meeting last month, and Parsons hung on his every word—he had no obvious cause for complaint.

But if Nora wasn't the only one bulldozed by Parsons Press—if every author felt this way, even their most successful ones—it felt like validation that maybe she wasn't the problem. She bit the inside of her lip and waited for Andrew to respond. Reminded herself that no matter what he said, she wasn't there to commiserate with him.

Andrew settled back in his seat. "Authors know enough."

"So that's the reason you don't want to sign the contract?" she asked. "You think Parsons is flailing?" She eyed him closely as he fiddled with a button on his sleeve. This was what Rita wanted from her: figure out why Andrew was stalling and solve it. But did she want what Rita wanted? Did she know yet?

"Maybe."

She wasn't there to commiserate, she told herself again. This wasn't a rant session with Beth. This was dinner with an author who needed a publisher. A publisher that might not be Parsons.

Her mind turned to Lynn, how proud she would be if Andrew signed with Weber. But the thought made her squirm.

She studied Andrew, knew he was expecting a response.

"You haven't said no to the contract," Nora said, thinking aloud. "You haven't negotiated at all, which means you're waiting on another publisher. But you've only ever published with Parsons, so you don't know anyone else. I'd guess if you're this reluctant about Parsons, you only sent us your proposal because you knew the option clause from your last book said you had to. Now that you've fulfilled that obligation, I don't think you have a plan for who to approach next."

Andrew gave her a doubtful look, like he knew exactly who to approach next, thank you very much. She stared him down, waiting for him to contradict her. He didn't.

If she was right, and if he *was* looking for another publisher, that was a pro for Weber: Nora had another publisher in her back pocket.

Their food arrived. Nora leaned back as the waiter slid a pizza toward her. It sat on a square wooden board that did nothing to prevent the grease from spilling off the sides. Next to the board, the waiter placed a silver pizza cutter. She picked it up and stared at it. She noticed Andrew also eyeing it in confusion. His halibut was presented normally. On an actual plate.

Nora gave in and slid the cutter along the pizza. As she cut, she thought more about Andrew and Parsons.

"I'm sure keynoting would have gotten attention from other publishers here," she said, "except this is a small conference, and the only publishers that come are Parsons and Friedman. And even then, the editors don't come. It's just me and Other Me."

Andrew looked at her quizzically, but she picked up a slice of pizza and kept going, her mind filling in the pieces. "And that's why you were free for dinner tonight. You were leaving it open, in case an editor from Friedman wanted to talk to you."

He shrugged. "No comment."

Nora took a bite of pizza and used her cloth napkin to wipe the grease running down her hand. She couldn't stop the next bit from coming out. "There's nothing wrong with talking to other publishers. But I don't think anyone's listening."

"Ouch." Andrew twisted his face into an expression of mock hurt, but his eyes betrayed his interest. He was waiting, she noticed, to hear what she was going to say next.

"I just mean you probably don't have contacts there, so you've submitted a manuscript to the slush pile like everyone else. Those manuscripts will sit in an editorial assistant's inbox for at least a month before they even look at them. Then, because you've got an impressive record, they'll show it to their editor whenever they actually have time to look at proposals.

"That editor will review it and want to publish it. But it'll take another few weeks to get to the proposal stage, maybe a couple weeks of contract talk. So then you have two problems: you want to act fast because you're"—she flourished the pizza cutter in his direction while his eyebrow quirked—"I guess *big* right now, and you don't want the buzz to die down. But by then, Parsons will have withdrawn your contract." Nora was certain this wasn't a thing, not at Parsons. They wouldn't have the guts to withdraw contracts, least of all from an author they were desperate to sign. But if he didn't know that, it was a pro for Parsons: a ticking clock might be all the push he needed to sign.

He hadn't picked up his fork since she'd been talking. She

leaned in to say the next part. "How sure are you that this other publisher will offer a contract?"

He didn't speak for a moment, just sat there thinking, watching, not ready to throw in the towel. "I could get an agent."

"Okay." Nora shrugged. "If you think Parsons will wait a month or two, go for it. You might land an agent, and you might even land a deal at a bigger publisher. But then you'll be left wondering how small a fish you are in all those big ponds." A pro for Parsons as well as Weber, both smaller than the major publishing behemoths.

Watching him process her argument, another thought occurred to her. If she took him to Weber, they'd pass him off to Lynn. Andrew was a game changer, and they wouldn't want him working with a part-time freelance acquisitions editor.

If she signed him with Parsons, it would be different. She would be his assistant editor. She could have him for herself.

Another pro for Parsons.

Andrew was looking off to some distant place behind her, like he was doing mental math that didn't add up. "What's wrong with weighing my options? Is it a crime to want my book to do well?"

This was her moment to tell him what to do. She took a sip of water, eyes roaming everywhere but Andrew as she ran through her options. If she dragged out the tired Parsons argument to convince him to sign, it might not have much of an impact on an author who was already looking elsewhere. But coming forward with Weber was a major risk. She'd have to admit her ties to Weber and trust him with her secret—a career-ruining secret. Her stomach clenched at the thought of what could go wrong.

Parsons was safer.

Her gaze shifted to Andrew. "There's nothing wrong with wanting your book to do well," she said. "But...we want that too." They were a *we*, she and Parsons. Tonight they were, just long enough to gauge how much she could push him toward Parsons. She could always divert his attention to Weber if he couldn't be convinced.

"We want your book to do well too," Nora continued. "And I'm telling you, you won't find terms better than ours." Before he could open his mouth, she added, "I mean, yes, if you sign with one of the really big publishers you will, but you'd need an agent for that. And agents take time."

Now he was shaking his head. "I don't care. You guys laid off Tom."

"You think I'm not mad about that?"

His expression softened. "In general," he said, "layoffs suggest a business is in trouble."

That PhD was really working wonders for him.

"Or that they're streamlining," Nora said. She was practically quoting from the CEO's emails now. "In the last year, Parsons has taken steps to start focusing on a few big projects instead of a bunch of little ones." This was definitely plagiarized from everything anyone with an executive tilt at Parsons had ever said, thought, or breathed.

But this wasn't: "You would be a big project."

Andrew nodded slowly, taking it in. "What does that mean?"

"We've already offered you our max on royalties, which is more than you're getting now. We're publishing fewer books a year so we can market them all aggressively. We actually added someone to our team recently." She chose to leave out that the *someone* in question was a twenty-two-year-old editorial assistant.

"And I don't mean you," Nora added, shooting him a pointed look. "Your book-selling skills are questionable at best."

He laughed. "I have to say, I do like that you're not as, uh, polite to me as everyone else at Parsons is. That meeting the other week would have been a lot more fun if you were there."

Nora shrugged. "Someone had to deliver your death sandwich."

Another laugh boomed out of him. "I could never forget my attempted assassination." He picked up his fork and speared an asparagus stalk. "All right, I'll think it over."

"Do what you want. I wouldn't want to talk contracts or anything." She gave an exaggerated shrug, and he smiled at her over his glass of water.

"And you said you're not sure about working in publishing? That doesn't compute with what I'm seeing."

Nora shrugged again and ran a finger along the edge of the pizza cutter. She did feel powerful talking to him like this and being taken seriously. But that didn't happen very often, considering all the author meetings she wasn't invited to.

"But if you are uncertain," Andrew said, looking at her thoughtfully, "I think that's okay. I love my job, but it's not something I always planned on becoming."

"What did you want to be?" Nora asked.

"Truthfully? I wanted to work at one of those ice cream shops where they sing when you tip them."

Something swelled in Nora at the thought of Andrew scooping ice cream and bursting into song. It was a fitting aspiration, based on what she'd seen of him thus far. He was good at captivating an audience. Just not through song, apparently.

"So what happened?" She rested her arms on the table and leaned forward.

"My sister told me no one wants to tip someone who can't sing. I know," he said when Nora solemnly shook her head. "It was tough. I cried. But the point of my tragic backstory is that seven-year-old Andrew learned how to find a new dream. And another, and another, until he found something that worked out for him." He picked up his water glass, paused when it was midway to his mouth. "Does that help any?"

Nora nodded, her stare distant. "So you're saying I'm seven-year-old Andrew?"

"Yes. But you're cuter. He had a very unfortunate haircut." He grinned and shoved a wad of spinach in his mouth, leaving Nora to process the unexpected compliment. She busied herself with a bite of pizza, pretending she couldn't feel his words from her cheeks to her toes.

"So what's on the agenda tomorrow? Another day of bookselling?" he asked, folding his napkin on his plate as the waiter brought the check.

She signed the receipt and tucked her credit card into her wallet. "Of course."

He pushed his chair in and gestured for her to walk ahead of him. "If you need a break, let me know," he said. "I'm a seasoned bookseller now."

She laughed. "That's questionable."

"I mean it," he said. "I'm happy to help out if anything comes up tomorrow. I'm sure it's not easy running the booth by yourself. In fact," he added, pulling a receipt from his pocket and fishing around in his laptop case for a pen, "I'm giving you my phone number. If you ever need help, text me."

She watched him scribble numbers onto the receipt, touched and disbelieving at the same time. "It's just six hours."

"A lot can happen in six hours." He handed her the receipt.

"I have made it through this conference alone for the last four years."

Andrew picked something off his tie before looking back up, unimpressed. "That's because your other authors suck."

She laughed. She found she couldn't look away from him, wondering what he might say or do next. He'd already gone so far off the usual script.

The elevator arrived. Andrew held the door open and motioned for her to get on first. It was a gesture she disliked ordinarily, but when Andrew did it, she didn't mind.

They reached her floor first. She stepped off, turned around to face him. This was Andrew at the end of a long day, still proper in his suit and tie, but small signs showed the person behind the keynote speaker. His tie was off-center. His hair was disheveled, a few strands curling in ways they hadn't this morning. The dark circles under his eyes hinted that he might be as tired as she felt. But he was smiling, dimples and all, and she hated that she could see it now, how charming he was. She remembered the Swedish professor, the way he blushed when Andrew talked to him. Thank god for Nora's unblushable brown skin.

"Have a good night," she said.

"You too." She watched the doors close on him and his charm.

Alone in her hotel room, Nora pulled out the receipt and stared at the blue ink written in his scribbly, uneven hand. She entered the numbers into her phone and saved him as a contact. She wasn't planning to use it, but she liked that it was there. Like a piece of him was hers.

CHAPTER ELEVEN

Nora was starting to take offense at how slowly time was moving. From her seat at the Parsons booth, she watched attendees drag their suitcases down the carpeted hallway. She checked the time again: five minutes to noon. Then it would only be two more hours before she could put Conference Nora to rest for another few months.

She ignored her growling stomach and focused on the fact that another minute had passed, bringing her slightly closer to two o'clock. More people dressed in their business casual-best wheeled suitcases down the hall in droves. A lunch session was starting. People tended to like free food, even if it meant listening to an hour-long panel. She wondered what food was being served, wishing she had time to abandon the booth to grab lunch somewhere. She checked the time again, then her email. Her Weber inbox showed a new message from Violet.

Great feedback on the proposal. That's exactly what we needed.

She smiled, basking in the praise, and relaxed into her seat. It felt like a sign that she'd made the right choice, embarking on this shadowy Weber path.

Emily had sent the group a proposal about creating a culture of innovation. Last night, after dinner with Andrew, Nora went through the proposal, thinking back to every innovation-related manuscript she'd skimmed over the years. Sitting on her hotel bed, bleary-eyed but determined, she emailed the group some suggestions on how the book could be better fleshed out—sidebars, case studies, research about the link between diversity and innovation. And perhaps they might consider a chapter on fostering innovation for teams, considering the Wharton School's research on the topic? Oh, they hadn't read that? Sure, she could send it along.

Nora reached under her chair for the conference program and flipped through it. The lunch session happening in the next room was a panel on diversity and inclusion. A Parsons author, Vincent Cobb, was on the panel. The book he'd written for Parsons about designing surveys for the workplace had not sold well in the decade since it published. They'd only brought it to this conference in case he showed up looking for his book (which he did not, presumably out of shame)—and even then, they'd only brought two copies, so confident they were that it wouldn't sell. Which it didn't.

But if his new thing was diversity and inclusion, that could sell, especially because his bio indicated he had a long relationship with the association running the conference. If they could copublish the book with an association, they'd have a built-in audience—and built-in revenue, because associations were big on buying copies of their copublished books to resell. And that made Vincent Cobb an author with promise.

Despite the four hours of sleep she'd gotten the night before, Nora suddenly felt full of energy. She circled Vincent Cobb's name and imagined approaching him and pitching the idea of writing a book for Weber. The thought didn't make her squirm like the prospect of luring Andrew to Weber had last night—a good sign. No one at Parsons would notice if Vincent Cobb, forgotten backlist author, signed with Weber. She could do this.

While googling Vincent Cobb to see if he'd done anything else noteworthy, Nora spotted Andrew emerging from the lunch session a few doors down. She looked up as he approached, expecting to meet his eye for a quick nod while he passed. But he headed right for her.

"I stole you a lunch," he said, glancing down at the two white boxes stacked in his hands.

Nora followed his gaze, then looked back up at him. He wore a friendly grin as he held an offering that once again challenged everything she knew about authors. "Really?" Her voice came out quieter, softer than she'd probably ever spoken to him.

He shrugged. "I just wanted to thank you for buying me dinner last night."

"I didn't, really. It was Parsons."

"Well, I didn't buy this either. Free meal for a free meal." He lowered the boxes to Nora's level.

It was all she could do not to stare at him, completely dumbfounded, as she reached over and took one. "From one freeloader to another, thank you."

His expression grew serious as he surveyed the exhibit hall around them. "Do you need a break?"

"I—" She did, actually. It would be nice to not have to pull out her hastily written *Back in five minutes* sign and come back to a forlorn book-browser acting like she'd left them at the altar. "Okay, but just for a couple of minutes. Don't sell books," she added, pointing a finger at him. "Don't touch the computer."

Andrew shrugged, as though he'd never dream of it. "Of course not."

She eyed him suspiciously, then closed the laptop just in case.

When she returned, Andrew was sitting at the booth, peering into his lunch box. "The lunch kind of sucks," he said.

"Are you ever happy with the lunches you're given?"

"At least there's no avocado this time," he said, darting a pointed look her way. He tucked the cardboard lid back into the box and stood. "Are you all set? Is there anything else you need?"

She eyed him, hesitating. She shouldn't ask, but she did anyway. "Do you mind if I listen in on the session for a minute?"

He tilted his head in the direction of the room. "Go ahead."

"I'll just be a minute."

"Go wild. Take two."

Nora hurried down the hall, following the sound of voices coming from the room. She slipped in quietly through the door. People sat at tables, cardboard lunch boxes in front of them. Only half were actually watching the panel; the others concentrated on their food or their phones. Nora crept to the back wall.

"Individuals typically don't have the power to bring about change in an organization," Vincent was saying. He sat between two panelists at a long table on the stage. He was a little older than his picture in the conference program showed; his black hair was graying now. But his wire-rimmed glasses—and even his pinstriped blazer, if Nora's eyes were right—were the same as the ones in his picture. "That's why we have an inclusion council. Ten people, different backgrounds, different departments. All leaders, or close to it. They meet four times a year to discuss the issues they've seen, and what's been brought to them. They make recommendations to senior leadership for actions they can take to make the workplace more inclusive. We've found it's been very effective. From the surveys we've sent—"

Christ, him and his surveys, she thought, slipping back out of the room. He'd better not send anyone to her booth to buy his boring survey book.

She returned to find Andrew eating a bag of potato chips and reading the conference program. He looked up when Nora drew closer.

"How was your minute?" he asked.

"Pretty good." He was still watching her, like he expected her to elaborate. "Just seeing what's what," she added.

"Just trolling for authors, you mean?"

Nora's breath caught in her throat. She studied him, wondering how he knew about Weber. But the glint in his eyes told her she was overthinking it. He clearly meant trolling for Parsons authors and didn't see the need to specify.

Nora gestured for him to move out of her chair. "Believe it or not, you are not the only author in the world."

As she settled into her seat, he bent his head back and tilted the chip bag, dumping the last of its contents into his mouth. It was the least dignified thing she'd ever seen him do. He grinned at her, crumbs lining the corners of his mouth.

"Judging from the way everyone was all over me at the Parsons office last month, I'd have thought I was," he said through a mouthful of crumbs.

That was pretty accurate, actually. But she couldn't blame Rita and Candace for fawning over their money-maker. She lifted the lid on her box: a ham and cheese sandwich, a bag of potato chips, a pickle spear, and a cookie. For Nora, who hadn't counted on lunch at all, it felt like a feast.

"Don't you have to get back to the session?" she asked, peeling wax paper off the pickle spear.

"I was just about to." He leaned past her to get his lunch box, and Nora ignored the warmth in her face. He gave her a parting nod before turning for the hallway.

"Thanks for lunch," she said.

"Thanks for dinner," he called over his shoulder.

Nora bit into her pickle. As she chewed, she noticed chip crumbs on the table. Fucking Andrew, she thought, fighting back a smile as she wiped them into a napkin with a sweep of her hand.

She bent to toss the napkin into the garbage bin at her feet, and when she sat up, she spotted a woman heading for her booth. Nora slid the lunch box under her table.

The woman picked up books one at a time from a few different sections: nonprofit, leadership, human resources. She read the back of each one, then set it down and moved to another.

Nora didn't like to bother people who were browsing, but this woman didn't have the leisurely pace of a browser. "Can I help you find something?" she asked.

The woman looked up, fifth or sixth book in hand. "Do you have anything on corporate social responsibility?"

These questions used to terrify her, like spontaneous pop quizzes she could fail any time. Her first year here, she read Parsons's catalog cover to cover on the plane and still couldn't answer every book-browser's questions correctly. But now it was different.

"This one is about developing employee volunteer programs."

Nora stood and plucked a book from the edge of the booth. "This one's a little bit broader," she said, picking up one of the books the woman had held earlier, "but it has a chapter on sustainable business practices." She handed both to the woman, then returned to her seat to let her flip through them. She didn't have to wait long.

"I'll take both."

Nora perked up and processed the order. She sat a little taller as she watched the woman walk away. Little interactions like this didn't make up for the travel and long hours, but there was satisfaction in helping someone find the perfect book. If transactions at the booth could always be like this—one-on-one conversations instead of chaotic lines or unplanned signings—she might actually like conferences.

At two o'clock exactly, Nora leapt into action. Teardown took less time than setup, and within an hour she'd packed everything neatly into ten boxes of unsold books destined for Parsons's warehouse. She watched the hotel staff cart them away. The hallway was fairly empty now, most booths packed up.

When Nora reached the top of the escalator, she spotted him standing in the hotel lobby—graying black hair, glasses, ratty pinstriped blazer.

Vincent Cobb had never met Nora. His book had been published before Nora's time, and he'd never written another. She would get to introduce herself to him as an honest-to-goodness employee of Weber.

As she shook Vincent Cobb's hand, preparing to ask if he'd ever considered writing a book with Weber, she saw Andrew smirking at her from across the room. His knowing comment about trolling for authors came back to her. She couldn't help it—she extended her arm out, low to her side like she was just stretching, but she innocently raised her middle finger.

Andrew broke into a laugh. Nora focused all her attention on Vincent then, listening to him talk about inclusion initiatives. When Vincent reached into his wallet for a business card, she let her eyes dart back to Andrew once, just to check. He was still there, though now he was looking off to the side, like he wasn't paying her any attention. But his quick glance in her direction betrayed him. This time, it was Nora who smirked.

CHAPTER TWELVE

Friday morning found Nora at her desk, jet-lagged and yawning while her inbox loaded two days' worth of unread emails. She spotted a message from Andrew, sent that morning. She scrolled past the many unread emails in her inbox and clicked on his.

Hi Nora,

It was great seeing you at CEF. Thanks again for dinner. You were kind enough to remind me that I hadn't signed the contract yet. I'm reviewing it now and should be in touch soon.

Thanks for your patience!
Andrew

The tone was oddly formal for someone who stole a lunch for her. She wasn't sure why he'd recapped their dinner conversation, but another glance at the email explained it. He'd cc'ed Rita.

The next email was just from Rita to Nora:

Way to go! I can't wait to hear how the conference went!

Rita dropped by later that morning to thank Nora for moving the contract along and ask about the conference. Nora gave an abridged version of what happened. It didn't seem necessary to mention Andrew's failed foray into book sales.

Once her inbox was mostly in order, Nora checked her voicemail and sighed as soon as the message played.

"Hi, Nora, this is Henry Brook. I took a look at the tip sheets you sent me, and I wanted to go over a few things. Can you call me back ASAP?"

Of course he was the type of person who said things like ASAP. Of course he wanted to communicate by phone. And of course after the two hours she spent last week, looking up each book in their antiquated content management system and downloading its tip sheet, he wasn't done with her.

Feeling confrontational, Nora picked up the phone and dialed his number.

"Nora, hi! Thanks for calling me back!" He had a cheerful, friendly voice that took her by surprise.

"You're...welcome," Nora said, stunned into confusion by his cheer.

"Thanks again for the tip sheets. I just had some pointers for next time."

"Next time?"

"For your future edification," he clarified without clarifying. "A lot of the way this description copy is written...it's pretty dry. There's no hook."

Hook?

"It's…internal marketing copy," Nora said. "No one outside of Parsons sees it." *And I didn't write it*, she wanted to add.

"I know. But it's what the copywriters read when they're writing the copy that goes on the back of the book. You see how it works? There are levels to this. If there's no hook in the internal copy, how can you expect what's on the back of the book to be any good?"

With every word he spoke, Nora's face contorted more and more into confused spite. She blinked several times, took in a breath, let it out.

"Right," she said.

"I made some edits to the tip sheets for the books coming out next year. Can you enter them into the system?"

"You didn't make the edits *in* the system?" Nora meant to ask it innocently—curiously—but she couldn't hide the quiet sigh lurking beneath it.

He chuckled the chuckle of someone with far too much confidence. "Normally my assistant would take care of this, but I'm between assistants right now." It was hard to believe, truly. "But take a look at my comments. It might be a good learning experience for you."

Oh, to have the ability to vomit through a telephone receiver.

Nora ended the conversation by responding to his every word with a series of patient hums that weren't quite grunts, just enough to indicate that she heard him without giving him something else to latch onto and explain to her.

The conversation with Henry Brook was enough to put her in a prolonged state of annoyance, striking her keyboard at full force with every edit she entered into the system. But a text from Beth helped Nora forget him for a few moments.

How was the conference?

The text brought a smile to Nora's face at first. She missed her post-conference ritual of rolling her chair to Beth's cube to complain about everything.

But Nora soon realized, as she drafted and deleted possible replies, that she had no idea how to share that she'd gone out to dinner with an author Beth called *daddy Santos.*

She decided on a one-word reply: Unexpected?

Beth replied instantly with a row of question marks, leaving Nora to once again figure out a response.

I had dinner with Santos.

But that alone wasn't unexpected. No use playing it coy. Nora added the murkier parts she was still trying to decipher.

Also he worked the booth for a bit.

Also he gave me his number.

Also he brought me lunch the next day.

She bit her lip and waited. Beth sent two texts in a matter of seconds.

NORA OH MY GOD

I technically have a happy hour thing at 6:00, but I am going to have to INSIST that you meet me for drinks at FIVE SHARP

Nora laughed quietly, feeling a wave of sentimental joy wash over her. Beth's assurance on her last day at Parsons—that she and Nora would still see each other—started to feel a little bit truer.

Nora was even more glad for these plans when Andrew emailed her later that day, just as she was preparing to meet Beth. Rita wasn't cc'ed on this one.

I had a couple of questions about the contract. What's

the best way to discuss them? I'd be happy to get on a call next week.

She was surprised to feel a touch of disappointment at seeing that his email was strictly business. But the fact that he was seriously looking into his contract was a good sign. She pulled up her calendar, then replied to let him know her availability.

Nora checked the time. She should shut down her computer now. Beth had insisted pretty adamantly on meeting at five sharp.

But she wondered if Andrew might respond instantly. A minute later, he proved her right.

That sounds good. I'll call you Monday at 2:00 if that works for you.

Thanks! I hope you have a great weekend. Hopefully no bookselling involved :)

That one little happy face and the weird things it was doing to her heartbeat. She tapped her fingers on her desk and considered her reply.

No bookselling! Not that you'd know anything about it.

She debated adding a smiley face and decided against it. Her reply was already bordering on flirtation; a smiley face would just be shameless. She sent the email, then checked the time again. Ten minutes to five. Any longer and she'd definitely be late. Nora closed out of her inbox, fighting the urge to open it back up again to check for a reply.

Her mind raced as she rode the elevator to the lobby. How quickly they'd devolved from professionals scheduling a call to happy faces and banter. What did that mean?

Beth would know, she told herself for perhaps the tenth time that day. Beth would know what to make of it.

Beth waved as Nora approached her table. Beth still had her same smile, her same shoulder-length brown hair, but she was wearing a T-shirt—blue with a drawing of an elephant. The dress code at Parsons stretched the limits of business casual, but not to the extent that graphic tees were common. Nora was used to seeing Beth in sensible blouses with cute patterns. But Beth didn't work at Parsons anymore.

"Hey," Nora said, sliding into the chair across from her.

"Hey yourself." Beth's eyebrows waggled obscenely.

Nora laughed. Ignoring Beth and her suggestive eyebrows, she tried to cling to a semblance of normalcy. "How are you?"

"Nice try. Tell me about the conference." Beth brought a bright-pink drink to her lips and kept her gleaming eyes on Nora.

Nora sighed, but out tumbled every interaction she'd had with Santos since the Sandwich Incident. Weber she kept to herself, unsure how someone with no money troubles would respond to an act of desperate duplicity, but the rest she laid bare. When she finished, she traced a finger on the beads of condensation forming on her margarita as she waited for Beth to piece it together and tell her what it meant.

Beth, who had listened to the entire explanation with a grin that she was getting worse and worse at hiding, now assumed a serious air. "Am I invited to the wedding?"

"You're invited to the funeral I'm going to throw you if you don't get serious."

"Why should I be serious?" Beth asked through a laugh. "Why should you?"

Nora heaved another sigh. "Because I don't know what it means!"

At this, Beth got as serious as Nora could hope for, in that she was not actively laughing. "It means whatever you want it to mean. If you think he was just being helpful at a conference, leave it at that. If you think it might be something more...you have his number." Beth gave a pointed glance toward Nora's phone on the table. "I personally think there's no harm in texting him. The worst that could happen is he's not interested. But that's up to you."

Nora followed her gaze. Her phone had never looked so intimidating. "Okay," she said, as if she didn't have a thousand more questions. She took a drink of her margarita and breathed a sigh. "Now will you answer me if I ask how you're doing?"

Beth agreed to the change of subject like she was doing Nora a favor, which she probably was. Nora could only talk about Santos for so long before she started to feel like her face was melting.

"I'm good," Beth said. "The job is still new, but good. Everyone's really nice. Some of my coworkers are getting together here at six."

"Cool." Nora ignored the stab of jealousy in her chest. Beth already had work friends she went to happy hour with. And Nora had patronizing calls with Henry Brook.

"I'm also looking into moving into a studio. I toured a place last weekend."

Beth showed Nora the photos, a large room with bare walls and polished floorboards. Nora swiped through them, called the apartment beautiful, and was reminded, again, why she couldn't tell Beth about Weber. Beth didn't know that every photo sent a pang in Nora's gut, mocking her with a life she couldn't afford. Beth, with her sufficient salary and shiny new studio, wouldn't be able to fathom Nora's bleak reality. Confiding in her would permanently change the way Beth saw her. Nora had seen enough change lately.

When Beth's coworkers arrived, she stood to give Nora a hug and advised again that she text Santos. Nora returned to her seat and drained her margarita. She twisted her empty glass in place as she watched Beth settle into a large table in the corner with a gaggle of people their age. Beth had said the worst that could happen was that Santos wasn't interested in Nora, but it was messier than that. It would almost be a relief if he wasn't interested—then she would know for sure that their time at the conference was purely work related, and she could stick to trying to sign him. But if he *was* interested, it would mean navigating more than just the signing conversation. Much more.

Nora looked down at her phone. It couldn't hurt to check her email.

Her heart skipped when she saw a reply from Santos.

Ouch. That's fair. But I swear the credit card was defective! You try swiping a faulty card!

She typed out a reply before she could change her mind.

I could out-swipe you right now, and I'm not even sober.

She knew it wasn't a good idea to admit this to an author via company email. But she didn't care. And really, Parsons probably didn't care either. Beth's *Seinfeld* torrenting was proof of Parsons's lax IT policy.

Nora refreshed her email every few seconds, touching granules of salt from the rim of her glass and bringing them to her tongue as she waited. Over an hour had passed since his last email. He probably wasn't online anymore.

But a few minutes later, as she was preparing to throw in the towel and go home to another evening of counting the blades of her ceiling fan, a new email appeared.

Drinking and working? Parsons must be fun.

She blinked at those words. She tried fighting through the thoughts in her head to find the words to explain just how wrong he was, but they got lost.

Nora bit her nail, tasting salt. She wanted to tell him it wasn't fun. She knew she couldn't, but at the conference, he'd been so concerned for her, so willing to help. Nora remembered his dark-brown eyes focusing on her each time he asked if she would be all right at the booth. The way he stole her lunch. The way he asked her if Parsons was what she wanted to do.

Right now, what she really wanted to do was see him.

But email didn't seem like the right avenue for that. Beth had said there was no harm in texting him. Nora scrolled through the contacts in her phone, and there he was, toward the bottom: Santos.

She crafted a text that she hoped was breezy enough not to betray how carefully she weighed every word. Or how her heart pounded when she hit Send.

No longer working! I'm at a happy hour thing if you want to get contract stuff over with now.

Where did he live again?

No matter. She'd already sent the message.

A minute passed. Then two.

Nora scrolled through her recent texts. One to Rita about revenue from the conference. One from Verizon about her cell phone bill. One from her roommate Allie, asking for her mother's Netflix password. She went back to her text to Andrew, wondering if there was some way to salvage the situation. She couldn't think of one.

Her phone vibrated on the table, intimidating as ever. There were two texts from him:

You just want a reason for Parsons to pay for your drink.

Oh, that would have been a good cover.

And the next:

I can stop by. What's the place?

CHAPTER THIRTEEN

Nora ordered a plate of nachos to keep her company while she waited. And, she told herself as the waitress walked away with her order, Andrew could have some if he wanted, so really she was being a provider.

Until the nachos arrived topped with a mound of guacamole and she remembered his avocado allergy. He probably had a case for premeditated murder by now.

As each figure passed by the window, Nora turned her head, waiting for a glimpse of brown skin and a confident stride. After several disappointments, she returned to her phone. She should probably let Beth know he was coming. Give her time to temper her response.

I texted Andrew and he's on his way here be cool

Nora lifted her eyes to Beth's table across the room. Beth, engrossed in conversation, took a minute before she looked down and tapped on her phone. Immediately, she turned to Nora with wide eyes and an ecstatic expression.

Nora stifled a laugh, shrugged at Beth, and ate a chip.

"Nachos?"

Andrew stood in front of her, a messenger bag on his shoulder. He looked from the plate to her, then shook his head like she couldn't possibly be serious.

Nora darted a glance behind him. Beth was now pointing at Andrew, as if Nora couldn't see him. "They're for me," she said. "I'm not trying to kill you."

He sat down across from her. "Just observing," he said, eyes crinkling.

Just to spite him, she took a chip and dragged it through the guacamole before taking a bite. "How have you been?"

"Since you saw me yesterday?" he asked.

"That was in Baltimore. How's San Francisco Andrew?"

"Tired," he said, stretching his arms above him. "I flew back today."

"Today?"

"I had a meeting."

"Oh, was it with a publisher?" she asked innocently.

He opened his mouth to correct her, then stopped. His lips curled into a smile. "I could get a meeting with a publisher."

Nora shrugged and used a chip to scoop more guacamole. "Right. You're meeting with one right now. Congratulations."

"Other publishers could have me."

"You're absolutely right," she said, keeping her tone indifferent enough to be maddeningly unconvincing. She ate a chip and chanced a glance at Andrew, whose glare might be considered open contempt if not for the laughter in his eyes.

"Do you want a drink?" He looked at the menu above the bar, written in chalk.

"A margarita, I guess." Happy hour was not part of her budget, but she had two salaries now, after all. And she could use something to nurse as she tried to navigate this strange new situation.

When he stood, Beth was once again in Nora's immediate line of vision. She put a hand to her chest like she couldn't be prouder.

Nora looked away to keep her face from heating. She ate another chip, eyeing him across the bar. He put his elbows on the counter and leaned forward, talking to the bartender. He seemed to have such a firm grasp on what he was doing. That was the quality that made him such a successful author and strong speaker—she assumed. The bits of his speech she heard through the occasional open door sounded confident and intelligent, anyway.

Andrew returned, plunking down a salt-rimmed glass for Nora and a short glass of something amber-colored for himself. Was it scotch? Scotch was such an adult drink. He was so much better at life than she was.

"What's the occasion?" he asked.

Nora looked up from studying his scotch for secrets of adulthood. "What?"

"For happy hour?"

"Oh. Just meeting a friend."

Andrew glanced from Nora to the no one else at their table. "An invisible friend?"

Nora felt her cheeks burn. "No. She had to get to a work social thing. She's at the other table over there." Nora immediately cursed herself for gesturing, because then Andrew turned around, and Beth, who must have been watching, gave him an enthusiastic wave. Andrew lifted a hand in return. Nora gulped her drink.

"She seems nice," Andrew said.

"Yeah, she—oh god," Nora sputtered, seeing Beth walking toward them.

"I just wanted to come say hi," said Beth. She beamed at Andrew. "I'm Beth Bodine. I used to work at Parsons with Nora."

"Really?" Andrew acted like it was the most normal thing in the world, being ambushed like this. "We may have emailed at some point. I'm Andrew Santos."

Beth even pretended to look surprised, raising her eyebrows like his name was any kind of revelation. "That's right! I made those flyers for your book."

Nora, meanwhile, shrinking more and more in her seat, wasn't sure she had a neck anymore. Neither of them noticed.

"Thank you!" he said. "I pass those out at every event I go to. I'm that annoying presenter who puts flyers in everyone's seats before my session starts."

Beth laughed a little too loudly. "Perfect! Why stop there? You could go door-to-door and hang them on everyone's doorknobs like takeout menus."

A jovial laugh erupted out of Andrew. "Genius! Maybe that'll be my next move."

Beth allowed herself one more moment of unabashed staring before she said, "Well, I've got to get back. I just wanted to say hi. It was nice meeting you."

As Beth returned to her table, Nora slowly sat up straighter. Beth had at least played it sort of cool, though the wink she gave Nora as she took her seat was decidedly *not* cool.

"I'm glad she stopped by," Andrew said. "Definitely an improvement over the invisible friend I thought you had. I guess we have her to thank for promoting my book."

"Uh-huh," Nora said with as straight a face as she could manage. He knew full well that Beth's flyers, designed in Microsoft Word, were not the reason for his book's massive success. "It's you we should thank. Our books don't usually get widespread media attention like yours did."

He scoffed. "It made a list or two."

"Which is amazing. I mean it," she said when he didn't react. "You don't think so?" She picked up her margarita.

He took a sip of his scotch, didn't even make a face at the taste like she would have. "No, it is. I'm just always hoping for better, you know?"

Optimism. Jesus.

"I think it's just something my mom came to expect," he continued. "I still don't think she's impressed with me."

"I thought the PhD would have helped."

"She has a doctorate too. She's a nurse practitioner."

A picture of Andrew began to form in her mind. Someone encouraged to do better.

"What about your parents?" he asked, turning it around on her like an inquisition—or, she realized, like a date.

Nora shrugged. "My dad's an electrician, and my mom's a paralegal."

"Do they have high expectations for you?"

She shook her head. They did, but not in the way he meant. They didn't care when she wanted to major in English. They told her many times over that they wanted her to be happy—which seemed like it should have been the easiest benchmark but was somehow the one Nora couldn't figure out how to reach.

What a bizarre, nebulous concept happiness was. Her father didn't become an electrician because it made him happy. He didn't wake up excited to lay cable. He did it because, as he told her once, *it made sense*. It was what he knew, a career path he started down at seventeen because it was a practical way to make money on limited opportunity.

But now there was supposed to be more to it than that. She had the opportunities. She was told to take those opportunities and find her dream job, something that would fulfill her. It was internalized now, this idea of fulfillment. It made her feel weak to put this much stock in something her parents couldn't even consider. They had managed just fine without tying their entire existence to their careers. She had the privilege to prioritize happiness, and she was getting it all wrong.

"Do you wish they did?" he asked.

Nora thought about it, her gaze wandering. "No," she said, eyes coming to rest back on him. "I wish *I* had higher expectations for myself sometimes."

"What do you mean?"

It surprised her that he was taking this so seriously, the musings slipping out of her. "I think I have a tendency to accept what I'm given instead of asking for what I want."

Andrew's inquisitive stare never left her. "What's stopping you?"

"It's…" Nora trailed off, unable to articulate what was standing in her way. "Everything."

"Okay." He didn't even call her on her vague, hyperbolic nonresponse. "And what do you want?"

She didn't have a good answer for that either. She could only handle a few seconds of eye contact before she reached for her drink. What did she want? To not have to work two jobs to afford to live. To not have to use him in a ploy to get a better position. To know what he wanted. She flicked her gaze back to him.

"If you want some blanket unsolicited advice," he said, leaning back, "I would say that whatever the situation, it never hurts to ask."

Nora nodded. This kind of advice was good in theory, but messy in execution.

"You don't believe me?" he asked. "I'll prove it. Do you want to talk shop for a minute?"

"You mean the contract?" When he nodded, she asked, "Did you bring it?"

"I did, actually." He bent and unzipped his messenger bag. Nora drank more of her margarita. She set down her glass when Andrew sat back up, papers in hand.

Nora sat up straighter, too, trying to shift her whirring mind from Andrew to Parsons—what they'd allegedly come here to discuss. She watched the papers in his hand. One signature, and she'd be an assistant editor. It would be at Parsons, on business books, but it was miles safer than the idea she'd considered at the conference. Signing him to Weber for a shot at a job she was six months away from maybe getting—and then having to spend those six months at Parsons, hoping no one caught on to her scheme— was too dangerous. She could sign other authors to Weber, like Vincent Cobb. Andrew, she would sign to Parsons. She'd get the promotion; he'd get his book deal. Maybe they'd even find more excuses to have meetings like these.

"Can you give me higher royalties?" he asked. He shuffled through the loose papers. Nora watched him, entertained. Any bravado conveyed by the directness of his question was muted by his inability to find the page he was looking for.

For all his modesty about his royalties, he wanted more. It was an alien concept for Nora—wanting more when you had so much already—but she supposed no one wanted to be taken advantage of by a greedy publisher. Guilt pinched at her when she wondered if she, too, fell in that category. She wasn't motivated by greed, exactly, but could she truly say she had Andrew's best interests at heart?

She couldn't stand watching him fumble through the pages anymore. Nora reached across the table and took them. She quickly examined the top line of each page, stopping at the one with the royalties section.

"This is the highest we offer," she said, setting the page down in front of him. "We only offer bestselling authors this rate. I'll take your question to Rita, but I can't remember a time we've gone higher than that."

"Okay. Thanks," Andrew said. He lifted his eyes to meet Nora's. "Notice how the world didn't implode when I asked for something."

Nora raised an eyebrow. "Noted."

"One more thing," he said. "What do you think about the advance?"

"What do you mean?"

"It's weirdly small, wouldn't you say?"

She reached over the table and flipped to the correct page to confirm the number she already knew. "It's more than what you got for your last book."

"Yes," he said, "but I've done a hell of a lot with my last book, and I think you all know that."

"Of course." Nora stared him down. "You had a call with Rita about this, didn't you? A couple of weeks ago?"

"Yes," he admitted.

"My answer won't be any different. Our advances are pretty conservative across the board."

Parsons's official line was that low advances left room for aggressive marketing, and that this, combined with a decent royalty structure, ensured authors were fairly compensated. In truth, Parsons framed authorship as an act of generosity. *Sharing knowledge with your peers is the best way to contribute to the profession*, their author guide read. The implication, Nora thought, was that writing a book expecting to profit from it would be ghastly. For Parsons's authors, many of them professors looking to pad their curricula vitae with a book, being an author was enough. It was why they didn't seek agents, why they rarely pushed back on advances. Parsons cultivated a beautiful lie that authors didn't need to be paid much for their labor.

Andrew had believed the lie when he signed the contract for his first book. Nora guessed he knew better now.

"Really?" He took a drink, eyes never leaving her. "You're telling me Hank Boyle gets a conservative advance? Horace Archibald? Chip Dixon?"

She could have applauded him for seeing through the bullshit. There was a point when Parsons cast its norms aside and went all in on authors, building brands and franchises around them. Each author Andrew named had carved out their own corner of Parsons. Hank Boyle had published a conflict resolution book in the '90s that spawned several follow-ups and a series of courses. Horace Archibald's bestselling guide on negotiation tactics had been translated into at least fifteen languages. Chip Dixon's book on accountability became such a standard that some companies bought it in bulk to give a copy to every new hire on their first day.

"Let me put it this way." Andrew set down his glass and leaned in. "Why do I have a feeling that if I were thirty years older and a hell of a lot paler, Parsons might want to invest in me the same way they invest in those guys?"

This deserved an *amen*. It was incestuous how Parsons's executives invested and reinvested in the same old, tired authors over and over again, never stopping to consider that perhaps the formula that made a few of their books massively successful didn't dictate how all success should look. Andrew—his passion, his drive, his youth, his perspective—was so counter to everything Parsons's circle of elite authors represented that no one could see how much he could do for Parsons if they actually threw their full weight behind him.

An impulse bubbled in her to tell him about Weber, so new they didn't yet have an established circle. Andrew would fit right in. But that would mean trusting him with a secret that could ruin her, betting on a job she might not even get, and risking getting exposed if Candace heard she'd effectively killed the Santos contract. She held still, buried the impulse back down, and gave him a grim smile.

"Why do I have a feeling you didn't say all of that to Rita?" she asked.

"That would bode well, would it?" he asked, raising his eyebrows. "Give me a higher advance because of racism?"

Nora shrugged. "Someone once told me you never know until you ask."

"Hey." He pointed at her in a show of amused sternness. "Do not use my own advice against me. I did ask; I just didn't drag race into it. You know why."

"I do," she said, feeling seen for the first time in a while. It was rare that she got to have this sort of shorthand about race with someone. After her years at Parsons, it was rare to be around someone who wasn't white.

Andrew sighed and looked down at the pages between them. "What else?" he asked, watching her intently. "Is there anything else I should be aware of?"

He wasn't asking Nora, editorial assistant. He was asking Nora, conference friend, fellow freeloader, and now drinking buddy.

"Is there anything else you want?" she asked.

He held her gaze for several moments. "I think we're all set," he said at last.

"How are you feeling about it overall?" she asked, nodding her head toward the contract.

He took in a breath, released it like a sigh. "I don't know." He rubbed his eyes and looked up at her, chin resting in his hand. "You want me to sign it," he observed.

Nora shrugged and twisted her glass on the table, feeling his eyes on her as she feigned innocence. "I don't care what you do."

"Right." Andrew watched the glass, then her. "You'll withdraw the contract if I take too long."

"That's right."

"Okay. Well, let me know what Rita says about the royalties."

"Will that make a difference?" she asked. He didn't say anything. Nora stacked the papers against the table and handed them back to him.

He took the stack, eyes still on her. "I didn't think you'd text me," he said.

"Why's that?"

"You didn't text me at the conference."

"Is it okay that I texted you after?" she teased. "You didn't turn into a pumpkin at midnight or anything?"

"Are you saying I was a stagecoach before?" he asked.

She thought of him at the conference, signing books and telling jokes at the booth. "Yes."

"Which means I'm a pumpkin now?"

She met his eyes, warm and brown, and saw the soft smile on his face. "No. You're a stagecoach now too."

He looked down at his scotch, then back at her. "That's the weirdest thing I've ever been flattered by."

Nora couldn't even play it cool, just kept staring at him, his kind eyes, his earnestness. "You're welcome."

"Does that make you Cinderella?" he asked.

This was such a stupid conversation, but it had her smiling anyway. "Both my shoes are accounted for, so I'm gonna say no."

"Happy to hear it." Andrew checked the time on his watch. "I have to go in a few minutes. Can I ask you something?"

Her heart beat faster as she met his eyes and contemplated at rapid speed the countless directions his question might send this conversation barreling into—some more dangerous than others.

"Sure."

"Who's paying for this?" He gestured a finger at their drinks and the death nachos.

"What do you mean?" she asked.

"Well...there's me. There's you. Is there Parsons?"

She hadn't planned to admit it, but it came tumbling out of her mouth anyway. "No, Parsons isn't paying for this."

He nodded. "I take it they don't know about this?"

More words, tumbling. "Only Beth, but she doesn't work at Parsons anymore."

"Okay," he said. "How about I pay for this, and we both reserve the right to tell Beth?"

Nora smiled. Come to think of it, she wasn't sure she'd ever stopped. It was an unusual feeling. Her cheeks hurt. "Deal."

While he headed for the bar to pay, Nora washed her hands in the bathroom. She studied her face in the mirror, examining the traces of her ridiculous smiling before they faded away. Two small indentations still curved around her lips, one on each side. They framed the corners of her mouth, her own set of parentheses illustrating Andrew's effect on her.

When she returned, Andrew stood and hoisted the strap of his bag onto his shoulder. Nora spotted the contract papers still on the table.

"Forgetting something?" she asked, picking up the pages.

He shrugged. "No."

Nora looked down at the contract in her hand, pulse racing. It would be distasteful to check now, in front of him, to see if he'd signed it. He probably didn't need the pages anymore, only brought them to reference for his questions. But it didn't stop her from clutching the loose-leaf stack like they held her future— and his, she remembered. If she got him to sign the contract even though they knew full well that Parsons didn't see his value, that would make her as bad as Parsons. Worse, even. She fiddled with the pages, suddenly not sure whether she wanted to see a signature.

"You ready?" he asked. She nodded, not sure what would happen next. "You headed to BART?" he asked. Again she nodded, and he walked beside her. Neither of them spoke on the walk to the BART station.

He waited until they reached the entrance to 16th Street

station. They made their way around the colorful railings surrounding the escalator, and Nora started down the stairs. She paused a few steps down, realizing she was walking alone. She turned around.

"I'm heading that way," he said, gesturing behind him.

So he'd walked her to BART, even though he wasn't going there himself. That seemed date-like.

"I'll let you know about the royalties," she said.

"Good. And this...was good."

She nodded. He stood there at the top of the steps, hands in his pockets, looking entirely comfortable while towering over her. On the BART station's wall of colorful tiles behind him, metal hummingbirds drank out of metal flowers, framing Andrew in birds like something out of *Cinderella*. She needed to stop associating him with *Cinderella*.

With a parting nod, Nora turned and continued down the stairs. She wondered if he was still there, watching her, but she resisted the urge to turn around and check.

Nora waited until the ride home to examine the contract. She traced the water ring on the first page with her finger, then slowly flipped to the signature page. She took a shaky breath when she saw the signature above his name.

No, she realized, peering closer at the blue scribble. Not a signature. Nora exhaled in equal parts disappointment and relief. And then she made out the words. He'd written *Lunch sometime?* in cursive.

She would have rolled her eyes if she weren't so pleased.

CHAPTER FOURTEEN

Nora was getting used to her new Monday routine: coming in, working at her desk for an hour, then retiring into the phone room until well past lunch. It was like she was holding office hours, open to all except Parsons employees.

The weekly call took less than an hour, but she tried to schedule her calls with Weber authors around this time too. Better to get all her Weber calls for the week done in one chunk than raise suspicions darting back and forth all week.

That was the idea, anyway—until Rita walked past while Nora was updating Violet on her progress with authors. Nora froze. Rita looked right through the window as she passed, eyes lingering on Nora like she had questions about what kind of lengthy private call Nora was having. Nora's throat tightened. But Rita passed on by without knocking.

Nora recovered, stammering an apology to Violet and pretending she'd accidentally hit the mute button. She spent the rest of the call watching the window, waiting for Rita to burst in and catch her in the act.

Maybe staggering calls throughout the week was the better

option. But she had a call with an author in five minutes, and it was too late to reschedule.

Nora stayed put and went through her phone script, eyes watching the window for any signs of movement. The author, someone from Tom's old list, was receptive to writing a risk management book proposal for Weber. After the call, Nora gathered her things, heart thumping in her throat, and bolted for her desk.

She'd have to work on the proposal materials when she got home. She used to leave work behind when it was just Parsons, but now it was becoming a nightly ritual, coming home from work and doing more projects for Weber. Last night, she'd stayed up until past 2:00 a.m., compiling a list of potential authors who might be able to write the book Violet wanted on the science of productivity. And when she sent Violet the list at nine this morning to avoid drawing attention to how late she'd stayed up working on it, Violet replied with, *Great! Can you start contacting them?*

That would be her project tonight, she supposed, rubbing her eyes.

When she blinked the bleariness away, she noticed a new email from Lynn.

So exciting that Vincent Cobb is on board! Violet told me the other day that you've done such an impressive job so far, and I couldn't agree more!

Nora read and reread Lynn's words, confidence growing inside her. Vincent Cobb had already submitted his proposal, and Violet was gearing to offer him a contract—all because Nora had walked up to him at the conference and sold him on Weber. It was like being a new EA again, still in the dazzling honeymoon phase, the unparalleled pride in hearing praise. She typed out a reply, a quick thanks and a happy face, but her finger hovered over the Send button. She pictured Andrew and the ease with which he asked for higher royalties. His casual, unassuming manner when he asked her to lunch.

She added a line break under her smiley thanks and typed:

I was wondering if you needed any help in the fiction department. I'm happy to focus on acquisitions for business, but I'd love to help out in fiction as well if there's anything you think I can do. Just let me know!

A thrill ran through her when she sent it. And then Nora waited, watching her inbox with anticipation that edged into dread the longer she waited. Finally, she gave in and closed the window. Andrew would be getting an earful when they had lunch this week. Just because things worked out for him—just because he was the perfect, brilliant, nice-smelling, successful author who floated through life, always getting whatever he asked for...

Unable to help herself, Nora checked her Weber inbox half an hour later.

There was an email from Lynn.

I'm glad you asked! I wonder if you might be interested reading through the attached? I'll be sending editorial feedback to the author in a few weeks, and I'd love to know your thoughts.

Nora clicked on the attachment so aggressively that it opened in two separate windows. She scrolled through one of them, letting out a breathy sigh at the sight of it: the first fiction manuscript she'd ever laid eyes on. Character names. Dialogue that wasn't part of a clunky corporate fable. No exhibits, appendices, or references. Only prose—prose meant to transport and entertain, rather than instruct and patronize. She hoped, skimming through the pages, that the words wouldn't blur together for her this time, in the same way they'd been doing lately whenever she tried to read for pleasure. Maybe the fact that this was something work related—an *exciting* something work related—would negate her recent lack of focus.

She dragged her eyes from the manuscript and went back to Lynn's email. Farther down was a description of the project: dystopian with a side of apocalypse. Nora didn't read much dystopian fiction, but she was willing to declare it her favorite genre if it meant she got to work on a novel for the first time.

Her fingertips flew over the keyboard as she typed out a reply to Lynn, deleted part of it, added more, deleted some, added more, until she composed an email whose tone could no longer be described as worryingly ecstatic.

She sent the email and sat back in her seat. Andrew possibly had a point after all.

She knew tonight would be another 2:00 a.m.-night, possibly later. But now that it included this beautiful, fictional thing, it was work she couldn't wait to dive into. For the first time in years.

And the late nights were paying off. She'd received her first payment from Weber that morning. She was so used to her twice-monthly ritual of logging into her bank account and checking on her Parsons income that she was taken aback at first to see the extra money in there—money that hadn't already been accounted for and earmarked for immediate deposit elsewhere. Money that, at least for a few moments, was entirely hers.

She'd told her mother about it to stop her from worrying, and there was something satisfying in that too. She'd smoothed the edges and glossed over the details; Nora was simply earning extra money on the side doing a completely above-board job for a vague company. Her mother just asked whether Nora was making enough money now, whether Nora liked the work, and then her dad got on the phone to describe the drama unfolding in their neighborhood over a rebellious ficus.

Even so, she couldn't help the pride that swelled in her when she saw it, this proof of what she'd earned. What she was capable of.

"Any updates on Santos?"

Nora stopped typing and turned to see Rita leaning against her cubicle wall, holding a publication schedule. Ever since catching Rita's eye in the phone room yesterday, just seeing her made Nora twitchy. She crossed her legs, as if that might make her seem more natural.

"No." Saying it was like admitting defeat. "But I think he might be coming around," she felt compelled to add. It wasn't a lie. He *was* coming around. For lunch.

Rita nodded. "That's great." Nora started to turn back to her email but paused when Rita opened her mouth again. "Did you know a few of our old authors have signed on with Weber?"

It was clear from Rita's hesitation that she was asking, not accusing. Nora's gut twisted anyway. She'd planned for this question, though. She would simply play ignorant. Why would she know what authors were up to? She was just an assistant.

"Really?" Nora did her part to frown a little.

"I've seen a couple of our authors making LinkedIn announcements about how *very* excited they are to sign with Weber," Rita said with a dry disdain Nora knew well. She eyed Nora thoughtfully. "You're close with Lynn, right?"

This question she hadn't been anticipating. Nora gripped her armrest to steady herself. "Yeah, I guess so."

"I don't suppose she's mentioned anything like that to you?" Rita asked. Before Nora had another chance to lie, Rita spoke again. "I don't know why I should be surprised. Of course her authors want to go back to her."

True, they were Lynn's authors. But Rita didn't know there would soon be another crop of Parsons authors signing with Weber—and these ones would be Nora's doing. She thought of Vincent Cobb and his looming contract, then looked at Rita and prepared another lie.

"I guess so," Nora said. "I hadn't heard about that."

"Yeah." Rita tossed the publication schedule into the recycling bin. It scraped against the plastic as it fell in. "Let me know when you hear about Santos, will you? We need to make sure we hold onto him if our authors are going to be leaving like this."

"Yes," Nora agreed weakly. "I will." She tried to focus on breathing and blinking the way a normal person might, but Rita's probing stare sent goosebumps along her arms. Finally, Rita turned and started for her desk, leaving Nora to control her breaths in peace.

She hadn't realized how quickly the departures of Parsons's

less-lucrative authors would be noticed. This was precisely why she had to make sure Andrew signed with Parsons. To hell with Andrew's doubts about them. To hell with the way he asked her to lunch, the non-signature that made her smile. This would be a work lunch. She'd get back on track. Whatever it took to clear her name of suspicion and keep her job.

CHAPTER FIFTEEN

"Why aren't the book titles in all caps?"

Calls with Henry Brook inevitably left Nora speechless.

"It's a publication schedule," Nora replied. She switched the phone to her other ear and clicked on the spreadsheet she'd just emailed him. "It's downloaded from the Parsons database. I can't change how it spits out information."

"I know," he said, having the gall to sound as patient as Nora was pretending to be. "But book titles should be in all caps. It's the convention in publishing."

Nora took in a long, deep, quiet sigh. "*I know.*" Like she could spend five years in publishing without knowing the conventions of publishing. Book titles shouted like her grandmother's Facebook posts. *TK* inexplicably standing for *to come*. The unnecessarily plural *permissions*. Publishing was full of conventions that made no sense.

"It's easier to see the titles that way," he said. "But I don't have time to retype every title myself. Is that something you can do?"

She sent him the seventy-eight tip sheets he asked for weeks ago, and she couldn't get rid of him. He'd latched onto her like a leech, asking her to complete mundane tasks for him because he was, as he said so often, between assistants. He'd even set up a weekly call with her just so he could have a dedicated window of time to ask her to do things. But she tried to be as difficult as possible.

"If you have thirty seconds, you have time," Nora said. "You can do it with an Excel formula."

"I don't know about all that."

She wasn't going to let him get out of this, not without taking the opportunity to condescendingly explain something to him. Consider it revenge for their last call, when he'd explained to her how hashtags worked.

But he was undeterred, even after Nora did a screen share and demonstrated how applying an Excel formula would indeed capitalize the titles in a matter of seconds. Because after her demonstration—which should have blown his minuscule mind—he said her computer desktop was too cluttered and spent fifteen minutes explaining his process for keeping his desktop clean.

They didn't hang up until Nora promised to declutter her desktop, middle finger digging into her palm.

Her phone rang not one minute later. She ignored it at first, until she realized caller ID existed and this was not Henry Brook circling back to explain oxygen to her.

"Hi, Nora," chimed their receptionist, Sarah. "Andrew Santos is here to see you."

"He's…here?" They did have lunch plans, but she'd expected a text when he arrived, not a parade around the Parsons office.

"Yeah, he wasn't on the visitor list, but we let him up."

"Oh. I'll come get him. Um, thanks."

Nora hurried to the lobby. She could hear his voice as she rounded the corner.

"I don't know, I just think *Leading Lingo* would look really good right there," he was saying. "You could put a cardboard cutout of me next to it. People would love it." Nora quickened her pace and saw him standing far too comfortably at Sarah's reception desk. He turned at the sound of her footsteps. "Nora!"

"Hi," she said. Lecturing him in front of Sarah, who was nodding at him with all the politeness she had in her, wouldn't be the best move. "You're here."

"Yeah," he said. "I learned I have to be on a list to get up here." He said it like it was a secret of the universe.

"Which you're not." Her intention to lecture crumbled as she looked at him. Seeing his utter lack of chagrin at learning that he was technically trespassing—how it had no effect on his cheerful air—made her envious of Andrew's worldview, how he must saunter through life, totally unapologetic of his own existence.

Andrew stuck a hand in his pocket. "A learning experience for us all."

"Well, just you." The pointed look she gave him was enough to elicit the reaction she was hoping for, and there it was in full: the narrowed eyes and disdain all over his face. Nora couldn't hide her satisfied smile. Andrew, she could tell from the way the corners of his mouth tugged upwards, was close to breaking too.

"Are you ready for lunch?" he asked, gesturing toward the elevators.

"Sure." As he headed for the elevators, Nora leaned in toward Sarah and whispered, "Sorry." Sarah dismissed it with a wave of her hand as the elevator sounded.

"Andrew?"

Nora turned. Rita, stepping off the elevator, stopped when she recognized Andrew, then noticed Nora behind him. Two surprises for the price of one.

"Rita!" Andrew exclaimed. "How are you?" He extended an arm out to hold the elevator.

"Good, and you?"

"I'm great. Just thought I'd take Nora out to lunch to thank her for all her help at the conference. Nora?"

Nora saw the thoughts coming together in Rita's head: first, confusion. There was no need to take an editorial assistant out to lunch to thank her for selling books at a conference; that was part of the job. Then, as Nora walked past her into the elevator and gave her a shy smile, a dawning realization that maybe Nora was working on getting a signature. This sort of wooing was normally done via calls or emails, or an elaborate meeting like the one Andrew had with the team a while back. For Nora to swing lunch with Andrew Santos just to talk contracts was, as far as Rita knew, a testament to her abilities.

"Have a good lunch," Rita said at last, smiling wryly like she knew a secret.

"Thanks!" Andrew retracted his arm and the elevator doors closed. "Did she know we were having lunch?" he asked, turning to Nora.

"No," she said, "but it's no big deal." She couldn't explain that it was a good thing Rita saw them, that it meant Nora was doing her part to sign him for a promotion. "So where'd you have in mind?" she asked.

"There's an onigiri place I've been curious about."

"Oh, on Kearny?"

"Yeah."

"I've been there. It's good." She looked down at her flats. Something about being this close to him, alone in an elevator, made her unsure where she should look. They'd shared an elevator in the conference hotel, but that was different. She hadn't known, then, that after that dinner they would fall into this nebulous thing she was still trying to figure out. But to ask would shine a light on it, and she wasn't sure she wanted to.

Her gaze moved across the elevator carpet to his shoes—brown leather Oxfords—then slowly up the rest of him. The blue gingham button-down looked good on him, sleeves rolled up as he apparently needed to do with every shirt he wore. She'd just mentally cataloged his forearms when the elevator sounded to announce they reached the lobby.

It was easy to avoid looking at him on the walk, but standing in line at the crowded restaurant, sitting across from him at a table so small she had to angle her knees to keep from touching his, was impossible.

While they waited for their orders, Andrew asked, "Should I not have come to the office?"

Nora sipped her plastic cup of water and thought about how to phrase it. "It's just…it's a big deal when authors are around. We have to dress differently, act differently. No one wants that sprung on them."

"But no one has to do that around me. I'm a cool author." He said it with a straight face, too. It was almost adorable.

"Oh, Andrew." Nora couldn't help the amused pity that clung to her voice. She bit back a smile and gently broke the news. "What you were saying to Sarah, at reception? That's what every author does."

"What?" He leaned back a bit, as if insulted. "We were joking together."

She shook her head. "I'm sorry to tell you this, but you were making the same tired jokes every author makes, about how your book should be in the lobby. Authors know two jokes: either pretending they're obsessed with their books or pretending they hate their books. Do you know how often Sarah hears that? That's like pull-my-finger-grade material."

For a moment, he didn't say anything, just stewed in the stench of his bad jokes. Their number was called before he could respond, and he shot her a defiant look while untangling his legs from under the table. "You know what," he said, "when I'm a famous comedian, you are not invited to any of my shows."

"Thank god!" she called out after him. She watched him sidle through the crowded restaurant on his way to the counter. But as much as she grew tired of those stupid author jokes, she had to concede it was always the nice authors who made them.

Andrew returned with two cardboard cartons. He set them down as he less-than-gracefully took his seat at the tiny table. Nora kept an eye on him as she pulled her carton toward her. This, now, was the moment to bring it back to Parsons.

"How are you feeling about the contract?" she asked.

He looked up from his rice balls, feigning shock. "Are you just here to talk shop with me, Nora?"

"Humor me."

"But you said no author jokes."

"Ha," she deadpanned. Even her sarcastic laugh brought a triumphant smile to his face.

"See, I'm funny."

"Mm."

"You are no fun. Don't go withdrawing on me yet. I'm still thinking about it. Did you ask about higher royalties?"

"I asked," she said. "Like I thought, Rita said you're already earning the bestselling rate." She didn't add that his advance was still, as he'd pointed out, far from what Parsons's top authors were given. It wouldn't help her case to tell him she believed he deserved more. She was here to save her job, not lose it. Nora forced herself to say, "I think it's a good offer, all in all."

She kept her eyes on Andrew as she waited for his response. She bit into her rice ball and savored the combination of warm sushi rice, earthy miso salmon, and seaweed.

"All right, well, my advice still holds," he said. "It never hurts to ask."

All that effort to get the words out, and he let them roll right off his back. But she couldn't deny there was a truth to the sentiment.

"You're right," Nora agreed, thinking about the dystopian manuscript with calm satisfaction. Since receiving it on Monday, she'd been reading a little each night, finishing her Weber work and curling up in bed with her laptop glowing dimly beside her. It was the first time in months that she actually looked forward to going to bed, instead of dreading how it brought her closer to another day of work. There were still moments when her mind wandered—last night she'd finished a page but couldn't remember anything she'd read, and she'd had to scroll back up and reread it. It was probably more her fault than the manuscript's, even if she hadn't quite taken a liking to the main character yet. But it still felt like taking a step toward becoming more of herself.

"Sorry, what was that?" he asked.

"I said you're right." Her mind was still back in bed with the manuscript. It wasn't until she looked up and saw him grinning smugly at her that she realized what he was doing.

"Could you say that again? Something about me being right?"

Nora stared him down. "I hope you choke on your onigiri."

He bit into an edamame pod and stared right back, unfazed. "Are you this sweet to all the authors you want to sign, or just the handsome ones?"

Instantly, she was brought back to their dinner at the conference, when he'd called her cute. This was different—he was calling himself cute, really—but its effect was the same. She was used to sidestepping the line, lobbing jokes and insults back and forth, but Andrew, for whatever reason, seemed to delight in walking right up to the line, planting his feet on it, and daring her to respond.

Calling himself handsome was a trap. If she disagreed, she was rude, she was lying, and she was acknowledging that she thought about his looks. If she agreed, she was admitting something she wouldn't dare.

There was no way to win. Nora took a bite of her onigiri, eyes roving everywhere but him, and begrudgingly accepted the loss with her silence. When she finally did look at him, she rolled her eyes at his knowing smile.

"Now I have a question for you," he said. She stopped chewing. "How are things at Parsons?"

Nora pretended to focus her efforts on chewing as she tried to think of a response that wouldn't kill her chances at a signature. "Are you asking as an author who's trying to decide whether to sign his contract?" She'd have added an *or* to that statement, but she wasn't sure what to call him—or what she'd want to call him.

Something like understanding crossed his face. "No. Not as an author."

Nora took a drink of water, knowing he was still watching. He'd stepped out of his author role and probably expected her to do the same, to set her editorial duties aside and answer him honestly. But she didn't have that luxury.

She opened her mouth, closed it. "Things are great."

She had a feeling he wouldn't let her get away with it that easily, and sure enough, he had a follow-up. "How great?"

Nora played with one of her edamame pods, twirling it in place. "A normal amount."

"Paint me a picture."

"I'm not much of a painter."

Andrew shrugged, undeterred. "Quantify it. Scale of one to ten."

He was relentless. She gave him a wary look over her cup of water. "You ask too many questions."

"Okay." He set his rice ball down and considered her with keen eyes and a scheming smile, like she was a puzzle he wanted to solve. "Since asking as myself got me nowhere, what if I asked it as an author?"

Nora shook her head, unable to resist smiling. "That depends, author. How would you rate your likelihood of signing the contract? Scale of one to ten, please."

"Five."

She liked the way his teeth slid up his bottom lip when he said it. Like he was biting his lip in slow motion. But it was inappropriate to read this much into the way he said a number. She drifted up to see he was already watching her.

"I'm glad you had a number ready, but not everything can be quantified," Nora said.

"Anything can be quantified—risk, worth, success. Did you know there's a global happiness report that ranks countries by average happiness level?"

It didn't surprise her that Andrew Santos, actual sunbeam except for whenever she had him scowling at her, read such a thing as happiness reports.

"Dare I ask what your happiness level is?" Nora asked, slightly afraid of the answer. He didn't disappoint.

"Ten."

Nora paused. "Out of ten?"

"Yeah."

"So…" She squinted at him. "You're the happiest person in the universe?"

"No, it's more that…I'm healthy. I have a job I love. I get along with my family. I make too much money, as you've been kind enough to point out. I have no reason to complain. So why not ten?"

It made perfect sense that he would have this outlook. Possible teasing remarks cropped up in her mind, but they all seemed trivial. A wistful ache burrowed inside her as she faced the idea that he was this content and she was so very not.

"I think that's nice," Nora said.

He gave her the curious stare he seemed to use when he couldn't tell if she was joking. "What about you?"

She couldn't say the first number that came to mind: three. A brash, unavoidable three. Not after Andrew's speech. Nora didn't have the money, or the job, but she had everything else going for her, didn't she? Why should her number be so low? How could it?

Nora swallowed, tongue thick in her mouth. She steeled

herself, putting on an expression of cool indifference. "I maintain that some things aren't quantifiable."

Andrew lowered his chin in grim disappointment. "That's a cop-out answer."

"I need to hear more about your ten." She rested her elbows on the table. "Is there anything you would change about your life? At all?"

"Of course. But it doesn't mean I'm still not a ten."

"What would you change?"

A faraway look came over him. "My family's mostly in Pittsburgh. Ideally, they'd live closer—my nephew especially, because he's five and he forgets me every time I see him. I take it very personally."

"As any well-adjusted person would," she said. It was so easy to imagine Andrew, in all his playfulness, making faces and playing games with a five-year-old.

"Anything else?"

A flash of hesitation. "You won't make fun of me?" he asked.

"No promises."

He grunted his disapproval, but he spoke anyway. "I don't have a lot of friends here." He paused, gaze flickering to Nora as if expecting a retort. When she didn't reply, he continued, "It's so easy to get into a routine of *work, home, book* that I let it suck up all my time."

Nora nodded, trying not to react visibly. She never would have guessed that this man, who had people lining up at the conference for a smile and a signature, who could make someone blush with a joke, had the same trouble as Nora when it came to making friends.

"Glad to help you shake up your routine," she said.

He chuckled and picked up another rice ball, expression relaxed as he regarded her. "What about you?"

She should have known he would lob this back to her. Now that she knew about her three, she couldn't think of anything else. It sat on her chest like a lump of lead.

Ignoring it, Nora shrugged. "I guess I don't have a lot of friends either."

Andrew's eyes glinted. "Does that make us best friends by default?"

She tried to keep a straight face but found it slipping. "It does not."

"I'm kidding," he said. "Obviously my nephew is my best friend."

"Obviously," she repeated. She watched him, unable to help the smile on her face. But when Andrew grew thoughtful, she suspected he'd find some way to bring the conversation back to happiness. She couldn't have him unearthing another dormant truth to make her question herself even more. She'd done enough soul-searching for the day.

With a couple of carefully placed questions, she got him talking about the research he'd done in grad school. While editing his last book, Tom had had to talk Andrew off the ledge of spending an entire chapter on his very specific dissertation topic. In the end, Tom had bargained him down to a sidebar. Tom knew how to do that—how to tell authors something they didn't want to hear and convince them to do something they didn't want to do. Not because he'd persuaded them to come around to his side of thinking, but because they trusted that he knew best.

Nora knew if she got Andrew to trust her, it would be for all the wrong reasons. It would be leading him to Parsons when their offer wasn't what he deserved, all because she wanted a promotion. Even if she had the courage—and the job security—to lead him to Weber, her main motive would be the coordinator position. If she truly wanted to help him, she'd stop trying to influence his decision. But that would leave her exactly where she was now: an overworked, underpaid three.

She walked him to the Montgomery BART station afterwards, pitiful three still on her mind. When they reached the station entrance, she stared up at him, not sure what was going to happen. Not sure what she wanted to happen.

He leaned down to hug her. She knew it was a possibility, but it was unexpected all the same. She wrapped an arm around his back, the other extended awkwardly with her onigiri box. For a moment, she let herself lean into him, pressing her cheek into his shirt. He smelled like cedar and citrus.

Nora watched him disappear down the steps into the BART station. As she walked back to the office, she could feel where his arms had been. She still felt like she was being hugged. Every part of her, right down to her lead-weight three, took comfort in that feeling of being embraced.

When Nora returned to the office, she walked directly to Rita's cubicle. She knew that if she didn't, Rita would pop up ten seconds later, eager to hear how the lunch went.

"Hi," Nora said.

"Hi! You took him to lunch, did you? Any updates there?" Rita's optimistic expression didn't leave room for disappointment, but Nora didn't have a choice.

"I told him we only offer bestselling authors that royalty rate, like you said. He's still thinking about it." Nora kept her voice upbeat, as if there was any good news in stasis.

"All right." Rita's smile wilted a little, but she seemed to accept the lack of news. "Keep me posted."

Nora walked to her cubicle feeling like she'd let Rita down, even though she'd made a genuine effort to tell Andrew it was a good deal. Even though she'd given Rita an immediate status update on the lunch. Even when she tried to do the right thing, apparently, it didn't matter when she was only doing it to cover up something worse.

Nora sank into her chair. She meant to put her leftovers in the fridge, but she found herself starting a text to Andrew. She typed out the question growing louder in her mind, just to see how it looked written out. What does it mean if I'm a three on the happiness scale?

Andrew would know. He would have an answer. He would cite research, come up with an action plan. Tell an anecdote about when he was seven years old, because that was apparently the age when he was most relatable to Nora.

Nora deleted the text before she could send it.

CHAPTER SIXTEEN

Something was wrong.

Nora woke to silence instead of the violent buzz of her cell phone. Her eyes opened easily, readily, instead of the reluctant prying weekday mornings required. She saw the laptop next to her, knew she'd fallen asleep no earlier than 3:00 a.m. pulling together proposal materials for Weber, and felt the dread billow in her stomach when she pieced these clues together and realized she'd overslept.

She felt around for her phone lying uselessly on the nightstand and peered at the screen. It was nearly ten o'clock.

A marquee of obscenities scrolled in Nora's mind as she tripped around the room, flinging clothes on—yesterday's jeans crumpled on the floor, the olive tunic on top of her clean laundry pile. In the bathroom only to splash water on her face and brush teeth fast enough to taste iron, and then she slipped into flats and sped out the door.

A train was waiting when she pressed her card against the reader at the BART station. She scrambled past the fare gates, pounded up the stairs, and came to a halt at the top, where she had an excellent view of the train taking off without her.

Nora rubbed her eyes and plodded to the San Francisco side of the platform. She checked her Parsons email as she waited. A cover mechanical she needed to review for errors before it went to print. An email from one of Tom's authors asking for an extension on his deadline. A couple of emails from Rita asking her to make updates in the content management system. Some bullshit email from Henry Brook she wasn't in the mood to open. Nora took a deep breath and let it out. This was all fine. Usual morning activity. No one asking where she was, no need to explain the oversleeping. She would arrive in half an hour, she would stay late to make up for it, and it would be fine.

Nora glanced up at the platform screen. Four minutes until the next train. She opened a new tab to check her Weber email.

A flood of emails awaited her, all with the same subject line: *Re: Interest from Irene Nichols*. All replies to the email Nora sent last night.

Her pulse raced as she clicked on the most recent message and scrolled down the thread. There, at the bottom, was her unsuspecting email that had started it all, announcing to the team that one of the potential authors she'd contacted—Irene Nichols, a prominent voice in psychology, according to Nora's research—had replied with enthusiasm to Nora's email asking if she might be interested in writing a book for Weber on the science of productivity.

Violet was first to reply, ten minutes after Nora's email:

We really don't want to publish anything from Irene Nichols. She got in hot water recently for some comments she made about the Black Lives Matter movement.

Another email from Violet, sent a minute later, had a link to an article about the incident.

Nora's cheeks burned. She scrolled through the rest of the email chain, in which others from the team helpfully added additional links with information about the situation. It then turned to theorizing, with someone positing that Irene Nichols probably leapt at the chance to write a book for Weber as a way to combat the bad press. Then, in emails sent this morning, they'd made a couple of gleeful jokes about how disappointed Irene would be when she learned Weber wasn't interested in her after all.

The last email, sent from Lynn to only Nora, was a kind offer.

Let me know if you need help crafting your response to Irene. I've had to rescind a few invitations in my day and it's never fun!

An approaching BART car sounded its arrival. Nora shoved her phone in her pocket as the car roared toward the platform, but she pulled it out again when she took a seat on the train. Already too much time had passed without acknowledging her mistake. She hit Reply All on the last email with the team and wrote a message that no one would suspect was typed with shaking hands.

Thank you for letting me know—I had no idea. I'll reach out to Irene ASAP and let her know we aren't interested after all. Sorry about that, everyone. I'll be sure to re-search potential authors more carefully going forward.

She'd email Irene this afternoon, when she had more distance from her failure. She tried to think of something else—anything at all to distract herself with—but she couldn't move past the shame of being so wrong and being told how wrong she was in front of everyone she knew at Weber. Just when she was starting to feel excited about work, getting praised for the authors she was bringing over, this happened. She wondered how slip-ups like this factored into the six-month timeline. If six months would become seven, eight, nine months, or however long it would take for them to forget her mistakes.

Nora made it to her desk, started her computer, and replied to enough emails to show she had a pulse. At last, the only unread email remaining was from Henry Brook. She gritted her teeth and opened it.

> These are the slides for a presentation I'm giving next week. Pls make sure the text and images are aligned.

> thx

Ordinarily, this might invoke the usual amount of annoyed obedience. Now, fresh off the Irene Nichols mistake, Nora read his words with a clenched jaw and knew she could not obey Henry Brook today. She remembered Andrew telling her there was no harm in asking for what she wanted. Best-case scenario, Candace might approve Nora's proposal to murder Henry Brook. She stalked to Candace's desk, not bothering with pleasantries. Nora had no pleasantries to give.

"Why does Henry Brook think I'm his go-to person for everything lately?" Nora asked, trying to keep her voice even. "I thought I'd just be sending him those tip sheets that once, but he's got me doing other stuff. Updating copy, formatting documents...I don't know why he keeps coming to me."

Candace, nodding along with this, said, "He said he's been mentoring you."

Nora tensed, almost laughed, died a little and came back to life. "Mentoring?"

"Didn't you say you had an interest in marketing? I thought it must have been something to do with that."

She had said that once, before she hated everything. Nora chose to pivot away from that.

"Can someone else help him? Between Tom and Lynn's titles, Rita's titles, and admin stuff, I don't have a lot of time."

"I know," Candace said. "As soon as he gets up to speed on the team—or replaces his assistant—he'll stop bothering you." She looked at Nora and sighed. "I'm sorry. If it was anyone here pulling this crap, I'd end it in a second, but..." Candace shook her head grimly. Nora knew where she was going. This was someone in New York, who outranked their highest-ranking person here, and Candace's hands were tied. And so, it seemed, were Nora's.

Nora decided Henry could wait to hear back about his slides. Instead, she gave in to her growling stomach and stopped in the café on the corner for a breakfast sandwich. Oversleeping meant no time for the toast she usually had at home. She would allow herself this one comfort: a warm bacon, cheddar, and egg sandwich to wolf down as she replied to emails at her desk.

Her order number, she realized as she waited for her sandwich, was zero. It was hard not to find significance in this receipt. Her three had felt so small yesterday, but today she was so far from a three. She may as well be a zero. She stared at the number with weariness that faded into resignation.

It was never devastating events that sent Nora's mind spiraling toward a place that scared her. It could be a major change that slowly gnawed at her, or several insignificant moments that piled up and sent her right back to the thoughts she tried to avoid. She felt sometimes that her mind was always in some state of interacting with these thoughts, whether it was gravitating toward them, trying to move away from them, or pretending they didn't exist. But they were always, always there.

The first time it happened, Nora was twelve. Her mother flew to Wilmington to help Nora's aunt adjust to daily life after a car accident left her unable to care for herself. The weight of her mother's absence had filled Nora with a heavy sadness she hadn't known existed. In class, she spent her time looking at her student planner, counting the days until her mother would be back. March 14 was so teasingly far away, in new territory of blank, unwritten pages. She would flip back to the current date in disappointment, seeing the pages of weeks she had to get through first.

As Nora was drying off after a shower on another lonely evening, wondering how she would get through the many days ahead when it took so much effort to get her through just this one, she realized she could just...not. If she weren't alive, she wouldn't have to work so hard to get from one moment to the next. The lonely moments would end.

It scared her, the seriousness with which she considered it. In that moment, as she stood in the bathroom staring at the wall and piecing it together, it was the most tempting thought in the world, to have it be over. She knew it didn't make sense, that it was a far too permanent solution to a temporary problem, but under the weight of her loneliness, it seemed so easy.

But she shook herself out of it. She hung up her towel, put on her pajamas, and retreated to her bedroom. Knowing she would need a distraction, she pulled out *The Lion, the Witch and the Wardrobe* and immersed herself in the comforts of a faraway yet familiar world.

That had gotten her through the remaining couple of weeks, reading book after book in a series she'd already read. She stayed up reading until her eyes were so heavy that all she had to do was close the book and switch off her flashlight, and she'd fall into a dead sleep. In class, she stifled yawns and read snippets of the book in her lap when she could. She spent every moment absorbing the words on the pages, knowing that if she stopped, if she gave herself a chance to think about anything besides Narnia, the missing would come back. And with the missing would come the other thoughts.

Since Nora's first introduction to the allure of suicide, it kept coming back to her. Whenever she faced something even slightly difficult or felt that pinch of despair, it crept out of the dark corners of her mind to remind her it was still there, willing to talk whenever she was. Nora began to think of life as a battle between herself and this creature. It lurked in the shadows of her mind, always watching, always waiting for a moment when she was vulnerable enough to listen to what it had to say.

She felt it coming closer when the layoffs started. Seeing Tom and Lynn—who she thought of sometimes as her work parents—suddenly leave and realizing one of the few comforts she had left at Parsons was being taken away from her had made the creature perk its ears, sensing an opening. She ignored it.

Beth's departure widened the opening. Beth had become the one bright spot left in Nora's workday. She felt the weight of

Beth's absence, the dread of knowing what it meant. The creature crawled closer.

When her pay was cut, Nora pushed the thoughts down, found a way to make rent, and let the challenge of a new job distract her. But distractions were never enough. The spinning blades on the ceiling fan were never enough. The creature would always return.

As it did now. Standing in a café, staring at a receipt that told her she was nothing. This unsuspecting receipt fluttered on top of the pile in Nora's mind, on top of Henry Brook and his incessant requests, on top of the Irene Nichols mistake, on top of oversleeping, on top of the guilt of the lies she told at Weber and Parsons, on top of how conflicted she felt whenever she spoke to Andrew, all resting on the shaky foundation of layoffs that Parsons execs built. The weight of this insignificant receipt sent the pile tumbling down, tearing through floorboards. The creature pulled itself up through the hole this pile left behind. It smiled at Nora and said hello.

It didn't matter that she threw the receipt away when her number was called. It didn't matter that she ignored the creature while she sat at her desk biting into an egg sandwich she couldn't taste and reading cover copy until her vision blurred. It would be waiting for her when she got tired of fighting. And she was so tired of fighting.

As the day wore on and the office grew quieter, Nora couldn't take the silence anymore. It was a silence that would only grow louder when she went home and laid down to stare at her ceiling fan.

The alternative to persistent silence was finding someone to avoid it with. She glanced at her phone and wondered what Beth was up to tonight—if she was available or if she'd have plans with her gaggle of new work friends. Nora wound and unwound a curl around her finger, playing out the scenario in her head. If Nora saw Beth tonight, there would be faking involved: smiles, laughter, cheer. The thought was enough for her to start retreating from the idea, except that would leave her to contend with her ceiling fan.

Nora tugged her finger free from her hair and tapped her phone awake. Beth was always a comfort, and faking fatigue was better than whatever her ceiling fan was doing to her. She pulled up a text to Beth.

Drinks after work?

Nora realized too late that she should have clarified. Beth hadn't caught on to the *I hate everything* subtext and saw fit to turn the occasion into a social event, inviting a couple of Parsons coworkers Nora didn't know very well—Julie, associate editor for the psychology team, and Eric, a project manager for the journals division. Nora used to think of them as the people with whom she competed for Beth's attention, fully aware that the competition was only in her head. Now, even after Beth left Parsons, the competition was apparently still ongoing.

They sent Nora a chat late in the day, saying they'd be meeting at the elevator to head to the pub. And Nora, reluctant to walk four blocks with two people she hardly knew, had caught their new editorial assistant Kelly in the kitchen and asked if she wanted to join her on a happy hour outing. As Nora walked off with Kelly's acceptance, she thought about how she might have felt guilty at one point about the way

Kelly lit up at the invitation, how Kelly didn't know the offer stemmed more from Nora's desire for a buffer than interest in Kelly's friendship. But maybe Nora was beyond guilt now. Maybe a month of lies had finally made her immune. How fortunate.

Their party of four slid into a booth at the pub. When they put in their drink orders, Nora's phone buzzed with an apologetic text from Beth, about how something at work had come up but she'd get there soon. That sounded about right for today.

While Julie recapped a call with an author, Nora slumped forward onto the sticky table and rested her chin on her arms. She was starting to think this outing changed nothing. Her thoughts were still there, demanding to be heard. She elbowed her beer aside to make more room for slouching. Next to her, Kelly moved her cider out of the way.

Julie paused. "Something wrong?" she asked.

Nora tried to think of a way to reframe her thoughts. "What—" She paused, searching for a euphemism. "What keeps you going?"

"Like, in life?"

Nora nodded. What she'd really been thinking about was her mental list of reasons to live. It was one of her tricks whenever the thoughts came to haunt her: thinking of a reason to live, any reason. The sweet, nutty flavor of hazelnut gelato melting on her tongue. The waddling pig she'd see walking on a leash in her neighborhood, with its wiry black hair and the small, snuffling noises it made when it sniffed in the grass. She always told herself that the next time she saw it, she'd gather the resolve to talk to its owner and pet it. She couldn't kill herself if she had a pig to pet, could she?

She ran through her list again: gelato; pig; Gilroy garlic mac and cheese from Homeroom; the smell of books in City Lights; and the comfortable, rubber-soled boots she'd just bought and the silent footsteps they gave her. If she could add to this list— put something more significant on it—she might be more than a three on a good day. More than the zero she was today.

"Well…" Julie drank her cider and leaned back in their booth. "I've always wanted to get my poems published. When I get tired of Parsons's bullshit, I focus on that."

Nora lifted her chin and sat up. "You write poems?"

"I had a few published in literary journals back when I wrote and submitted stuff in college, but I haven't done that in a while. I started teaching, and then I just kind of stopped writing."

The revelations kept coming. "You *teach*?"

"I did. I was an English teacher for, like, five years."

It was hard to imagine Julie working in a field besides publishing. It was hard to imagine any of them anywhere but Parsons. But Julie and Eric were a little older, maybe midthirties. It was only natural that they had lives before Parsons. Most people didn't come straight out of college like Nora and Beth.

"What happened?" Nora asked.

"It was too much," Julie said with a shrug. "Teaching all day, grading homework all night. Meeting with parents and getting yelled at for doing my job. It sucked. So I found a job that suited me better, and now I have time to write poetry again. I just need to get back on it."

"Wow." Nora studied Julie—her feathery, lavender-blond hair; her floral dress; her bomber jacket—and tried to picture her in a classroom. She could see Julie the teacher. She could see Julie the poet. Maybe this was all Julie's innate effortlessness, though, because Nora could imagine her fitting in anywhere. "How'd you know publishing suited you better?"

Julie laughed. "I didn't. I was just looking for jobs and applying to anything I thought I could do. I got to the final round of interviews at a place that was looking for a corporate trainer, and I was feeling kind of *meh* about it. But then Parsons called me to interview for an editorial assistant job, and as soon as I got there, I just knew."

Nora knew this hunch. She'd come away from her Parsons interview with a similar feeling, brought on by how kind and welcoming everyone she spoke to was. Even the temp she'd shared an elevator with had taken the time to give Nora a rundown of her two months at Parsons and wished her luck on her interview, all while balancing two drink carriers filled with coffee cups.

Over time, the appeal of that kindness had been dulled by the administrative work, the restructuring, and the departures of her favorite coworkers. But Julie was probably a better judge of what was a good fit for her, coming off several years in another career. For Nora, then just out of college, it was all guesswork. She wondered if, now that she had a little more experience, she might be a better judge of what suited her next time. Julie was proof that it was okay not to know right away. That you could get it right the second time around.

Nora turned to Eric, now wondering what secrets he held. He always waved at her when they passed in the halls, but she couldn't remember ever having a conversation with him. All she really knew of him was what she could see at a glance: horn-rimmed glasses, stocky frame, and a decent hallway wave paired with that awkward, close-lipped smile everyone gives when they're in a hurry.

"What about you?" she asked him.

"What keeps me going?" he asked. She nodded. "I'd be remiss if I didn't mention my husband and our kids—which means being able to sleep in one day is a big dream of mine." Nora forced a chuckle and waited for him to continue. His expression grew pensive. "I guess...I've always wanted to travel more. I haven't even been outside the U.S. Maybe when the kids are older, we could go...everywhere. Sydney, Rome, Tokyo. That would be cool."

This was new, too, the knowledge that she had him beat in something. She'd only been to one other country—Mexico, on a cruise with her parents—but it counted. She wondered what onigiri was like in Japan and added *Tokyo* to her mental list.

"Kelly?" Nora tried.

"Pass."

Nora laughed. "What?"

"I don't know!" Kelly said. "For the last year, I've been working toward graduating and getting a job in publishing. Now I've done that. I don't really know where to go from here."

"You sweet little newborn," Julie said. "I forgot how young you are."

Kelly just shook her head. She didn't say anything for a few moments, but then she brightened and sat up straighter. "Okay, I have one. I've always kind of wanted to move to New York. I went there once when I was a kid and—I don't know. It just seems exciting." She looked from Eric to Julie to Nora, awaiting their response.

"Cool," Eric said.

"You'd have your pick of publishing houses over there," Julie said.

"Yeah," Nora agreed. "That's a great one." She played with her coaster on the table but paused when she saw Eric watching her.

"Your turn," he said.

She took in a breath. "There's a cute, fat pig in my neighborhood, and I really want to pet it."

They laughed. Nora answered their questions about the pig as well as she could, but she was relieved when the conversation turned to debate about ordering another round. No matter how much she tried to cling to her list, she knew everything on it was minor. It was supposed to distract her from not having a greater purpose in life, but Julie's poetry ambitions and Eric's future family vacations and Kelly's New York dreams put everything back into a daunting perspective. She needed more than her list of scraps to cling to. She needed to be more than a three.

It was around then that Beth flew in, all apologies as she pulled up a chair to the booth.

"I'm so sorry," she said, still out of breath. "A client call went long, and then there was something wrong with a marketing package we were sending them and we all had to rush to fix it, and it was chaos." She settled into the chair and tucked a few flyaways behind her ear. "What are we talking about?"

"What keeps you going in life?"

Nora gave Eric a grateful look for taking up the helm.

Beth hesitated, as if awaiting further instruction. "Can I get an example?"

"Traveling the world," Eric said, gesturing to himself. He went around the table, pointing at everyone. "Publishing poems. Moving to New York. Petting a pig."

"I didn't realize we were so philosophical tonight." Beth shot a teasing look around the table. "I don't know. Is it cheating to say more than one thing? I feel like there's a lot, probably. Write a book. Run a marathon in under four hours. Give someone a black eye."

Laughter erupted at this last one. Nora realized too late that she should have laughed too. But now Beth was looking at her.

"What's the story behind the pig?" Beth asked.

The mood was getting too genial. Nora didn't miss her ceiling fan exactly, but being surrounded by happy people was starting to take a different kind of toll.

"I've got to head out, actually." She said the words before she could dwell on how odd it was to leave so abruptly. "I hope we can do this again," she said to no one in particular. She waved without making eye contact and sped to the bar to pay her tab.

It wasn't long before Beth sidled up next to her. "Hey."

"Hey." Nora afforded her a quick glance and went back to watching the bartender.

"Are you okay?"

"Yeah. I just have to get home," Nora said. She could still feel Beth's eyes on her. She shifted her weight to her other leg.

"Okay, I know. But I don't mean now, I mean in general. I don't think I've seen you post on BookTap in like two months."

Nora felt her stomach sink, like she'd finally been caught doing something she wasn't supposed to—and there were so many somethings to choose from.

She mustered her energy and faced Beth with an approximation of a smile. "Is this an intervention?"

Beth's eyes were too serious for that. "Do you want it to be?"

The bartender dropped off Nora's credit card and receipt. She signed it and tucked the card into her back pocket, then met

Beth's eyes with a sigh. "Okay, how would you rate your happiness on a scale of one to ten?"

"We *are* philosophical tonight." Beth's smile dulled when she looked over Nora's serious expression. "Sorry," she said. "Well…I mean, if I have food and shelter, who am I to say I'm not a ten?"

Nora wondered how it had taken her this long to realize Beth and Andrew had the same disturbingly sunny outlook on life.

"But really, I guess I'm an eight," Beth went on. "I think when I'm a homeowner with a dog, I'll be a ten, but that's a long way off." She went back to studying Nora. "Why?"

Nora looked down, playing with the pen on the counter. She was the one who raised the subject; she may as well see it through. "I'm a three." She searched for an explanation, something else to say, but there was nothing. She set the pen down and met Beth's stare.

It was a little unsettling to see Beth this serious—this speechless. "Why?"

"Now who's philosophical?" Nora said, giving a dark chuckle that Beth didn't seem to register. Realizing Beth wouldn't let her go without some kind of explanation, Nora said, "It started with the layoffs, and then it just kept getting worse. I thought I'd get out, and I haven't been able to, and it's all just a lot. But I'm fine. It's just exhausting to be around people sometimes." Nora kept her eyes on the menu above the bar, as if memorizing custom cocktails could free her from Beth's reaction. Aware that Beth was still watching her, Nora cleared her throat and attempted a bright, *nothing to see here* smile. "Anyway. I'll see you later." She turned and fled before Beth could respond.

As she walked to the BART station, Nora wondered if it had

been too much to lay on Beth—or if the way she did it, confessing and running, was unfair. But nothing about her three felt fair.

Her phone buzzed as she walked down the steps of the station.

Thank you for telling me. We're having lunch next week and it is nonnegotiable.

Unless I'm exhausting in which case I get it.

Beth's words pulled at something inside Nora, telling her it wasn't a mistake to be honest. She replied I can do lunch and tucked her phone into her pocket, then stared at the monitor of destinations and times. A Richmond train was coming in three minutes.

But what was waiting for her there? A Craigslist roommate and an empty bed. A ceiling fan to stare at. The creature.

She thought about the bar she'd just left, the crowded booth and the cheerful chatter flying around. She didn't want to go home, but she didn't want to be surrounded by people either.

Person, maybe. Person, she could do.

She pulled out her phone again and texted Andrew to ask where he lived.

CHAPTER SEVENTEEN

Nora stood in front of a squat blue apartment building surrounded by trees, staring at an intercom buzzer with a letter next to every button. Andrew had said he was in "number B." This man who didn't understand that letters weren't numbers was a published author.

She pressed the button for *B*, ignoring the moths fluttering around the light fixture above. The door buzzed, shrill and abrupt, and she grabbed the handle to let herself in. Stepping into the dimly lit hallway, she didn't have time to consider what floor *B* was on because there was Andrew, walking down the hall. In gym shorts.

"You found it!"

He folded her into a hug like there was no question about it. Nora closed her eyes and breathed in. He smelled like a cross between deodorant and sweat. She didn't mind it.

She stood back and let her gaze linger over him. "I like the shorts."

He glanced down at his clothes and sighed. "I just got back from the gym."

"You're usually fancier."

Now he looked her up and down. "You're usually quieter."

She ignored him. "Where's *B*?"

"That would *B* this one right here," he said with far too much amusement in his voice.

She wouldn't *B* surprised if he'd chosen this apartment specifically for the puns.

Apartment B turned out to be a cluttered one bedroom. Most spectacular was what *wasn't* there. She didn't know anyone who lived without roommates in something bigger than a studio. Granted, she didn't know a lot of people, but the point remained. She knew better than to bring up the benefits of royalties, so she stood in the living room and took it in: the gray fabric couch half-covered with clothes, the TV stand cluttered with cords and playing cards, the overstuffed IKEA bookshelf, the desk piled with papers and an open box of cereal.

It shouldn't have surprised her to learn he was messy, but he came off so composed, what with the graduate degrees and the professor job and the published book. It made her feel the slightest bit better to know now that whenever he emailed her, she could imagine him sitting at his cereal desk.

"I like your place," she commented.

"I cleaned up, believe it or not. In the time I had." He stood by the front door, gauging her reaction. He didn't seem to know where to put his hands. One played with the cord on his shorts while the other hung at his side.

"I know. That's okay. I didn't give you much time." Nora looked away, busying herself with trying to make out the titles of the books lining his bookshelf. Every passing second reminded her that she'd shown up here unannounced and probably unwelcome, and she couldn't expect him to fix her life just because she was here.

He stayed there, still gauging. "How have you been?"

A complicated question, if there ever was one. Nora ran a hand over her hair and turned to him. "How would you feel about pizza?" she asked.

"Nora."

"Santos."

He narrowed his eyes and gave her a puzzled look. "Are you a little bit drunk?"

"I would call it tipsy-adjacent."

Andrew rubbed the back of his neck, looking thoughtful as he considered Nora. "I would love pizza," he decided, breaking into a warm smile. "Why don't you sit down?"

That was all the invitation she needed. She sank into the couch between a tie and a pair of jeans, sending Andrew into a belated cleaning frenzy.

"I'll just grab those…and that," he said as he reached for them, but she pulled the tie from his grasp and worked her head through the opening. Once she wrestled it past her hair, her curls fluffed back into place.

"Can we have it delivered?" she asked. "Do you like pepperoni?"

Andrew conceded and ordered a pizza. Afterwards, he tossed his phone onto the couch but didn't sit down.

"Would you mind if I took a quick shower?" he asked. "On account of the gym and all?"

She dipped her head into a low, somber nod. "I will allow this."

"Okay. That's my phone. If the pizza deliverer calls, press five to buzz them in. And…here's a book," he said, looking around and grabbing one off his desk. "For your entertainment. I'll be back."

She examined the cover of the book: mint green with pink block letters, something about creativity. To its credit, it didn't sound as boring as some of the Parsons books she endured.

The sputter of a shower sounded in the background. Nora flipped through the pages and the book fell open at the halfway point. Marking the page was a piece of card stock cut roughly in the shape of a bookmark. At the top, in her handwriting, were the words *Keynote Speaker!!*

As the conference wound to a close, Nora had gone around plucking out the bookmarks to rubber-band together and take back to the office. Andrew must have gotten to this one first. If he'd seen her find this, she would have pretended not to see meaning in it. She would have teased him for being so self-involved as to steal a bookmark that mentioned him. But here, alone, she savored the feeling it gave her—that same whole-body warmth she got whenever he hugged her.

Nora settled into the couch, resting her head on the armrest and propping the book up on her stomach. Her eyes flitted over the words on the page, but they kept coming back to the bookmark.

She closed her eyes and let the book fall forward. At some point, the shower stopped running. Moments later came footsteps, drawing closer.

"What's this?"

Nora opened her eyes. Andrew stood above her, hair tousled and wet. He gestured to her, the book, her tie.

"You stole my bookmark," she said.

"It says *Keynote Speaker!!*" His finger poked the top of the bookmark. "I'm keynote speaker."

"That's what you want to be called, is it?"

"Yes. Bestselling author works too."

She laughed. He made his way around the couch, and Nora sat up to make room for him. He'd changed into a plain white shirt and jeans. She liked seeing him like this, more casual and approachable than the button-downs he usually wore. She could see his bare arms for the first time, the slight curve of muscle.

Now that he was sitting next to her, only inches apart, Nora didn't know what to do. She stared ahead at the TV that wasn't on. With each passing second, she was reminded more and more of her abrupt, possibly unwelcome appearance.

"Is it weird that I'm here?" she asked. It was better if she mentioned it. It was good to show self-awareness, maybe.

Andrew leaned his back against the arm of the couch to face her. "It's only weird if you make it weird."

Nora nodded, pretending to find meaning in his nonanswer. She turned slightly toward him. "Did you have plans tonight?"

"Only put off writing my manuscript—which you're helping me do right now, so thank you."

She forced a smile. Soon he'd ask why she was here, and she'd have to tell him about the three, and she knew she wouldn't be able to use the same blurt-it-and-run strategy she'd used on Beth. For starters, pizza was coming. And now that the looming number had been given voice, she knew she couldn't lock it back in. It pressed forward, already on the tip of her tongue.

He eyed her curiously. "Did you come from somewhere?"

"A work happy hour thing." Nora traced a seam on the side of her jeans. "It was at a bar a couple of stops from here, and I didn't feel like going back to Oakland right away, and—" She looked up, suddenly breathless, and let the words burst forth. "What if I'm a three?"

"A three?" he repeated.

"On that happiness scale. You're a ten. I think I'm a three."

"Oh." His brow furrowed. "Why?"

Nora found a loose thread on the seam and pulled it. "It's not one thing. It's just a lot of things. I feel like it was a slow descent. Like at one point, maybe a year ago, I was probably—well, not a ten, but whatever's normal for people who aren't you."

"The U.S. average was six-point-something, almost seven." Only Andrew Santos could spout happiness statistics from memory while managing to sound comforting.

"Yeah. I could have been a six-point-something a year ago. But then..."

"What?"

She cast an uncertain glance at him. He would surely realize the common thread connecting everything she was thinking of. But she'd come this far.

"I think it started when Tom and Lynn were laid off. I didn't like the work I did, but I loved working with them. I thought that even if it took me a while to figure out what I wanted to do in life, I would be fine with that because I loved my team. But then Tom and Lynn left, and suddenly I was doing the work of three people. I was fine because I still had Beth, but then she left. And—" Nora hesitated. This next part would be new information for him. Information that validated his suspicions about Parsons. But for the sake of her three, she needed to get it out there.

"They cut our salaries," she said. Andrew, who up until then had been listening with concern, frowned. "I could barely afford rent as it is, so I took a second job." That, she would have to be vague on. Telling him even this was messy enough. "And today was just one of those days where everything went wrong. At my job. At my second job. I just feel like I can't do it anymore. I'm so tired all the time. So," she said, straightening her posture, "is there something in that happiness report of yours that can tell me what to do?"

Andrew looked physically pained now. She wasn't sure why until she heard his whispered confession.

"I didn't read it."

"What?"

"I didn't read it," he repeated, eyes wide. "I read an article that summarized the findings, and I downloaded the report because I wanted to read it, but it was two hundred pages. I should never talk about reports before I've read them. I clearly misconstrued the information somehow when I was relating it to you, and now it's led to this."

Nora wasn't sure what to expect from her honesty, but watching him panic about his reading habits was not on the list. She'd been wrong, she realized, to think he might know what to do. Her three was apparently beyond even his optimistic capabilities. "It's okay," she said, giving him a weak smile. "Your failure to read an article has no bearing on my three." Still, she could see his mind working overtime as he looked around the room.

"I could read it right now," he offered. "I'm a fast reader." He said it with such hope, eyebrows raised so high his forehead wrinkled.

Nora's small smile grew a little. "Please don't."

He was still looking around, less frenzied than before. But his gaze steadied when he settled his eyes on Nora. "I'm sorry you're having a hard time."

Just this acknowledgment brought relief, let her crawl out from under the weight of pretending everything was fine.

"Thanks." She stared back at Andrew, wondering what he might say next.

He opened his mouth just as his phone chirped. They glanced in its direction, startled. Andrew reached for it. "Pizza's here," he explained. He disappeared into the hall, returning with a pizza box that he set on the coffee table.

Nora was two bites into a slice when he emerged from the kitchen with plates. She relished the way he shook his head when he saw she'd already started eating. It was like things were settling back to normal after her confession. If they had a normal.

"Is there anything more you want to talk about?" he asked, taking a slice of pizza. "About what you were saying before?"

"No." Getting the words out was catharsis enough. Andrew's panic was a clear sign that he wasn't in any position to help her anyway. Nora took another bite. "You?" Follow-up questions about Parsons had to be coming.

Andrew considered as he chewed. "What's your second job?"

"Working in an ice cream shop. I'm an excellent singer." She lifted a brow just enough to let on that she was teasing.

He stopped chewing and delivered a frown. "You are unbelievably cruel."

Nora laughed, swatting the crumpled napkin he threw her way.

But the effect of her confession still lingered, like wisps of smoke hanging in the air around them. Nora reached for a second slice, trying to think of a topic that could bring them back to familiar ground.

"How's the book coming along?" she asked. Andrew let out an uncharacteristic grunt. "That well, huh?"

"I haven't been writing for it."

"Why not?"

He shrugged and drew circles in the crumbs on his plate. "I haven't wanted to. I have it outlined and it's partly written, but when I sit down to write it, I just...don't."

Apathy and inaction, she could get behind. "Why?"

"It just seems...boring," he said.

It *was* boring, because all business books were boring, but she didn't want to bring him down any further.

"Boring how?"

"It's not the book I pitched." He ran a hand through his damp hair and pursed his lips almost bitterly. "You know what they told me when I came to the Parsons office? They wanted me to broaden the topic. Water it down. I wanted to write something based on my dissertation, but they said it would be too narrow."

Nora must have given herself away, because he fell back as if she'd wounded him. "Don't tell me you're on their side, Nora."

She did her best to look unamused, but she felt a smile creeping through. "I'm on the side of logic. Parsons books have to appeal to a broad audience if they want to sell. I think it's good that you expanded your topic."

"That I went from boring and specific to boring and broad?"

She liked seeing him like this, as despondent as he'd ever been. Part of her wanted to bring him down further, find the depths of his misery and swim in it, revel in their mutual unhappiness. In no longer being alone in her unhappiness. But she knew, watching him play with the crumbs on his plate, that it wasn't the same, his unhappiness and hers. He could leave his behind.

"Hey." Nora nudged him in his side and he looked up. "No one would find you boring," she said, thinking back to his keynote, the line of people waiting for his signature at the conference.

"Why do you think we're after you? We don't publish books that won't sell." Actually, they did—a lot—but they always thought they would sell at the time, which counted for something.

It worked. She caught a glimpse of a dimple, just for a moment, before it faded.

"Thanks." He put a hand on her knee. It tingled at the touch. "I do want it to sell—I want it to sell better than my last book. Not because of royalties," he added before she could say anything. "Just...Arthur Moore wrote most of the last book. I just contributed."

"You contributed in a way that blew the last edition out of the water," she reminded him.

He shrugged. "Still, this new book is all me. It's on me if it fails, and it's on me if it succeeds. I want people to read it. I want them to love it. If it doesn't sell as well, I'll feel like a failure. But I still want it to be me. I don't want to just...water it down, slap my name on it, and make money. That's not my idea of selling." He sighed and leaned back against the couch—hand, Nora noticed, still on her knee. "Now that I'm saying it, it sounds so trivial."

"It's not," she said. She couldn't deny that Parsons's approach of publishing broad, easily marketable books was smart from a business perspective. But knowing that Andrew wasn't swayed by the company logic made her feel like she wasn't alone in seeing more than marketability in books. She glanced at him, didn't even look away when he met her gaze. "If it matters to you, it's not trivial." Her order number that morning was glaring proof of that.

"What matters to you?" he asked.

It disappointed her that the only thought that came to mind was *Not Parsons*. Books might have been her instinctual response ordinarily, but that was what led her to Parsons in the first place and look where it had gotten her. Now she had no response. Only a fear that whatever mattered would lead her down a murky path, just as Parsons had.

Nora studied him, searching for an answer. She could say something simple, like "You," and then they'd move closer on the couch and add a physical component to this thing they'd been dancing around for the last few weeks.

She couldn't, though. That would complicate things. There was no good reason to pull him in deeper with this version of Nora, with pieces missing inside her. She missed them. She missed herself. The Nora who giggled with Beth over silly jokes instead of tolerating them with forced laughter. The Nora who spent weekends devouring books instead of working or staring at the ceiling. The Nora who didn't hide from sincerity or truth. That Nora had been gone for a year now, since the layoffs hit her team and sent her retreating further and further into her unhappiness.

But that wasn't any kind of answer to give.

"You."

He held her gaze, surprised but pleased, and she leaned in to kiss him before he could speak.

There wasn't a plan with the kiss. It was meant to distract him—and her—from her swirling thoughts. But it worked. On both of them.

She leaned closer as they kissed. Andrew felt around for their plates, clumsily setting them on the coffee table before pulling her forward to lie on top of him. She'd never been this close to him, this flush against him. His hands stroked her back, her sides. She wanted more.

It was Nora who led them to the bedroom, a move she considered bold only because she didn't know where it was. While she wandered past the couch, fingers threaded between his, she hoped she didn't accidentally lead him to the bathroom.

The room was dark, door ajar, but she made out the shape of a bed and stepped toward it. Andrew drew ahead of her and started throwing things off the bed—shirts, shorts, a towel; he really did believe anything could be a closet if he wanted it to be. She watched him do one last sweep with his eyes, and when he seemed sure there were no more clothes lurking about, he reached an arm out for her to join him. She wanted to say something sarcastic, something like, *You sure it's safe?* and then he could say some kind of retort, but she realized it was pointless to pretend they weren't both already here in his bedroom, finally ready to admit what they wanted. She skipped the remark and joined him on the bed.

She liked the way he looked at her when he took the tie off, the one she'd tipsily wriggled herself into on the couch. It was a look of amused reproach, a raised eyebrow and a smile. He was careful when he took it off, guiding it up her neck and navigating it past her curls.

After he tossed the tie aside, he gently smoothed down her hair, looking so concerned and maybe even content that she had to do something to stop it. She kissed him again, harder this time, to remind him they were not there to exchange romantic gazes.

It worked. She wiped his gazes right off the map, had him squeezing his eyes shut, taking ragged breaths, gripping her hips. She allowed herself to watch him like this, the sheen of sweat on his forehead, the tension in his jaw, because if he didn't see her staring, it was okay.

But it was only temporary. Afterwards, after he'd started getting dressed and she'd stumbled into the bathroom to pee, she came back to find him sitting on the rumpled sheets, half-dressed in his shirt and boxer-briefs, still gazing.

She looked away and picked up her shirt. He waited until she reached for her jeans before speaking.

"Do you need those?"

"I'm not sure they'd let me on BART without pants."

"I mean, you could just sleep here."

"I'm not big on sleepovers," she said. "I should get home, anyway."

"Okay." If he felt any kind of way about it, he didn't let on. Nora appreciated it.

Jeans zipped and buttoned, she went to the living room to gather her things. Andrew followed behind her.

"Thanks for the pizza," she said, glancing at the box on the coffee table, their two plates hastily stacked next to it. "And for letting me come over," she added, meeting his eyes.

"You can always come over," he said. "Even when you're not coming from a bar."

"Okay." They were standing near the door now. Nora bent to put on her flats, then glanced up at him. She stood to kiss him, her reward for breaking that barrier—no more awkwardness and uncertainty upon their hellos and goodbyes. All it took was telling a few truths. Something occurred to her then, and she pulled away.

"You know that what I said about Parsons—I'm not supposed to—"

"I know," he said. "I won't tell anyone."

She nodded, picked up her purse, and started for the BART

station. She walked quickly, partly to escape the darkness of the quiet side street and partly because it was drizzling. Gentle raindrops speckled her feet with cold and she thought about her boots at home, wished she were the sort of person who checked the weather before getting dressed. The sort of person who thought anything through at all.

Whatever lightness she'd felt from her partial honesty was obfuscated by the ways she'd managed to complicate the truth. She'd told Andrew things an author should not know about Parsons, which would surely complicate her ability to sign him and get the assistant editor promotion. And if she couldn't sign him, Rita's suspicions might grow, putting Nora's job at Parsons in jeopardy—and Parsons might be her only option if she continued to make mistakes at Weber. Worst-case scenario, this spontaneous visit might cost her both her jobs and her only real shot at happiness.

She'd also told him unequivocally that he mattered to her, when she was struggling to see past anything besides her fog and her three. And her honesty wasn't even all that honest. He didn't know about the creature and how it warped her mind.

And so she couldn't even feel proud about taking one step forward in search of happiness. Not when she had reason to fear where that step would lead her next.

CHAPTER EIGHTEEN

Andrew waited an entire thirty-six hours before broaching the subject. Nora suspected what was coming when he texted her Sunday morning to ask if she wanted to meet for coffee at the ferry building. When she pointed out that she preferred not to make her weekday commute across the bay on weekends, he invited himself to the East Bay, undeterred.

He even suggested the place, a café on Piedmont, where they sat now: Nora with Earl Grey and what remained of a sesame bagel, Andrew with a half-drunk coffee and a slice of quiche he hadn't touched.

"I was thinking about what you told me the other night," he said right after she'd taken a particularly large bite of her bagel. "I'm sorry I wasn't more helpful."

Nora looked up from her plate, still chewing. "Hmm?"

He raised his eyebrows, like she couldn't possibly forget showing up on his doorstep with a moment's notice and confessing that she was a three.

She hadn't. But now, in daylight, she didn't want to dwell on it. Nora washed the bagel down with a sip of tea and met him with an even stare. "That's fine. I just had a crappy day. Thanks for letting me come over. It helped. It was nice." She tried a smile. The word *nice* was almost offensive in its inoffensiveness, but she couldn't let herself think about it, about Andrew being anything more to her than *nice*, when there were bigger problems lurking in her mind.

"I can help more," he pressed.

"I'm sure you can," she said. "Any soup kitchen would be lucky to have you." Andrew rolled his eyes and Nora smiled. "I appreciate the offer, but I'm really okay."

"I don't want to brag, but I have my life figured out pretty well. That's expertise you don't have."

"That's true," Nora admitted.

"So I read the happiness report."

She searched his face for signs that he was joking. She came up empty. "You said it was two hundred pages," she said.

"It was mostly graphs and charts. It wasn't a big lift." He dug into his quiche, leaving Nora to watch him with what she guessed was a very stupid look on her face.

"You didn't have to do that."

He shrugged and shoved another bite of quiche into his mouth. "It's no big deal. I highlighted some parts I thought might interest you. I can email it to you if you want."

"Okay," Nora breathed, unable to think of a clever response. "Thank you."

"I got you a book too."

"What?" She was almost dizzy from his barrage of kind gestures.

Andrew reached under the table and pulled out a small paper bag. He slid it across the table.

Nora swallowed and took the bag. She peered inside and brought out a hefty paperback. "A career book."

"It's supposed to help you figure out what you want to do with your life," he explained a little too excitedly for her comfort.

She turned it over and read the back. She wouldn't tell him career books had never helped her in the past, not when he was looking at her like this, mouth hung open, eyes fixated on her like he thought she might get an epiphany just from touching the thing. Not when she was still reeling from his kindness.

"Thank you," Nora said. "You really didn't have to do this."

He shrugged. "I wanted to." He was still looking at her with such earnestness that she didn't know what to do. "I want to help you be more than a three. If not a ten, then at least the U.S. average. Let's get you to six-point-something."

It shouldn't have been surprising that Andrew came prepared with books, research, and a goal in mind; it was everything she'd hoped for the other night. But it still touched her to know he put this much thought into her three.

"No guarantees," she said. "But thanks. It's really nice of you." There it was again, that word that said nothing.

"Of course. I want you to be happy. I think it's clear by this point that you're not just an editorial assistant to me. You're... more than that."

"I know. Thanks," she added, smiling what little she could. She knew he was waiting for her to say more, to read between the lines and reciprocate, but it was too much to expect her to feel anything when she couldn't feel at all. And it was too soon for this, wasn't it? No one had confessed feelings to her or anything like it since her last boyfriend in college. Which wasn't to say she'd been closed off since then—every now and then she tried her hand at dating apps—but she was never looking for anything serious. Her last arrangement had been rather ideal: she'd reactivated her account last December to distract herself from her gnawing sadness, and she met someone who wanted to distract himself from his seasonal depression. They had dinner, they had sex, but they never talked feelings. She stopped hearing from him when winter melted into spring, and she supposed he didn't need a distraction anymore.

Now, looking at Andrew, Nora wondered how he'd take it if she told him he was the best distraction she'd ever had. Even in her haze, she couldn't stop herself from thinking about him, texting him, inviting herself over. She wanted to bicker with him, walk beside him, make him laugh, lie next to him, and never ever acknowledge anything serious. If she could just press pause on him and come back when her mind was clear, it would be different.

But here, now, she couldn't let him into her fog. It would be too much—too overwhelming—to talk about. He'd hear the word *suicide* and panic, but for Nora it was what everything always came back to.

Deciding to change the subject, she asked, "How's your manuscript coming along? I know you said you haven't been writing for it. I don't suppose you got any writing done this weekend?"

His frown called her a traitor. "I buy you a book, and you shame me for not writing mine?"

Nora laughed. "No. But if you're helping me, I want to help you if I can. My dad used to give me a sticker every time I did my chores. What if I got you some stickers?" Nora decided there was no victory greater than a glare from Andrew. "Or I could read what you've written, if you need a second opinion."

This sparked his interest. He considered her thoughtfully. "I thought you said you didn't read Parsons books."

"I could make an exception for you."

"Mine's terrible so far."

Nora shrugged. "I love terrible books."

His self-deprecating reluctance gave way to a smile. She had to admit his smiles—especially these ones, so small his dimples didn't even show—were almost as appealing as his glares.

"Maybe," he said.

"Let me give you my email address," Nora said. "My non-Parsons email." This felt like another step toward something. She tried not to think of the ways they were weaving into each other's lives. He was in her phone, she'd been in his apartment, and now he would be in her personal inbox, where she received job rejections and newsletters from her favorite bookstores. It would be ideal if she could have the weaving without him ever asking what it meant—or what it could lead to.

After entering her email address into his phone, he asked, "Would you be reading it in a Parsons capacity?"

"What's a Parsons capacity?"

Andrew twirled his fork between his fingers. "Would you be reading it with an eye for what Parsons wants it to be? Watered-down and bland?"

"No." Nora watched the fork spin in his hand. Here was an opportunity to plant a nudge about signing with Parsons. He was the one who brought it up, after all. "How are you feeling about Parsons, anyway?"

The fork stopped twirling. Andrew set it down and raised his eyes. "I've decided I'm not publishing my book with Parsons."

Nora tried not to react as she struggled to come to terms with this. She busied herself with taking a drink. Warm, bitter tea went down her throat to join the disappointment coiling in her stomach. This decision closed the door on her fantasy of being an assistant editor and working directly with Andrew and authors like him, that appeal of earning enough money that she wouldn't need to work two jobs anymore.

"Okay," she said, keeping her voice even. "You're sure?"

"You're not going to try to get me to change my mind, are you?" Andrew asked.

She looked up, not realizing he'd been watching her. "No," she said.

"You're disappointed," he observed.

Nora gave him a defiant look. "No, I was just wondering how long you knew you weren't going to sign the contract and didn't tell me."

Andrew shrugged. "It was just something I'd been thinking over for a while."

"Right." She studied him with narrowed eyes.

"It's true!" he insisted. Nora could see he was starting to break, though. A smile tugged at his serious expression. He pressed his lips together to hide it.

"Right." Nora continued to stare.

"Fine!" Andrew threw a hand up in the air. "Let's say we're back at that conference. I tell you I'm definitely not signing the contract. Do you still invite me to dinner?"

"Yes," she said before she had time to think. "There's more to you than just your book." She knew this was the screaming truth, but she felt like a hypocrite for saying it. No matter where her thoughts were, her motives told a different story.

Andrew studied her with serious eyes. "Really?"

"Really." As his expression softened, Nora added, "I'm in it for the royalties."

He didn't bother hiding his grin this time. "I can live with that."

She stared into her tea, thinking about what this meant for her. If Parsons was out, she could switch gears to Weber—once she worked out how to confess her ties to Weber in a way that wouldn't make him think she was using him for his book. Again.

"Will you tell Rita?"

She looked up. "Hmm?"

"Will you tell her I won't be signing with Parsons?"

Nora could already picture Rita's face at hearing this news, the downturned mouth, the disappointed eyes. Nora played with a sesame seed on her plate, used her fingernail to slice it in half. "Yeah, I'll tell her." She'd just need to figure out how to do it in a way that didn't raise more suspicion.

"Thanks." He let out a relieved sigh. "It sounds stupid, but I've always kind of had this idea in the back of my mind that my book is this thing between us. Once that's off the table, we could actually be…us." He only held Nora's gaze for a few seconds before looking away.

Nora ached to tell him she would like that too. But his book *was* between them. It was the buoy to get her somewhat on track, a step out of her foggy mind and back to everything she used to be.

All she could do was find something else to focus on. She picked up the parachute book and flipped through the first few pages. Andrew went back to his quiche.

"Learn anything?" he asked.

Nora glanced up. Andrew was looking at her expectantly.

"It must be exhausting to transmit this book to production."

She held up the copyright page. "Look at all the copyright dates. It must be so boring as an EA to transmit essentially the same manuscript over and over again and try not to miss permissions on any new stuff. Do you think he just highlights the new stuff so it's easy to catch?"

Andrew's mouth formed a thin line of disappointment. "You ruin books for me," he said, "as an author and a reader."

"You gave me this book!"

"Yes! I wanted to help you find out what color your parachute is."

"What does that even mean?" she asked.

"Maybe if you read past the copyright page, you'd find out."

She flipped through the book, stopping at the last page. "Oh, this is cool. There's a page where you can submit requests for revisions for next year's edition. I wonder how that works."

"You know what, you don't deserve to know your parachute color." Andrew reached for her book, and she laughed and held it out of his grasp.

"I do appreciate the book. Thank you."

"Will you actually read it?"

She smiled. "I will."

"Good."

They didn't part ways immediately. They walked down Piedmont Avenue until it became Mountain View Cemetery, and Andrew recalled a 5K he did through the cemetery a few years ago. He showed her where the route began and pointed out notable graves along the way.

It felt silly that she'd never been here despite living just a couple of miles from it. It didn't feel like a cemetery. Amid the joggers, the hikers, the people sitting on benches and lounging on the grass, the land that stretched on for acres, the only sign it wasn't a park was the gravestones scattered throughout the grass.

"You could be a chocolatier," Andrew suggested when they passed Domingo Ghirardelli's grave.

"How does one become a chocolatier?"

"I said I'd help; I didn't say I'd do everything for you."

He led them through the twists and turns along the path, bypassing the longer, hillier trails to direct them to the exit. If she wanted to be polite—or perhaps *forward* was the better term—she could have taken him to her apartment. But she didn't like the thought of showing him her home, her bedroom with no decorations whatsoever, introducing him to Allie and having him know a little bit more of the nonwork part of her life. They'd crossed enough boundaries as it was.

But she did walk him back to MacArthur station. There, under the bridge, as the roar of the freeway above drowned out everything else, she kissed him goodbye. Like it was something they did all the time.

Nora leaned against her headboard with the parachute book in her lap. She glanced at *Kindred*, still on her nightstand untouched. It was joined by the Dorothy Dunnett book Lynn had lent her at lunch, also unread.

The career book counted as reading, sort of. She sat back against her pillow and opened it.

A few chapters in, the book described a self-inventory exercise that would help her design her career around skills and interests. That hadn't worked out so well the first time around, when she went all in on books in a straight path to publishing, but maybe there were other options. Still, once she pulled a half-used notebook from her nightstand and turned to a blank page, *books* was the first word she wrote down. Her pen hovered over it as she tried to think of another.

Her phone chimed. Nora let the parachute book fall shut and checked her messages. An email from Andrew, two attachments and two words: *Be nice.*

The first was the happiness report. She skimmed it, spotting bright yellow highlighted text every few pages, saw the charts and the descriptions of regression analyses, and concluded it held no secrets.

She opened the second attachment. The first page to greet her read only *Untitled by Andrew Santos*. She scrolled through the pages, seeing he'd written five chapters. She recognized three of them from the proposal he submitted to Parsons. In the couple of months since then, he apparently hadn't written much else.

Nora skimmed the first chapter. His writing was approachable without being condescending. The chapter was about how effective communication was a cornerstone in the workplace and made its point simply, without grandiose hyperbole. Parsons's books often overstated their importance. Andrew's was quieter, more focused on letting the information speak for itself.

As she read, she could see where he got carried away in later chapters. While Parsons's books were light on research, relying more on examples, anecdotes, and practical advice, Andrew dove a little too deeply into the research. Citing a study to support an idea was one thing; going into detail about the study methodology and quoting from interviews with the study author was quite another. But she knew it was Andrew's passion coming through, his belief that everyone must be as interested in a topic as he was. Nora went through and added comments, praising the parts where he struck the right balance and noting the areas where he needed to dial back the research.

It was tricky, giving authors advice when they had subject matter expertise Nora lacked. Parsons often relied on other professionals in the field to provide in-depth feedback on manuscripts when needed. Making comments in Andrew's manuscript based only on her own thoughts was new territory. She was surprised to find she had any feedback at all, but it was a good sort of surprise. It made her feel like an editor. She felt this way when she read through the Weber dystopian manuscript and made comments in the margins too.

Thinking about the pride she had when commenting on the manuscripts, how good it felt to offer ideas, she opened her notebook to the page with the parachute exercise and wrote *input*. It was vague and hazy, but it was something. One more clue to what a future, non-Parsons job might hold in store for her. And if Andrew wasn't signing with Parsons, her need for a non-Parsons job was getting a little more urgent.

CHAPTER NINETEEN

Nora chewed the cap of her pen as she sat in the Parsons phone room on Monday morning, gathering the resolve to dial in to the Weber meeting. Approaching the wrong author last week was not a terrible offense, but for Nora, who needed to be flawless if she wanted any chance at getting the full-time editorial coordinator position, one error was already one too many.

She dialed the meeting number, entered the code and, after taking a breath, pressed pound to connect to the call. Instantly, the small room filled with pre-meeting chatter. She could make out Emily recapping her weekend hiking in Lands End.

After a few minutes, Emily called the meeting to order and the team went around giving updates about their titles.

"And your updates, Nora?" Violet said.

Nora cleared her throat and looked at the notes she'd jotted on her Post-it. "I've been checking in with John Skalnik on getting his manuscript in. He says he thinks he'll be able to have it in by the end of August, which is only four months past his deadline." She relaxed a little when she heard their chuckles. She moved on to the next item and braced herself. "And I have a call with Wendy Altman this week about possibly authoring the science of productivity book. She's a psychology professor with a background in business, and I think she could be a good fit."

She chewed on her pen cap, waiting. Bringing up the science of productivity book could invite them to mention Irene Nichols, the last author Nora approached about it. They could ask how it went telling Irene Nichols they weren't interested after all (fine, in the end; Nora had sent her a vague email saying the project would be moving in another direction and received no response). Or maybe a verbal reprimand about how wrong Nora had been, in case the email thread wasn't enough. A second passed. Another.

"That's great, Nora," Violet said. "Keep us posted. Donna?"

Nora's breath slowly left her as Donna launched into her updates. She could hardly even hear Donna, so preoccupied she was in telling herself everything was okay.

Until a knock sounded at the door.

Nora looked up. Rita peered through the window and gave a quick wave, mouth in a tense line.

Heart thundering, Nora waved back and looked down at the phone while Donna continued her updates. She took the call off speakerphone, then pressed the mute button. Hopefully no one would ask Nora to chime in on anything for the next thirty seconds.

Nora stood, straightened her shirt, and twisted the doorknob. Rita, phone and laptop in her arms, gave her an apologetic smile.

"I'm sorry to interrupt," Rita whispered. "I have an author call in a couple minutes, and all the phone rooms are full. Is there any chance you'll be out of this one soon?"

"Yes," Nora blurted out. "Sorry, I was just on a call with"— her mind scrolled through possibilities, but only one name came to mind—"Andrew."

"Oh." Rita's eyebrows shot up. She peered into the phone room behind Nora, as if Andrew might be perched on the table, awaiting her return. "How's that going?" The hope in her eyes was soul-crushing. Nora couldn't tell her that just yesterday, Andrew had said he definitely wasn't signing with Parsons. Not now.

"He's still—uh—thinking it over." Nora caught her gaze wandering off to the side. She forced herself to look at Rita, see the hope drain out of her eyes. "He just wanted some input on one of his chapters." Nora rattled off some details about the draft he sent her yesterday, leaving out that she'd reviewed it in a *non-Parsons capacity*, as he put it. "But we're wrapping up in just a minute. I'll be right out."

Nora backed into the phone room and closed the door, knees trembling. Rita's eyes never left her, even as she slowly shut the door in her face.

Feeling like she was putting on a performance, Nora fell into her chair and brought the phone to her ear. Silence. The meeting must have ended when she was talking to Rita. She would just have to hope they hadn't asked her anything. Otherwise, that would be another strike against her for seemingly checking out.

In case Rita was listening outside the door, Nora had a fake one-sided conversation, apologizing to nonexistent Andrew for stepping away and asking if there was anything else he wanted to discuss. She cleared her dry throat and bid pretend-Andrew a cheery goodbye before hanging up. She picked up her laptop, though her wobbly arms threatened to drop it.

Nora opened the door to find Rita leaning against the wall. She gave Nora a tight smile and murmured a *thanks* on her way inside. Nora watched the door close on her and wondered how long Rita had been standing outside before she knocked. How much of the Weber meeting she might have overheard.

She continued to stand there until she heard Rita's muffled voice through the door. She took a step closer, straining to piece together words from the muted sounds, trying to figure out whether Rita could have overheard the Weber call.

The muffles began to take shape after a minute. ...*wouldn't worry about the structure comment. I thought the...takeaway was...*

Standing outside the room, imagining Rita hearing bits and pieces from Nora's unsanctioned call, she decided she couldn't tell Rita about Andrew's decision. Not yet.

Nora spent the rest of the morning in a daze, paranoid that every footstep she heard was Rita coming by to accuse her of treason. She messaged Beth to follow up on her lunch text and ask if she could do lunch today. She may as well have a meal out while she still had the incomes for it. Beth's reply was immediate, like she feared Nora might run off again. Which was fair.

Beth was already in the Thai restaurant when Nora arrived, perusing the menu, even though they never strayed from their usual orders.

Nora could feel Beth's eyes on her as she slid into her chair. There was a sort of timid intensity in her stare. "Hey," Nora said. She meant to be at least somewhat chipper to downplay her hurried three confession, but Nora couldn't be bothered anymore after her panic that morning. Maybe it was for the best to downplay nothing.

"Hey." Beth watched Nora like she was afraid to make any sudden movements. "How have you been?"

Lying would invite probing questions and curious looks, and Nora had more proof than ever today that she was terrible at getting away with things.

"Well, I think Rita may have overheard me having a meeting at my second job," Nora said. Beth's eyes narrowed into a question. The rest of it—all of it—came falling out: the pay cut, her bills, Lynn, Weber, the possible promotion, the lies. Andrew squarely in the middle of it all.

By the end of it, Nora was left watching Beth, waiting to see how this changed her view of her. Beth's *Seinfeld* torrenting must have seemed like an innocent lark compared to Nora's treachery.

"Shit," Beth said. "I'm so sorry."

Nora released a breath, felt her eyes water from Beth's concern alone. "I'm not sure what to tell Rita the next time I see her. We have the team meeting tomorrow, and she's going to ask about Andrew, and—"

"Well—yes, that sucks," Beth said. "And we'll get to that. But I think the most important thing to focus on is your three."

That sounded familiar. "I know," she said. "Andrew's determined to get me to six-point-something."

"Gotta love daddy Santos," Beth said, eyes delighted and dangerous.

Nora wrinkled her nose. "Please never call him that again."

"No promises." Beth's expression turned serious as she eyed Nora across the table. "I think six-point-something is totally doable. I think it starts with getting out of Parsons, and everything should get better from there."

"I'm working on getting out of Parsons."

"Are you, if you're still chasing the promotion? And this six-month-whatever thing at Weber doesn't seem sustainable." Beth speared a shrimp in her pad Thai. "The most important thing is for you to find a job that will get you out of this situation entirely."

"I've tried," Nora mumbled into her plate. It was sort of true. She *had* tried—until the BookTap rejection sent her down a darker path.

"I'll help you."

Nora looked up. Her second offer of help in two days. She took in Beth's steady gaze, the intent all over her face. As much as Beth's offer made her heart swell, she couldn't shake the feeling that she was beyond help. "Are you sure?"

"Yes. I'm very good at finding jobs someone in publishing can talk their way into."

"You do have an excellent track record," Nora agreed, giving way to a small smile. "One whole non-publishing job to your name."

"Exactly. It's foolproof."

Nora twirled a few rice noodles on her fork. "How do you like your new job?"

Beth grew pensive. "It's cool to finally have a say in things. I pitch to clients, I give presentations, I schmooze at conferences. It's kind of terrifying, but I like feeling like I'm actually doing something here."

"There's nothing you wouldn't change?" pressed Nora.

"Hmm." Beth chewed as she thought. "It's a lot of being available for longer than I'd want to be. Everyone has my cell, and they call me on it. I don't think the always-on part of this is really for me. But it's a change, and it feels kind of familiar, weirdly. Trying to impress clients feels a lot like trying to impress authors."

It sounded exhausting. Even the impressing part, which Nora's distaste for was growing. At Weber, she was constantly reaching out to potential authors, massaging egos before turning the conversation to whether a brilliant, talented expert like them might want to write a book for Weber.

The impressing wasn't new. She'd always known it, seen it, done it. The way people dressed up for author meetings, false smiles at the ready—it was standard for their line of work. And there weren't always egos to contend with. Plenty of authors were down-to-earth and easygoing. Nora's favorite author to work with, Dana Garnett, always asked Nora how she was doing when she emailed and actually seemed interested in the answer. Nora met her in person at a conference once and was touched that Dana's first reaction was to pull her in for a hug.

But her work at Weber—and the pressure coming from all sides about Andrew—was showing her just how stressful these interactions could be. How she'd rather not have them at all. Hearing Beth admit that she didn't like these aspects about her job either almost had Nora relieved. As wrong as it was to find relief in Beth's unhappiness.

"So now what?" Nora asked. Maybe Beth had a plan for what to do next. Maybe Nora could steal it.

Beth shrugged. "I'll stay here for the experience. And maybe next time, I'll get it right, but now I know how I feel about sales. That's something."

"Is it?" Nora couldn't imagine it being enough. Finding contentment in Parsons wasn't an option. She'd tried that already, and it just made her feel insane, trying to convince herself she wasn't feeling what she was feeling.

"Don't be so negative. Yes, it is. I'm out of Parsons, and I'm figuring things out. And so will you." She gave Nora a look of amused defiance, like she dared her to protest.

Nora knew what she could have said if she wanted to protest: that she'd gotten nowhere trying to figure anything out before. That, at this rate, she'd probably end up taking a third and fourth job to get out of the problems caused by her first and second jobs, and she'd never be free of the cycle.

But Beth's determination told her skepticism would not be entertained. That was enough for Nora to let herself believe it might be different this time.

CHAPTER TWENTY

Nora lay in bed the next morning, already dreading the Parsons meeting looming over her. She imagined sitting across from Rita in a few hours and telling her that not only had she not managed to sign Andrew, but that Andrew confirmed he wouldn't *ever* be signing with Parsons. Then, after dropping that failure bomb, she could give Rita the floor to ask questions about any and all suspicions she had about Parsons's authors mysteriously leaving for Weber. Who Nora talked to when she disappeared into the phone room every Monday at eleven. What Rita might have overheard yesterday.

She hadn't come up with a plan for how to approach it. Instead, she spent yesterday hiding in her cubicle, hoping Rita wouldn't come by, which she never did. Nora couldn't be sure if it was because Rita didn't suspect anything, or if she was biding her time.

Nora sent a text to Beth. We never said yesterday how I should handle Rita. The weekly meeting is today.

She carried the phone to the bathroom and squeezed a stripe of toothpaste on her toothbrush. Her phone vibrated mid-spit.

Be sick today. Cough, cough.

Nora waited for a follow-up, an indication that Beth was joking. Nothing. She brushed her teeth with one hand and typed out a reply with the other: I can't fake sick.

Secret second jobs are okay but you draw the line at faking sick?

Doooooo it. Apply for the jobs I sent you.

Nora spat in the sink, stood up straighter as she considered it. Beth, true to her promise at lunch, had emailed her half a dozen job postings yesterday evening. She remembered Beth's advice, the importance of focusing on the bigger picture—her three— and not getting caught up in the stresses of her jobs. Easier said than done, but the thought of putting off her worries for a day grew more and more appealing.

She reached for her phone and pulled up her Parsons inbox.

In her email to Candace and Rita, she wrote that she'd be taking the day off because she wasn't feeling well, which was true in an existential sense. She sent the email and logged off quickly, before any sympathetic replies could set off her guilt.

She swiped to her personal inbox to review the jobs Beth had sent her. Instead, she found herself opening the email above Beth's, an article Andrew sent her last night. *22 Science-Based Ways to Be Happier Today*. She doubted a clickbait article could change her situation, but the thought of him seeing it and thinking of her was enough to boost her mood a little.

Halfway down the list, she came across an item that struck something in her. *Revisit what used to make you happy*. Revisiting her old sources of happiness felt so much easier and kinder than what she'd been doing lately: berating herself for losing that happiness now. She thought about what used to make her happy, back before the layoffs. Before adulthood, even.

Nora spent her morning sitting in bed drinking coffee from her favorite mug and watching *Sister, Sister*. She walked through her neighborhood, noticing how much quieter it was in the later morning hours instead of eight o'clock, when she'd take side streets to avoid all the other commuters walking to the BART station. Today, she would not be lining up to pack into a train car, where personal space was a myth.

For breakfast, she parked herself in the booth of a diner she hadn't been to in a while. She breathed in the sweet, cakey smell of homemade donuts and scrolled through the Weber dystopian manuscript on her phone. Halfway through it now, she was noticing a pattern in the comments she left—namely, that not a single one was positive. It told the story of an astronomer who had failed to notice the signs of a world-ending asteroid and roamed the empty streets of New York in search of forgiveness and family. And, apparently, excessive confirmation of his sexual prowess.

Nora dug a fork into her waffle and looked up the author on BookTap. She still held a grudge against BookTap for the job rejection, but not enough of one to stop using their app. She hadn't heard of this author before. Lynn had included some background information in her email, but Nora had ignored it and gone straight for the manuscript in her excitement for fiction.

A search on BookTap turned up one result: a book he'd published with an indie press six years ago. Its rating was below average, but the book had clearly amassed a wide reach, going by the surprisingly high number of reviews. One, she noticed, was a two-star review from Lynn, posted four years ago. Lynn's review, which simply read *A little self-indulgent*, made Nora laugh. Lynn never would have guessed that four years later, she'd be working on his next novel with him—or maybe she did, and that was why Lynn's BookTap profile name was only LR, her initials.

It was all so familiar. Nora remembered being trained on reviewing unsolicited book proposals to assess whether they were worth showing to an editor. It came down to an author's platform, how marketable they were. The handful of times she pulled something from the slush pile to show Tom or Lynn, it was because the author had published a book before. And those, too, were ultimately rejected, almost always because their sales weren't strong enough. Nora would be left to send them a form rejection email, desperately wanting to add that she thought the content of their boring business proposal was just as good as all the other boring business books they published.

Fiction, she knew, was a realm where platform mattered far less. She'd heard the stories of famous authors who'd amassed hundreds of rejections when they were first starting out, only to be plucked from anonymity by one publisher who believed in their book. But that didn't mean fiction publishers wouldn't also latch on to established authors in the same way Parsons did. Publishing was a business, after all.

Nora knew there was nothing wrong with this. The revenue from a book that was sure to sell gave publishers the freedom to take chances on the less-marketable books, the ones that may not appeal to a broad audience. And Lynn, who clearly saw room for improvement in this author's first novel, might even enjoy the challenge of shaping his next into something better.

Still, Nora couldn't help the disappointment settling under her skin at the realization that the novel she'd been so excited to work on was, in a way, the fiction equivalent of the dull money-makers Parsons pounced on.

But she could be wrong. This manuscript was the only novel Nora had read at all in the last couple of months, distracted as she was by Parsons, Weber, and her mental state. Contrite astronomers with strong erections and a poor understanding of female anatomy might well be what the literary market was missing.

She remembered Andrew's mock outrage the other day, how he'd told her *You ruin books for me*. She had Parsons to blame for tainting her view of publishing, but her foray into fiction at Weber showed just how far the disillusionment had spread. Even in novels, now, she could see the nuts and bolts. The strategy lurking beneath.

After breakfast, Nora ducked into a bookstore across the street to be among books and forget, for a minute, how they were made. As she stepped through the doorway and breathed in the paper-ink smell, she tried to channel her childhood, the joys of trips to the bookstore—squished into a shapeless beanbag with a stack of books next to her, settling in to do the important work of deciding which two books she would get to take home. Preparing her arguments for why her parents should bend their rules and buy her a third as well. She won about half the time; the key was finding a book that sparked her parents' interest too. Her mother could usually be convinced by books with some sort of acclaim, best of all a Newbery Medal foil emblazoned on the cover, while her father was partial to silly plots or funny covers. There was a satisfaction in convincing her parents why a book was more important than their rules. It felt like she was letting them in on a secret: books were more important than anything.

Nora roamed the aisles, thinking about her childhood of negotiating and convincing. She read back covers of new releases and flipped through pages, bowing her head just enough to breathe in an inky whiff of new-book smell. She read the first page of every book she touched until she found one she didn't want to put down, written with a charming quirk that spoke to her. Nora carried it with her as she continued through the store. The only person she needed to convince to buy it was herself. Her argument against making the purchase was sound: she shouldn't buy a new book if she hadn't been reading in months. *But*, she protested to herself, *maybe this will be the one that gets you back into it*. The thought filled her with longing, had her studying the book in her hands like it was her best hope. How good it would feel to be herself again. Just like that, she won another argument.

In the kids' section, she found a roll of flower stickers. She thought of Andrew telling her last weekend that he wasn't making much progress on his manuscript. Her joke about motivating him with stickers had earned her a glare. She didn't know what reaction a gift of stickers might elicit, but she desperately needed to see it. Nora picked up the roll.

Next to this, she noticed a display of bookmarks. There, in the bottom corner, was a bookmark in the shape of an ice cream cone, a reminder of seven-year-old Andrew's first career aspiration. She grabbed that too, telling herself as she took these items to the counter that none of this meant anything. She knew better than to let herself feel hopeful about anything she was doing with him. Nothing good could come from a beginning forged on a desire to use him for a promotion.

And yet. She couldn't stop herself from it, taking her phone out of her pocket to ask if he was free tonight. It was cheating on her mission for the day, kind of. Seeing Andrew wasn't revisiting what used to make her happy. But if the theme of the day was happiness, Andrew certainly counted.

Dinner tonight?

You're really not good at planning, are you? **he replied.**

Or maybe you're bad at spontaneity, **she wrote.** I'll send a save the date next time.

You better. And I can do dinner tonight :)

CHAPTER TWENTY-ONE

Andrew's apartment was in the same state of intellectual sloven-
liness as before. An overturned box of crackers spilled onto the
papers on his desk. Books and plates cluttered the coffee table.
His jacket was thrown over the back of the couch.

She didn't, however, see Andrew anywhere.

"Hello?" she called out.

He emerged from the kitchen. "I just cleaned up my desk!"

She decided not to tell him about the crackers.

He gave her a greeting kiss. It was a pleasant surprise for a
second, and then it stirred guilt in her for letting them progress
this far. "Do you want anything to drink?" he asked.

"No, I'm good," she said, taking a seat on the couch. "And you
don't have to clean up for me."

He sat next to her. "I guess not. Why don't I show up at your
place sometime, and you can clean up for me?"

"I have a roommate."

"I know. It'd be nice to see where you live."

She couldn't imagine Andrew at her apartment. She didn't
want to imagine him there, the place where she spent more and

more of her time staring at the ceiling fan, thinking of reasons to live. His powers of distraction would be lost on her there.

"Maybe," she said, pretending to consider it. "But I like not having a roommate around here."

"It is a plus," he agreed. "I kind of miss it sometimes, though. Having someone around to talk to."

She studied him. He was looking at her in a way she couldn't place.

"How was your day?" he asked.

"I skipped work." A smile took over before she even finished speaking. This was possibly the most excited she'd been about any day in recent memory. She relished the way Andrew looked her over, like he was making a new discovery.

"Really?"

"Really. I watched TV. I had waffles in a diner. I went to a bookstore. It was a good day."

"What prompted this?"

"Um." Nora pretended to think. "It was Beth's idea to take the day off. And then, I guess—" She glanced at Andrew, knowing the thrill he would take in learning what his clickbait article inspired. "I guess in that article you sent me, there was something about revisiting what used to make you happy, and it wasn't a completely terrible idea."

Andrew saw through her lukewarm wording immediately, a satisfied grin crossing his face. "I knew you'd like that article. Do you want me to sign you up for their newsletter?"

She took in his exaggeratedly wide-eyed expression and tried to ignore the smile tugging at her mouth. "No."

"Add you to their mailing list?" He pulled his phone out of his pocket and held it up, a threat to make good on his promise.

"New topic," Nora insisted. Andrew begrudgingly set his phone down. "How's the manuscript coming along?" she asked.

He made a face. "Well, after I followed your advice and deleted some of the research-heavy stuff, I have even less of it, so thanks for that." He shot her a look of pretend annoyance.

"Always happy to help."

Andrew couldn't keep the act up for long. "Really, though, your notes were helpful. It needed some trimming. I did keep one interview snippet because it had a quote I really liked, but with the other stuff gone, I think it flows a lot better now. Thank you."

His words were like a hug, sending warmth blooming through her. She still hadn't sent Lynn her comments on the dystopian novel, so unsure of what she could say, other than she hated it. Between Henry Brook and his demands, and Rita asking about Santos at every turn, this small moment of feeling like she did a good job was something she didn't even know she craved.

"How'd Rita take the news?"

Nora hesitated. "What?"

"Did you tell her I'm not signing with Parsons?"

"No—but I will." Watching his gaze fall to his lap, she remembered his hopefulness in the café on Piedmont, his relief that the book between them wouldn't be an issue once it was finally off the table. His words, still ringing in her head: *We could actually be us*. "I will," she said again, more firmly. "I just haven't been able to get to it yet. We have more important things to do at Parsons than talk about you all the time."

"So you say." His brow arched playfully, but she could still see traces of disappointment in his eyes. She pushed away her thoughts of Rita, Parsons, and how to lure him to Weber, searching for something—anything—to chase the disappointment off his face.

"Oh," she said, suddenly remembering, "I got you something." She reached down for her purse and sifted through it, bringing out the small bag from the bookshop. "It's stupid. Don't get your hopes up."

Andrew's gaze lingered on her as he took the bag. He reached into it and pulled out the box of stickers.

"Stickers," he said.

"You said you hadn't been writing for your manuscript," she said in a rush, feeling the need to defend her silly purchase. "Stickers used to motivate me when I was a kid."

Andrew looked at Nora like she'd just told him a terrible pun. "I did work on it for the last three nights in a row," he said.

"All right, there we go. That's three stickers." Nora sat up and took the box from him. One by one, she peeled the flower stickers off the roll and placed them on Andrew's shirt while he watched patiently: one on his shoulder, one near his clavicle, the last over his heart. She leaned back against the couch to survey her work. "Do you feel motivated?"

He looked down at his shirt, looked back up with a smile. "You have no idea how much."

She felt her smile fading the longer he stared. A thought crossed her mind that this gift she thought too silly might somehow be more than she meant it to be. She still needed to bring him around to Weber, but she couldn't tear herself away from this moment here. Now. The sticker on his shirt and the pleased look on his face.

"There's one other thing in the bag," she said. Andrew stuck a hand in and took out the ice cream cone bookmark. "I thought your seven-year-old self might appreciate it."

He pulled the bookmark out of its plastic sleeve and set it

inside a book on his coffee table. "Every version of me appreciates it. Thank you." He was gazing at her again, maybe even meaningfully.

Nora looked away and scratched her elbow, thinking of a way to change the subject. "I started reading the parachute book. It has me doing this self-inventory exercise, making a list about what I want in a future job."

"I think that earns *you* a sticker," Andrew said, picking up the roll. Nora watched with interest as he peeled one off and stuck it over her heart. "How's the self-inventory going?"

Nora pried her gaze from the sticker on her chest. "I have a whole two items on it."

"What are they?"

"Um—" She paused, reluctant to voice them. Her two small words seemed so insignificant. "I want to work with books, and I want to have input on things."

"Perfect." Andrew peeled more stickers off the roll. "Books," he said, planting a sticker on her right shoulder. "Input." He placed another on her left shoulder. "Anything else?"

She watched the roll of stickers in his hands and sifted through her thoughts. Hearing Andrew say her feedback on his manuscript was helpful gave her a different kind of satisfaction, compared to how she felt making comments in manuscripts. It felt one-sided sometimes, sending comments into the void and never quite being sure how seriously they were taken. But talking it out in person stirred another feeling. There was a more personal element to it, a chance to understand their point of view and see how they felt about hers. Even her childhood bookstore persuasions with her parents were like that, picking a book she thought would be most likely to get her mother or father on board with bending their two-book-maximum rule, watching the interest flicker in their eyes as she stated her case. Gathering their feedback, listening and learning.

"I think there's something I like about working with people in person," she said. "I like that it's having input but also getting their response."

Andrew pursed his lips and eyed Nora like something didn't add up. "Interesting."

"What?" she asked, drawing back under his stare.

"You did not seem thrilled when I gave you an opportunity to work with people at the conference."

Nora thought back, then gave him a skeptical look. "You mean the unplanned book signing you ambushed me with?"

"Some might call it that, yes," he said, chin in the air in a show of haughty indignance.

"Then let me clarify that I don't enjoy stampedes. But I think I like working with people one-on-one. I think that's something else for my list."

"Another victory." A soft smile lit Andrew's features as he peeled another sticker off the roll and pressed it on her chest. Nora looked down at her stickers with more pride than she'd felt in a while.

Was it stupid to be touched by something she bought as a joke? If that was the case, Nora thought, looking from the stickers on her shirt to Andrew and the three stickers he wore with pride, they were both foolish, grinning idiots. And when he asked what she wanted to do for dinner—dinner was, she remembered, the whole pretense for coming over in the first place—she scooted closer and kissed him without a second thought.

He brought a hand around her waist, drawing her in. But as

the kiss became longer, slower, he pulled away. "Really, though, what about dinner?" he asked.

She kissed him again, crawling into his lap and playing with the hair at the nape of his neck.

"You had eight hours to figure out dinner," Andrew said. And, breath warm on her skin as he laid kisses along her collarbone, he murmured, "At least with the avocado sandwich you were *trying* to feed me."

Nora laughed into his neck and pulled back to take in this image of him, pupils dark and dilated, smile triumphant at getting a laugh out of her. She realized too late that this might count as some kind of romantic gazing, except that wasn't what she was doing, because that wasn't something she allowed herself to do with him. But if she *was* gazing—which she wasn't—it was only because of the goofy, idiotic mood the stickers had her in, and that wasn't her fault.

But she couldn't stay in the idiot bubble forever. Later, when the coffee table was littered with Chinese takeout cartons and the smell of scallions hung in the air, Nora looked over from the movie they were watching and saw Andrew yawn. His elbow rested on the arm of the couch, chin in his hand like he couldn't keep his head up on his own. The image jolted her into realizing it was nearly midnight. Before he opened his eyes, she sat up and said, "I should get going."

"You don't have to," he said, blinking a little sleepily, and that wasn't something she would dwell on either, how cute he looked when he was tired.

She stood and knelt by the door to pick up her purse. "The trains will stop running soon."

Andrew joined her, leaning against the wall. "There's a sticker in it for you if you stay."

She just shook her head, afraid that if she spoke, she'd stumble on her words and end up agreeing to something that would take them further down this precarious path she couldn't trust herself on. She knew—and had known—that she wanted more than a signature from him. But wanting him for distractions and banter was very, very different from the line she was walking tonight, the gifts and gazes that hinted at infinitely more. Going down this path when there was so much he didn't know about Parsons, Weber, and the fog in her head was reckless.

But still she stayed, lingering in the doorway, watching him. He brought her in for another kiss, cupping her face with his hands. When he pulled away, he stroked her cheek with his thumb, a gesture so intimate that it snapped her out of her trance.

She turned her head just enough to make his hand fall away. If he knew it was intentional, he didn't show it.

"Thanks for dinner," she said, mustering a quick smile. She left before she could change her mind.

Outside, the cold air put goosebumps on her skin. She looked down at her shirt, the stickers still on it. She was starting to feel, each time she thought about Andrew, that she was past forgiveness. But worse than this were the moments she thought about him as she was falling asleep, wishing he was next to her, wishing she met him outside of Parsons, in another time when she was more herself. This was worse than unforgivable. It was laughable.

CHAPTER TWENTY-TWO

The next day brought a return to reality: cramming onto a BART car as sweat glued her shirt to her skin, settling into her desk chair, and watching her inbox load a flood of emails like a personal assault.

One name appeared more than most.

The only thing more dangerous than a man with a bad idea was a man with the power to make it happen. Henry Brook was inspired, he told Nora in one of their calls a couple of weeks ago. After catching up on the business team's books—thanks to the decades' worth of tip sheets, proposal documents, and even full manuscripts Nora had sent him—he now knew what the business team's next move should be: conflict resolution seminars.

Conflict resolution was Candace's team's first—and biggest—success. It grew from a single book published in the early '90s into a full-fledged franchise. When the book sold surprisingly well, the author wrote a field guide. And then a workbook. And then a revised tenth-anniversary second edition, at which point someone—Nora wasn't sure who, but they deserved a special place in hell—decided *Why stop at books?*

Hence the course. The registration fees and franchise costs brought in revenue, but it never took off like Parsons wanted. A conflict resolution certificate from a publishing company didn't mean much, it turned out. The course died down after a few years, from what Nora could tell.

Henry Brook wanted to bring it back. And drag Nora through conflict resolution hell to do his bidding for him.

Nora typed out reluctant replies to the emails he'd sent her yesterday: yes, it would be ideal if the hotel could offer organic midmorning snacks at these seminars; no, she didn't have time to sit in on the weekly call he scheduled with the seminar instructor; yes, it was expensive to print a suite of office supplies with the conflict resolution logo; yes, Nora was sure she got his approval on the cost of the materials, if he could please refer to the attached email; yes, she understood how he might approve things without thinking when he was having a midafternoon caffeine crash; no, Nora did not have time to circle back to the vendor and ask them to retroactively lower their prices.

She scrolled up and came across an email that was just a subject line: *pls block Tues 12–3*. At least he said please. Or some of the letters in please, anyway.

With a sigh, Nora pulled up Henry Brook's calendar and blocked off his Tuesday afternoon. She noticed some meetings on his calendar she hadn't scheduled. She knew Henry didn't make them because spelling and capitalization weren't his strong suits.

Executive Assistant Interview (Summer St. Clair). Executive Assistant Interview (Robin Mays). Executive Assistant Interview (Alex Ortiz). All scheduled by HR, all for this week.

She might soon be free of his mentoring stranglehold. Then

Summer or Robin or Alex could put up with Henry Brook and his demands.

If she didn't have to endure calls with Henry Brook anymore, she wondered if she might be able to handle sticking it out at Parsons long enough for the full-time Weber job to become available. There would still be long nights and tired days, weekends spent researching authors and reading manuscripts, but if Henry Brook wasn't involved in any of it, it was possible that leading her double life for a few more months just might be a bit more bearable.

"Nora?"

She looked up, blinking her duplicitous thoughts away. Henry Brook getting an assistant would never fix the guilt Nora felt whenever she saw Rita.

"How are you feeling?"

A second stab of guilt struck her at the reminder that this was another lie Nora told her.

"Better," Nora said. "Getting some rest yesterday really helped."

"That's good." Rita's bright smile faded to something more thoughtful. "I was thinking about Santos. Has he said why he's not budging on the contract?"

"Um—" Nora frowned a little and looked off to the side, pretending to think back, pretending to be a good person. "I think he's just undecided."

Rita took a long sip of coffee and leaned against Nora's cubicle wall. "Okay," she said. "It would be great if we could get an answer out of him soon. Candace has a meeting with her bosses in New York next month to plan for the next fiscal year. Having Santos on board would have a pretty big impact on our budget."

Nora squirmed under the intensity of Rita's stare. "What do you want me to do?"

"Why don't we set up a call with him? If we can get him to talk about his concerns and feel heard, that might get things moving."

Except it wouldn't, because nothing could change his mind. And now Nora had to go back to Andrew and tell him he'd have to put Rita out of her misery himself—which he would happily do in his eagerness to take his book off the table, the book he saw as the only thing preventing him and Nora from being an *us*. Except for everything he couldn't see: the haze in her head that kept so many of her feelings bottled up where she couldn't reach them. The stain on her conscience for trying to make Andrew take a lackluster deal for her own benefit. The suspicion that would flare in Rita's eyes if Andrew leaving helped her connect another dot on the crooked line between Nora and Weber. Nora's growing exhaustion at working two jobs with no Parsons promotion to fall back on.

"Okay," Nora said. Her voice came out lifeless and empty.

Rita gave a satisfied nod, as if there was anything to be satisfied about. Nora watched her leave, dark hair swinging behind her as she walked. When Rita turned the corner, Nora swiped to her texts with Andrew. The text he'd sent this morning came into view: If the whole author thing doesn't work out, I think I have a bright future in computer repair. Next came a photo of a frayed computer cable, followed by a photo of flower stickers covering the exposed wire. Their texts had then devolved into the likelihood that Andrew would electrocute himself before Nora saw him next.

Somewhere in this joking, flirtatious exchange that had become so natural, Nora would need to bring the conversation back to his book when she told him about the call with Rita.

She could have typed it out now and been done with it—dropped the news and gone back to making predictions about his imminent electrical death. Instead, she chewed on her lip and tried to ignore the sinking feeling in her stomach. If she wasn't being paranoid, if Andrew turning down the contract would heighten Rita's suspicions and put Nora's job in jeopardy, she needed to go a more strategic route. Andrew closing the door on Parsons meant there was a different door she needed to coax him through.

Beth sent another curated jobs digest that morning: a handful of links, each preceded by a brief introductory line ranging from *I like the sound of this* to *Maybe* to *Not super exciting but not terrible*. Nora flagged the email and made a note to apply to them that night.

But unlike the last jobs roundup Beth sent a couple of days ago, this one had a question at the bottom.

Is your three the reason you haven't been on BookTap lately? I miss your reviews.

A touch of longing pulled at Nora. She missed her reviews too. Her main motivation for posting reviews of the books she'd read was mostly trying to make Beth laugh, because Beth was one of the few people who followed her on BookTap. But not reading the way she used to, too distracted to focus on anything but her three and her ceiling fan, meant having nothing to review.

She typed out a reply to Beth: Yeah, kinda.

There wasn't a simple explanation for it, really. Reading had always been her comfort, her escape whenever the creature had reared its head in the past. But it was different this time. She wondered if it was something Parsons was doing to her: driving her favorite colleagues away, burdening her with the work they left behind, and sending her home too frazzled to focus on words on a page. Too frayed to watch *The Great British Baking Show* with Allie and put on silly accents. Too overwhelmed to even figure it out on her own, clinging to Andrew and his book and his optimism and stickers as a buoy when really she was more his anchor than anything else. It left her with just enough energy to exist, and even then only barely.

Beth responded with a calendar invitation for 8:00 p.m. that evening, an event simply titled *Virtual reading date*. In the body, she'd written *We're going to read for an hour tonight. Show that three who's boss.*

Nora accepted the invitation, warmth rising in her chest at the thought of Beth taking charge to help Nora fight her three.

Just having it on the calendar was a help, somehow. It turned the act of reading from a cycle of defeat—wanting to read, being too tired to, berating herself for not reading—into an activity with a set time. It was okay that she only made it through a few pages of *Kindred* on the BART ride home because she had a set appointment later that night. It was okay that once home, she dove straight into her Weber work as she always did because she knew she'd be reading later. She didn't have to feel, as she edited her cover letter, that time spent applying for jobs was time stolen from activities she'd rather be doing, because she'd still get her chance. And at eight exactly, she fell against her pillows with *Kindred* in her lap and popcorn at her side, and for an hour she read. She let Octavia Butler transport her between two worlds, let herself get caught up in the horrors of traveling through time as a Black woman.

When her alarm buzzed to alert her that it was nine o'clock, she allowed herself to finish the paragraph she was on. She closed the book, wishing an hour of reading changed everything, wishing it meant that she'd regained her ability to escape for the long stretches she used to. But there was still Weber work to do—she had a manuscript to comb through by Friday. And as good as it felt to fall back into her usual habit again, part of it still felt forced—like she knew, deep down, that she wouldn't be doing this if it hadn't been on the calendar.

But it still had her feeling better about herself than she had in ages. Even if she only did it because of Beth and her invite, even if she didn't have the headspace to forget her surroundings and fall into a book for hours like she used to, she felt like she'd touched upon something good. Nora took a few minutes to put some additional reading appointments on the calendar for herself: an hour twice a week. And then she texted Beth Thanks for the reading date :)

Beth's response—three hearts—brought a grateful smile to her face.

As Nora opened the Weber manuscript to begin her work, she couldn't stop herself from sending a text to Andrew—a stupid and transparent question about how his writing was going. Only a few texts passed between them before he was asking if she'd be free for lunch on Saturday, and she leapt at the chance to see him again.

While they nailed down the details, she remembered her conversation with Rita that afternoon, remembered how she'd need to use this lunch to not only tell him about the call with Rita but also try to lure him to Weber. Her stomach coiled at the idea of trying to persuade him to sign with anyone.

She'd thought before that Weber could be a good fit for Andrew, and that was still true. But not like this—not this sneaky, slimy way where she tried to lead him to her best interests and hoped he wouldn't see her pulling the strings. Not when he deserved so much better.

CHAPTER TWENTY-THREE

Andrew, Nora conceded, was better at making plans than she was. He gave notice, for one. He picked a place instead of showing up on her doorstep and deciding they could figure out food later.

The place he chose for lunch on Saturday was a burger spot in the Mission. Nora weaved around tables of people talking and laughing over beers and baskets of fries. She spotted him at a table by the wall, contemplating his water glass. He looked up when she pulled out the chair across from him.

"Hey!" His eyes crinkled. "Glad this wasn't too far for you."

"Yeah, the twenty steps from the BART station really did a number on me."

Andrew sighed, giving her an unamused look that had her smiling. "I know, but you live in Oakland. You said before that you don't like coming to the city on weekends."

"True." She forgot somehow that this was usually the case. She almost never came to San Francisco on weekends, even if there were things here she still wanted to see and do. She wanted to get breakfast at the place with the cream biscuits and the beignets. She wanted to drink Irish coffee at the end of Fisherman's

Wharf. But the idea of making her weekday commute on her day off normally filled Nora with too much dread. Now, apparently, Andrew had her forgetting that dread, replacing it with something else entirely.

Her gaze shifted back to Andrew. "How's your week been?" she asked.

"Good." He said it with the ease of someone unburdened. "I got a lot of writing done."

"Yeah?" Nora felt another smile coming on. "Was it because of the stickers?"

Andrew gave a knowing nod, taking it all in stride. "It was entirely because of the stickers."

"I thought so."

"Will you read the next chapters if I send them to you?"

"Sure," she said quietly. She'd love to bottle this, the sense of purpose that ballooned in her chest whenever he treated her like her professional opinion mattered. Not so much the other feelings that arose when his manuscript was brought up. She remembered Rita standing in her cubicle the other day, suggesting the call like it might have an effect on anything except Nora's chances of keeping her job. She studied Andrew across the table and decided to get it over with.

"Rita wants to have a call with you." Nora tried to keep her tone light, but her gaze hung on Andrew, waiting for his reaction.

Andrew's eyes passed over Nora as he took this in. "So you didn't tell her?"

"I can't. She'll be disappointed, and she'll ask a bunch of questions, and I'd rather you be the one dealing with all that."

He chuckled. "Can't wait." He looked more relaxed now, a smile coming over him. Nora suspected he was having those thoughts again, about being glad to get the call over with. What he thought it would mean for the two of them.

Nora ran her finger along the tops of the condiment bottles on the table. "What are you gonna say when Rita asks you about the contract?" she asked.

"I'll just say I've decided to take the book in another direction."

She knew of another direction he could go in—the direction she *needed* him to go in if she wanted to make sure at least one of her jobs was safe. "Would you be interested in publishing your book with Weber?" she asked.

He regarded Nora with equal parts confusion and interest. "Why?"

"I know an editor there," she said. "Lynn Ralston, who used to work for Parsons? I thought Weber might be a good fit for you. Do you want me to introduce you?"

He searched her face, almost like he didn't know how to react. "You'd do that?"

"I would."

He broke into a slow smile. "Funny how you didn't think to mention it until after I said I'm not choosing Parsons." There was a hint of accusation in his voice, but his eyes flickered with laughter.

Nora knew it was a joke, like his trolling-for-authors comment at the conference. But it struck closer to the truth than he knew. She forced a laugh. "I can't be held responsible for the fact that I was doing my job." Another lie: her use of *job*, singular.

"I guess that's fair," Andrew said. Nora watched him, waiting for a definitive answer. "What?" he asked.

It was harder to sound casual when she was repeating herself. "So…do you want me to introduce you to the editor at Weber?" she asked. "Since I have the connection and all?"

"It means a lot to me that you offered," he said, eyes serious. She tried not to squirm under his sincerity. "But I think I want to try for a bigger publisher."

Her gaze faltered, but she tried to keep her expression even. "You do?"

The news that he wasn't signing with Parsons had been one disappointment, but she hadn't counted on him not being interested in Weber either. She'd already played it out in her head: introducing him to Lynn and Violet, hearing them gush over how impressed they were with her, watching them accelerate the timeline and offer her the coordinator job on the spot.

"Yes. Why?" He eyed her curiously.

"I just—" She thought back to their dinner at the conference, the arguments she'd used then. "I think smaller publishers can be nice. You don't want to be a small fish in a big pond." Was that the metaphor she'd used? It was hard to remember now. "They promise you one thing, and then all their money goes to their bigger authors, as it always does, and where does that leave you?"

"Swimming in my big new pond, apparently." The way Andrew was watching her started to feel more and more like scrutiny. "Why does it matter to you where I take my book?" His voice was guarded now.

"It doesn't." Nora twisted her face in offense, even as her stomach wrenched at this absurdity of a performance she was putting on. "I just think you should give Weber a chance. I think they could be good for you. That's it."

Andrew didn't say anything. She couldn't gauge his mood from the distant look in his eye. She looked away, too aware of the silence between them. She watched a couple a few tables over giggle with an ease she envied.

Their food arrived, burgers for both of them. Nora leaned back as the waiter set her plate in front of her. She replayed her words in her head, hating herself for every syllable. She watched Andrew squirt a blob of ketchup on his plate. He closed the plastic lid with a snap that seemed to ring in her ears.

Nora busied herself with unfolding a thin paper napkin in her lap. When she reached for her burger, she noticed Andrew sliding his pickle spear onto her plate. She looked up at him.

"You like pickles, right?" he asked.

Nora blinked away her stare. "Yes," she said. "Thanks." As she bit into her burger, she tried to remember when she ever told him she liked pickles. There must have been a moment when he said he didn't like them, she thought, watching him peel pickle slices off his burger. Here he was, committing her likes and dislikes to memory and using that information to benefit her, and yet even now, some two months after the avocado incident, Nora couldn't recall anything but his allergy. And even that she forgot sometimes.

"I'm sorry if I offended you," Andrew said. "I've mentioned before that I had this stupid fear that you were only in this to sign me, and hearing you talk about smaller publishers just had me worried this was all coming back to Parsons again."

He was apologizing. For doing absolutely nothing wrong. Nora swallowed a lump in her throat and forced herself to look at him.

"I'm the one who should be apologizing," she said. "You know what's best for your book."

He nodded, stare intently focused on her. "I'll meet with Weber if you think I should."

This, here, was her chance to do something right. She could

tell him to forget it, and she could put her weird, guilting manipulations behind her and move on. With Andrew.

But then she thought of Rita—pictured what might happen when Andrew told Rita next week that he wasn't signing with Parsons. Knew she needed to protect her Weber job before she screwed that one up too.

"I think you should," Nora said, meeting his stare.

He was looking at her differently now. Like he trusted her. "Then I will." He grinned like that solved it and shoved a fry into his mouth.

The cloud hanging over them was gone now, or at least Andrew seemed to think so. He slipped into anecdotes about work, his writing, his week. Nora only felt more isolated than ever, knowing he'd come close to uncovering her motives and she'd steered him around them with a lie. A lie that had him apologizing to her.

Andrew snatched the bill before she could grab it, holding it over his head like a prize. She went through the motions of offering to pay, pulling out her credit card and letting him push it away, because why not pretend she could afford things.

But maybe Andrew did sense the pall still, because when they left the restaurant, squinting in the afternoon sun, he said, "Let's go somewhere."

"Like where?" Her voice came out dull and defeated.

"I don't know. It's Saturday; we have the day ahead of us. You said you never come here on weekends, but you're here now. What do you want to do?"

She considered this, thinking back to everything she'd wanted to do in San Francisco but hadn't yet. She met his gaze, and his eager expression chased the reluctance out of her. "There *is* an ice cream place I've always wanted to go to."

"Name it."

Nora hesitated. "It's touristy."

It took Andrew all of two seconds to process what she was saying. "You've never been to *Bi-Rite?*"

"I live in Oakland!"

"Yeah, but you work here. Nora, that's pathetic!"

She laughed. "I'm aware." She'd known about Bi-Rite Creamery for years, how tourists and locals alike lined up for its unique flavors. She'd always meant to go one day. She spent a lot of time meaning to do things.

"And now you want to walk ten blocks and stand in a long line with every tourist in the world for fancy ice cream?" He gave a deep, exaggerated sigh that sent another laugh through her.

"Unless it would upset you too much to be around people living your dream?" she asked, looking up at him with a straight face. "I don't think they sing for tips at Bi-Rite, if that helps."

He was already walking ahead of her, but he turned back to register his offense. "I'm never telling you anything ever again."

In line at Bi-Rite, after recounting his adventure babysitting his nephew the last time he was in Pittsburgh, he asked Nora about her family. With no nieces, nephews, or siblings to speak of, she told him about her parents, found herself showing him a picture of them on their thirtieth anniversary last year, sitting at their favorite table in their favorite steakhouse, picture presumably taken by their favorite waiter.

"You have your mom's eyes," he commented as he handed her phone back to her. "Different color, but same shape."

Nora glanced up at him. "Everyone always says I look like my dad."

"Because your dad's Black?" he asked. Nora nodded, and he

bowed his head in a knowing nod. "I get it. My nephew's half white and no one ever says he looks like his dad. It's like they see which parent you get your race from and decide everything comes from them."

"Exactly," Nora said, so emphatically it surprised her.

He looked pleased with himself. "You do have your dad's smile, though." He said it matter-of-factly, like he'd already committed her parents—and her—to memory. And there went Nora, unintentionally reminding him what her smile looked like anyway.

They walked down Dolores Street with their cones. She couldn't take her eyes off Dolores Park when they passed it, the sea of people spread out on blankets as far as she could see, farther than she could comprehend.

"I don't know what I'd do if I lived near here," Nora said. She slurped on her scoop of honey lavender. It had a light, calming taste, the perfect complement to the salty, nutty black sesame flavor she'd gotten for her top scoop.

"You've never been here either?"

"I don't come this way. Except to see you," she added.

He turned to her, ice cream puddling in a corner of his mouth. She braced herself for more incredulity, but his expression was pensive. "There's a place I think you'll like."

The bookstore had brightly colored window frames that lined her view of the rows of books within. She stepped inside and was greeted by the familiar dusty smell of books. Bookshelves lined the walls, handwritten cardboard signs peeking between books to mark genre and alphabetical place. Nora wandered past the stacks of books on display, resisting the temptation to graze a hand along each one she passed. She took in the covers, titles, names of authors known and unknown.

"Do you like it?" Andrew asked, trailing behind her.

"I do," she murmured. It wasn't anything special, really. She'd been to bigger, more impressive bookstores. She hailed from the state where Powell's was founded, after all. But a bookstore is a bookstore is a bookstore. And there was always magic in that.

Nora dove into her bookstore habit of picking up a book, reading its first page, and setting it down in exchange for another.

"You know some books have more than one page?" Andrew said.

"The first page sets the tone." Nora skimmed a first page—gossip between neighbors—and set the book down. The next, a wry narrator's detailed description of a table's place setting, had potential. Nora turned the page.

"You found the second page."

She gave him a stern look and went back to the book. A family spat. An intriguing sort of conflict, described with humor. She closed the book and prepared to tuck it under her arm, but she hesitated. She still hadn't read the novel she bought at the bookstore last week. Ordinarily having an unread book at home wouldn't have stopped her from buying another—if it did, she'd have no books to her name—but this one wouldn't change her recent lack of reading habits. She didn't know yet how effective the reading appointments she'd put on her calendar would be. Taking this book home and letting it gather dust with the others was submitting it to a fate it didn't deserve.

"What?" Andrew asked. "Do you need a second opinion?"

Nora glanced at him, then at the book in her hand. "I was just thinking that…I miss seeing books for what they are, instead of how much money they'll make." It was the first lie to come to mind, except she realized as she said it that it wasn't even a lie. She couldn't unsee it, now that she had a glimpse of fiction publishing at Weber. Books—not business books, which she'd always known were bullshit, but her books, the ones in her home and in her heart—were a business like any other.

The image of her adult self that Nora had conjured as a child, working in publishing and gushing to Judy Blume about her book, was wrong. A more accurate depiction would have been Nora looking at Judy Blume and seeing not stars, but dollar signs. Much like how she sometimes looked at Andrew now.

"Do you still want to work with books?" Andrew asked. "Isn't that one of the things on your list?"

"Yeah." She looked down at the book again. "But I think it would be cool to work somewhere where it's not about business; it's just about books. Like a book-related nonprofit." She met his eyes, wondered if she sounded too idealistic. "Is that possible?"

Andrew's answer shouldn't have surprised her. "Anything's possible."

She used to think of his positivity as a punch line, but now she wanted to capture it, steal some for herself. Nora mentally added *nonprofit* to join *books*, *input*, and *one-on-one* on her list of clues for her future career.

"As for wanting to see books for what they are, I think you can get that back," Andrew said. "It starts with this one." He pulled the book out of her hand.

"What are you doing?"

"I'm gonna get it for you."

Nora grabbed at the book, but he held it out of reach. "You don't need to do that."

He raised his eyebrows, taunting her with generosity. "That's what makes it fun." Nora tried again for the book to no avail. "Do you want to see something?" he asked.

She turned but he was already gone, darting off between two aisles. She started after him but didn't get far because there he was, coming back, a second book in hand. A book she recognized immediately.

"It's me," he said, pointing to his name on the cover.

"How often do you come here to stare at your own book?"

"Not that often." He examined the cover. "I should put this back. Someone probably wants to buy it."

That old, tired joke authors liked to play about being obsessed with their books. It made her laugh anyway.

They spent a while there, most of it sitting cross-legged in the children's section, flipping through picture books. They'd started out joking about a cover they saw featuring a sophisticated French cartoon snail, but then Nora found a book with a Black girl on the cover, hair in two pigtail puffs like how she used to wear it as a kid, and Andrew found a book with a boy on the cover who he said bore a remarkable resemblance to his seven-year-old self, and they quietly flipped through them, these books written by and for people like them, these books that weren't around when they were young.

"You ever think about kids?" Andrew asked.

Nora looked up. "Having them?" When he nodded, she shrugged. "I don't like thinking about my future."

He frowned. "Why?"

Nora fiddled with a corner of the page between her fingers. "I just...I don't know. I don't really see it when I think about it."

"Why?"

She shrugged. "I just don't. I want to leave Parsons, but when

I try to imagine leaving…I don't see myself anywhere. I don't think I want to *be* anywhere."

"Why?" He closed his book and shelved it somewhere behind him, in what she was sure was not its proper place. He turned to face her, knees touching hers.

Nora looked down and continued to run her fingers over the page. "Just…" She let the silence stretch on. The page was starting to wrinkle.

"Something to do with your parachute?"

She nodded.

"Are you still feeling like you don't know what color your parachute is?"

She nodded again. He slid the book out of her hands, and she lifted her head to watch him shelve it (also in the wrong place).

"I don't think there's anything wrong with that." He leaned in so closely she could smell the milky sweetness of ice cream on his breath. "I think you're smart, and I think you can do anything you want to do." Andrew was staring now, waiting for his words to have some effect on her.

"But I don't think I want to do anything." She spoke slowly at first, but her words spilled out faster as she went on. "When I think I do, it turns out I'm wrong. I think I just don't have a parachute color. I don't even have a parachute. Maybe I'm not even on the plane. Maybe that happens, and maybe some people are fine with doing something pointless for the rest of their lives, but I'm not. If my life is pointless, that's not a life I want to live." Now she was the one staring, daring him to find a rebuttal.

He drew back, then leaned in again, eyes dark and serious. "Your life is not pointless."

Nora's gaze drifted to the shelf behind him.

"Nora."

"What's my point, then?"

"That's for you to figure out," he said. "You keep trying until you find the job that fits you. You *will* find it."

"You're psychic, are you?" she grumbled.

"Yes. I also do palm readings." He reached for her hand and Nora swatted it away with a laugh.

"Go shelve those books right."

Andrew grinned and turned to pull the books off the shelf. Before he reshelved them, he inched forward, leaning almost past her, and she was going to tell him that wasn't the right shelf, either, when she felt his lips gently graze her cheekbone. He pulled back, met her wondering gaze, and she leaned in to kiss his cheek, one chaste kiss for another.

"Where to next?" she asked.

She spent the night. She'd been so careful before, always made sure to leave before it turned into the intimate act of sleeping next to him. But this time, she couldn't stop it from happening. She didn't want to.

When she used his shower, she was mildly annoyed at forgetting to ask for a towel, dreading the moment of stepping onto the bath mat cold and wet and having to ask where he kept his towels. But when she turned off the water and pushed the shower curtain aside, she saw a gray towel folded neatly on the bathroom counter, where moments before there had been nothing.

She stood there, staring at it. It made no sense that this was what struck her and not everything he'd done before that, now running through her mind: watching the booth, stealing her a lunch, reading a happiness report, buying her a career book, standing in line for gourmet ice cream. For whatever reason, as she stood dripping wet, staring at his bathroom counter, it was this towel—which said more about his politeness as a host than his feelings for her—that made her realize she could depend on him.

Later, they sat on opposite ends of the couch, Nora reading the book he bought her and Andrew working on his manuscript, their legs tangled together, her feet resting on his thighs. Every few pages, she looked up from her book and watched him staring intently at his laptop. It was so easy with him, she was realizing, when she wasn't turning away at sincerity or lying when he asked how she was doing. Today showed that she could be honest with him, and he would listen. They could argue and they could make up. He could leave her towels and she could stare at him like everything was different.

There was more to tell him. He didn't know the reason she'd tried to convince him to sign with Weber was because she worked for them. He didn't know about the creature in her head. But she was starting to think he might understand. And then...she didn't know what would happen. But there would be a *then*. Maybe a lot more *then*s. And much more of this. It was coming together in her mind, forming a picture despite the haze.

It was on the tip of her tongue, all of this. But then he looked up and caught her staring. He smirked, her face flushed, and she dove her head back into her book.

He didn't bring it up again, the conversation they had in the bookstore, but she felt different. He held her while they slept, and she didn't mind—didn't try to escape it. She sank into it, felt herself craving it in the middle of the night after he'd rolled onto his back. She curved into him and was gratified when his sleeping form pulled her closer.

The next morning, she stood in Andrew's doorway and kissed him goodbye. When he looked down at her, hands still on her waist, he said, "I'm looking forward to getting that call with Rita over with."

"Me too," Nora said. It wasn't even a lie this time. He was right about his book being between them. Whatever was going to happen at Parsons would happen. And whatever might happen at Weber started to feel faraway and unimportant. Signing him didn't seem to matter as much anymore.

She kissed him again, pulled back, and stared. She could see him doing it, too, watching her curiously. She opened her mouth but couldn't say it, everything she was thinking.

She started for the BART station, mind whirring. This was different. Her head was still hazy, foggy, all of those things, but apparently Andrew Santos lived there now too.

CHAPTER TWENTY-FOUR

Nora spent Sunday evening cross-legged on her bed, browsing social meetup websites for networking opportunities. The parachute book was big on networking. And at this point, fresh off the confusing high of spending last night at Andrew's, she needed something new to focus on. A new avenue for finding another job and sidestepping the Parsons mess entirely. Because Beth was right: getting out of Parsons was the key to raising her three. The longer she stayed, the more the guilt would drag her down, and the more she'd stress over Rita's every glance. And if whatever job she got next didn't fulfill her, she would still have Weber to work toward. It was a dream she hadn't given up on yet, even if the first novel she got to work on was a dud. But it didn't mean she needed Andrew to achieve it.

The images on her laptop looked familiar—men and women wearing name tags and shaking hands; people standing in circles, holding drinks and plates with awkward smiles glued to their faces. All reminders of Nora's fruitless networking attempts a few months into her career at Parsons, the happy hour mixers for young professionals she'd attended in hopes of finding friends to replace those who had moved away after college.

But standing in a crowded bar struggling to find common ground with strangers had yielded no results. Then, when her drink tab came, she'd done a double take before pulling out her credit card and deciding she could not do this regularly. Slowly, as her hours increased and her salary stayed bullishly the same, *not regularly* dwindled into never.

But maybe she'd have better luck networking for job opportunities than she did networking for friends. Nora scrolled past more gatherings that had nothing to do with her—meetups for small business owners, women in tech, financial planners—when her eye caught the word *publishing*. Even now, after everything she'd been through at Parsons, the word still pulled her in.

If she was going to fling herself out of her comfort zone and network, this was the event for it. The conversations would be less likely to dry up because she'd actually have something in common with these attendees. And maybe someone Nora spoke to could connect her to a job, one that had nothing to do with Andrew, and then Nora wouldn't have to care where he took his manuscript. Maybe the job might be better than what was waiting for her at Weber, and she wouldn't have to wait around at all.

A women's publishing group is doing a happy hour on Wednesday, and I'm thinking of going, she texted Beth. Interested?

Even if Beth didn't work in publishing anymore, it was worth a try to have a friendly face to save her from awkwardly standing alone. As Andrew said, there was no harm in asking.

Ooh, is it Ladies Who Pub? Beth replied.

A good sign. Yes!

I have a ton of packing to do next week. I'm moving into my studio on Friday.

Nora hardly had time to register her disappointment before Beth sent another text, one that had her sighing.

But I bet Julie's going. She goes like every month. Let me check.

Attending an event with an acquaintance wasn't quite what Nora had in mind. She wasn't sure how much Julie's presence would save her from awkwardness when she was now already worrying about how they'd make conversation on the way to the event. Nora's thumb hovered over her phone as she tried to think of a polite way to retract her invitation. But she wasn't fast enough.

She's going! She'll meet you after work and you guys can head there together. Here's her number.

Nora typed a feeble thanks and saved the number in her phone. She should have known Beth, extrovert extraordinaire, would do something like this. She wondered if this was Beth's way of making sure Nora didn't back out. She couldn't blame her if it was.

She made it official and signed up for the happy hour through the event page, a current of satisfaction running through her as she did. Another step forward for her and her three. She pictured telling Andrew about it when she saw him next, imagined the pride in his voice. He might even put a sticker on her shirt.

She allowed herself a few moments to imagine it, feeling the beginnings of a wistful smile inching over her. She almost picked up her phone to text him, but she stopped herself. Mindless texting was gooey and couple-y, and they were neither of those things. Given how they started, what still remained between them—his book, her lies—she couldn't afford to complicate their situation any further.

But then, she thought, remembering how he kissed her in the bookstore yesterday and the way he held her while they slept last night, maybe they could find their way back from this. She could start unraveling the thread to uncomplicate everything, a little at a time, truth by truth.

She put her phone away, but it didn't keep her from daydreaming.

———————

Nora gave herself a mission on Monday: make choices that alleviated her guilt. There was too much of it from too many sources, and it was doing nothing to help her three.

It meant, for one, finally putting the call with Andrew and Rita on the calendar. She scheduled it for Thursday to give herself a bit of a reprieve from Rita's disappointment that would inevitably kick in after the call.

She texted Andrew afterwards, telling herself this wasn't mindless texting because there was a purpose behind it. It was simply professionally informing him about a call she'd scheduled. And if their texts then turned from the phone call to weekend plans, that wasn't her fault.

Another choice she made was taking her Weber call outside instead of holding it in the phone room. It wasn't ideal, dodging pedestrians or muting herself every few seconds to avoid traffic sounds and police sirens coming through on the call. And constantly pulling the phone away from her ear to mute and unmute meant she missed about a quarter of everything being said. But at least she didn't feel like Rita was watching her.

She also chose not to mention Andrew on the Weber call. Even though on Saturday he'd agreed to consider publishing with Weber, she knew his heart wasn't in it, knew he was only doing it because she thought he should. And she knew full well that she only thought he should because it would benefit her. It was clear to her now, after their Saturday together, that she should never have tried to use him this way. It didn't change everything she'd done so far, but it meant she felt a lot better about herself going forward. That counted for something.

When she returned from her Weber call sweaty and slightly out of breath, she saw an email from Henry Brook. She wasn't sure how this factored into her new mindset. In his email, he reminded her to ship him ten samples of the materials he'd had her order for the conflict resolution seminars: ten binders, ten padfolios, ten pens, and ten buttons, all emblazoned with Parsons's outdated conflict resolution logo from the '90s, four vaguely person-shaped blobs extending their arms in a circle. He was having a branding meeting for the conflict resolution seminars later that week, he reminded her. The executives needed to see the materials before the idea could be greenlit. Because of course Henry Brook thought it was worth investing in materials before anything was even decided.

Reading his email, Nora decided her new mindset didn't apply to Henry Brook. She imagined herself not sending the materials at all, letting him suffer while the executives he tried to impress called him irresponsible and inept, and it didn't incite any guilt whatsoever. It sounded glorious.

In that case, then, she listened to logic rather than her internal guilt gauge, because she was apparently incapable of guilt when it came to Henry Brook. Logic told her to do as he asked to avoid losing her job. Nora begrudgingly packed up the materials and set them in the mailroom for delivery to Henry Brook, but it didn't stop her from fantasizing about what would happen if she failed to send them and they both lost their jobs in a blaze of glory. It would be worth it for that.

But some guilts couldn't be avoided. Not long after scheduling the call with Andrew and Rita, a meeting invitation from Rita settled on her calendar for that same Thursday. It was titled *Check in about upcoming projects*, but Nora knew its actual purpose was to debrief after the call with Andrew, to discuss how it went and what next steps they could take to convince him to sign the contract. Nora guessed Rita would cancel the meeting once they had the call. Once Andrew made it clear that he wouldn't be signing with Parsons, Rita would know there wasn't a point to discussing next steps. There wouldn't be any next steps left to take.

Unless, Nora realized, a chill running through her, that next step had anything to do with whatever Rita might know about Nora's illicit activities.

She accepted the invitation, feeling silly about how confident she'd been that morning, thinking her new attitude would change anything. It didn't matter that she'd done nothing to add to her guilt today when she'd already made a mountain of things to be guilty about. Her mountain wasn't going anywhere.

Unless someone offered Nora a job on the spot at the networking event, she had a bristling feeling that something unpleasant was waiting for her on Thursday.

CHAPTER TWENTY-FIVE

Her excuses for texting Andrew were getting flimsier.

Two days ago, it was the notice that she scheduled the call with Rita. Today, sitting in her cubicle as the workday came to a close, it was a very unsubtle hint that she would be in his neighborhood within the hour.

Heading to a networking event in the Mission tonight. I'm leaving with a parachute even if I have to steal one.

His response sidestepped the hint entirely:

You're really running this parachute metaphor into the ground.

But his second text sent a wave of satisfaction through her.

Where's the event?

Less than ten blocks from his apartment—not that she'd looked it up already. But they would circle to that topic and its many implications eventually, Nora was sure.

They were drawing closer to it when Julie appeared at Nora's cubicle, ready to depart. On the walk to the elevators, Nora asked Julie how long she'd been coming to these events.

"A few years," Julie said. "I don't go to every one, but it's fun to meet other people. The panels they do sometimes are cool too. There was one on publishing career paths that was pretty interesting."

"Do you have a plan for your path?" Nora asked, stepping into the elevator.

"Editor, obviously," she said with a shrug. "Eventually publisher. I'd like to start my own education imprint one day. Publish the books I would've liked to have had as resources when I was a teacher."

Julie was first to get off the elevator, partly because Nora was too busy marveling at Julie's aspirations to remember to do things like move and speak.

"What about you?" Julie asked, probably not meaning to be cruel.

Nora caught up to Julie and met her stride. "I don't know. I always used to think it was editor, but I don't know anymore."

"Marketing?" Julie offered. "Production?"

"It might not be publishing," Nora admitted.

Julie shot her a sidelong glance. "And you want to go to a publishing happy hour?"

Nora shrugged. "Just keeping an open mind."

They entered the BART station and scanned their cards against the readers. While they waited at the platform for the next Daly City–bound train, Nora tried to articulate it. "If all my experience is in publishing anyway, it's worth exploring my options. Leave no stone unturned and all," she said, thinking of the rote guidance she'd come across in one of Parsons's books on developing a winning strategy. The book was less clear on what was supposed to happen once you turned over all the stones.

A short BART ride later and they were walking through the door of a brewery in the Mission. At the far end, Nora could see a group of women laughing and talking to one another. Some stood holding glasses of amber beer, while others sat at tables with *Reserved* signs and shared appetizers. Julie strode ahead while Nora trailed behind.

Julie stopped at a table scattered with blank name tag stickers and Sharpies. She uncapped one and wrote her name and, under it, *Parsons Press*. Nora picked up a Sharpie and followed suit. As she pressed the sticker over her chest, she saw Julie settle into one of the empty *Reserved* tables and pick up a menu. Nora slid into the seat across from her. It was so much better to have someone to follow at these events. Part of the reason Nora's bill was so high at the young professionals meetups she used to go to was that she inevitably ordered more than she should have, just to have something to do. Something to eat and drink, to have and to hold.

"You want to go in on the fries?" Julie asked.

"Yes," Nora said quickly. Fries came in large quantities. Lots of opportunities to hold something. Much better than the mozzarella sticks she got once. Five sticks of gluey cheese and that was it.

Order placed, Julie rose and headed for the cluster of women standing and talking by the wall. Nora watched them greet her warmly. A few said Julie's name without even glancing down at her name tag. With no fries to busy herself with yet, Nora edged into the circle.

"Did you do anything to celebrate?" one of the women was asking.

A woman whose tag read *Brenda* nodded, cheeks rosy. "Nothing wild. I just went out to dinner with some friends. They don't work in publishing, but they knew it was a big deal for me."

There were nods and murmurs of understanding. Julie leaned toward Nora and said, "Brenda got promoted to editor last week."

Nora looked at Brenda, understanding the excitement now. "Congratulations!"

Brenda's eyes shone as she thanked her. She looked about mid-thirties, with large round eyes and short dark hair. Nora fought the urge to pile questions on Brenda—ask her how long she'd been working in publishing; how often she changed companies, if at all; whether the editor title was everything she wanted it to be or if she'd lost some of her drive somewhere along the way. But this wasn't about Nora.

Nora practiced the skills she'd picked up from her young professionals happy hours: attentive listening face, polite nod, readiness to answer any questions batted her way. After a few anecdotes, she looked over her shoulder and saw the plate of fries sitting where she and Julie had been. Nora discreetly backed away from the group and piled some fries onto a small plate. Brenda may be an editor, but Nora would have a purpose. Specifically, to shove fries into her listening face.

Nora popped a fry into her mouth. She was chewing and wiping the grease onto a napkin when she heard a throaty laugh she knew well.

She froze and scanned the room. There, in a group by the bar, holding a glass of something clear and sparkling, was Lynn. Red glasses, blond hair in full frizz, laugh hearty and emphatic.

Nora turned away. She picked up the small plate of fries and walked quickly to the circle. There was still an opening where she'd been standing next to Julie and across from Brenda, but that would put her back to Lynn, and she needed to keep eyes on her.

"Sorry, excuse me," Nora muttered, wedging a shoulder into the group. The person next to her, whose name tag Nora was too stressed to read, stepped aside to create room. Nora leaned back, looking past the shoulders of the woman next to her. If she stood here, she could see Lynn's back. There were about fifteen feet between them. Lynn wouldn't be able to see Nora easily, even if she turned around. Still, Nora's heart pounded in her ears so loudly that she couldn't concentrate on what anyone around her was saying. And yet her hearing was somehow better than ever, because she swore she could make out Lynn's Southern accent over every other murmur in the room.

"Oh, fries are here?" Julie asked.

Nora followed her line of vision to the small plate of fries she held but hadn't yet touched. "Oh. Yeah."

"Do you want to go sit down?"

Nora glanced at the table where she'd been sitting with Julie. Lynn might be able to see her out of the corner of her eye if she sat there. "No." She looked up, saw Julie still waiting for an explanation. "I'm fine standing," Nora said.

Julie, asking for no follow-ups, headed back to the table. A couple of other women from the group trailed after her, leaving Nora with a smaller circle. Brenda and—she peered at the woman's name tag—Josie. Nora leaned back and looked past Josie. Lynn hadn't moved.

"How do you like it at Parsons?" Josie asked.

Nora snapped back to her shrunken circle of physical buffers. "Hmm?"

"Parsons," Josie said, gesturing at Nora's chest. "Do you work with Julie?"

She looked down. Of course. Her name tag innocently declared to the world that she worked at Parsons.

"Yes, I do," Nora said. "Julie's great. Excuse me." She backed away with a small smile. She'd seen a restroom in the corner.

Nora darted to the bar across from her and set her uneaten plate of fries on the counter, then followed the wall to the restroom.

Inside, Nora peeled the name tag off so quickly she left part of it behind. She peeled at the other half more slowly, noticing how her chest rose with each breath she took. Nora crumpled the sticky pieces into a ball between her hands, then threw it in the garbage.

She looked up and met herself in the mirror: panicked eyes and a visible sheen of sweat on her forehead, all from a few minutes of standing and worrying.

Nora pulled her phone out of her purse. She and Andrew were still circling. His last text asked her if she was getting anything to eat at the happy hour. They were almost there. She could say no and ask if he'd eaten yet; he could say no; she could mention that the event was ending; he could ask if she wanted to get dinner with him.

The sounds outside the bathroom were getting louder, clearer. Sharp taps on the ground. Someone was coming. Even though in her worried haze she knew they weren't Lynn's footsteps, knew Lynn didn't wear anything with a heel, the sound still sent Nora darting into a stall.

She went through the motions of using the bathroom: arranging a toilet seat cover, unbuttoning her jeans, sitting down. The woman in heels clacked into the bathroom and picked the stall next to Nora's. She watched the heels—a pair of sleek black pumps—move around the stall as the woman laid out a toilet seat cover and settled in.

Nora flushed the toilet and stood, fastening her button so quickly it only went in the loop halfway. She opened the stall door and washed her hands just long enough to be considered acceptable. She ran a hand over the automated paper towel dispenser. It lit up, but nothing came out.

The toilet flushed. Nora wiped her hands on her pants and turned for the door just as the stall clicked open. In the mirror, she caught a glimpse of the figure leaving the stall: a tall woman with hair styled in a silver bob. Nora opened the bathroom door and slipped out, but her mind was still putting the image together.

She'd shaken that woman's hand once, somewhere with an atmosphere of anxiety.

The Weber interview. Violet.

Nora did a quick scan of the brewery. Brenda and Josie were still standing where she'd left them. Julie was still at the table with the fries. And Lynn was nowhere to be found. She ran her eyes along the bar once, twice. No Lynn.

Nora pushed herself to keep moving, knowing Violet would emerge from the bathroom behind her at any second. As she walked, she became more obvious in her scanning, turning her head from side to side, honing in on every woman's face.

She didn't dare let herself hope Lynn had left. She had the feeling she got when she found a spider in her room, took her eyes off it for a second to grab something to use against it, and looked back to find it was gone. It was a feeling of skin-crawling uncertainty, the knowledge that the spider could be anywhere. Anywhere at all.

Feeling nauseous, Nora slid into the seat next to Julie. Julie was in conversation with a couple of women from the group, whose names Nora would check if she could focus on anything at all. She kept her head down and pulled out her phone. Circling be damned.

Can I come over now?

She bit her lip and stared at her phone, *say yes say yes say yes* pounding with each thump of her heart.

Three teasing dots appeared, stalled, disappeared, appeared again. Christ, he was typing something clever.

But she didn't need him in order to make an escape. Nora lifted her head and looked toward the door she'd entered through, some twenty feet away. All she needed to do was make it to that door without being spotted. If only she knew where her roaming spider was.

"Nora was in Baltimore recently, weren't you?"

Nora tore her gaze away from the perimeter of the brewery. "Yes," she said slowly.

"Amy grew up in Baltimore."

Nora turned to face Amy, the woman sitting to her left, enjoying fries like any carefree person would. "Oh. That's cool." She struggled to think of something else to say. "It was for a conference with long hours, so I never really got to leave my hotel to explore the city."

Amy seemed to accept this. She nodded with a polite smile and took a fry. Nora wondered if Julie was regretting coming with her, conversational dud that she was tonight. She looked up again, scanning, searching. Nothing. She couldn't sit around waiting for the spider to find her.

She rehearsed the words in her head twice and opened her mouth. "I've got to head home, actually. I wish I could stay longer. This was so much fun." She tried to approximate a smile but had a feeling it was coming out wrong. Every muscle in her face felt strained. "It was nice to meet you," Nora said to Amy and the other woman at the table, who she didn't actually meet. She turned to Julie. "Thanks for coming with me. I'd love to do this again."

"Sure." Julie's voice was pleasant, unsuspecting.

As she started toward the door, counting down the footsteps until she was home free, she felt her phone vibrate. Andrew and his clever response. He'd let her come over, and she'd relax into a puddle on his couch, and he'd make fun of her for never making plans, and—

"Nora!" a familiar voice called out, sounding so pleased and carefree. Nora tried to ignore it and keep walking, but Lynn would not be deterred. "Nora!"

Pulse racing, Nora paused. Turned. Her spider sat at a table facing the door. Violet sat across from her.

"Lynn," Nora forced out, voice coming out in a strangle. "Violet. It's so nice to see you!"

Violet's gaze fell on Nora. It seemed to take her a moment to place Nora, and she didn't blame her. This wasn't the calm, collected person who'd shown up to the interview, all black flats and dress pants, ironed blouse and hair neatly styled. This was Nora. Jeans and a wrinkled top. Tired eyes and tired curls. She'd tried to revive the latter by shoving her hair under the faucet that morning, furiously scrunching it in the two minutes before she had to leave to catch her usual BART. The results were questionable.

Violet recovered, a friendly smile washing over her. Lynn pulled Nora into a hug.

"I didn't expect to see you here!" she exclaimed.

"Me neither!" Nora said semi-truthfully. "How have you been?" she tried, which got Lynn talking about her adventures in repainting her bathroom. But it was shortsighted of Nora to ask, because then Lynn lobbed the question back to her, and Nora had to think of something that didn't involve ceiling fans, deception, or sleeping with an author. "I'm good."

Lynn nodded, waiting for Nora to continue. Nora didn't.

"Well—" Nora glanced at the door, but she stopped speaking when she heard Lynn start talking.

"Thank you for sending your comments on the novel." She turned to Violet and explained, "Nora gave me her thoughts on the Blake manuscript. She's interested in fiction."

Lynn was the best career wingwoman there ever could be, but now wasn't the time.

Violet fixed her curious gaze on Nora. "How did you like it? We saw a lot of potential in that one."

"Y-yes," Nora stammered. *Potential* was a good word. Something it had not yet achieved. "It's not a genre I typically read, but I can see why you acquired it. It's such a compelling premise." That was what Nora's email to Lynn had emphasized: a love for the premise. It was the best lie she could think of. She certainly couldn't declare a love for the protagonist, his regret, his unfathomable sexual escapades, or the entitlement dripping off the page.

Violet was nodding. Nora took it to mean that she was saying the right words. Lynn was looking at something behind Nora, which seemed like a good moment to take advantage of the distraction. Nora cast another obvious glance at the exit and mentally prepared her parting words.

"Is that Julie?" Lynn said loudly like she knew the answer.

Nora turned, dread pooling in her stomach, to see Julie standing at the bar, impossible to miss with her blond and lavender hair. Julie whipped her head around.

"Lynn, hey!" she exclaimed.

Nora watched, frozen. Lynn and Julie hugged. They asked after one another, gave brief summaries of how they were doing. Violet and Julie were introduced to one another.

Before anyone could mention Nora's place(s) of work, Nora opened her mouth, though a full second passed before she thought of something to say. "Do you come to these events often?" she asked. "This is my first one, but it seems fun."

Lynn nodded, smile bright. "I've been coming on and off for years, but now that I work at Weber, I love coming to the San Francisco ones. I miss having an excuse to go into the city."

"Right," said Nora, as if she didn't dread her commute each morning.

"We've actually hosted a few of these at the Weber office," Violet said.

"Yes!" Julie said, something dawning on her. "I think I've been to one. It was a panel."

Nora's phone buzzed again. She ignored it, watching Julie and Violet discuss the panel they'd seen at the Weber office, staring intently to make sure her name didn't escape their lips.

"Have you been to this brewery before?" Lynn asked. Nora, still watching Julie and Violet, still convinced she could learn to lip-read if she watched them long enough, shook her head. "I'm not one for beer," Lynn continued, "but they do this honeyed cheese that's incredible. I was just trying to convince Violet to order it. It's too much for two people, but what do you think? We're four now."

Nora turned to Lynn. "I have to pass, but that sounds delicious. Maybe another time?" Guilt plummeted through her. Ordinarily, when her worlds weren't on the verge of colliding and collapsing, she would have loved to sit with Lynn and share a mess of honeyed cheese with her.

"Absolutely," Lynn said.

"I'd love to have lunch the next time you're in the city," Nora offered. Her phone vibrated again, urging her to leave. She obeyed. "I've got to head out, but it was so good to see you."

Lynn wrapped her in another hug. Over her shoulder, Nora saw a figure come in through the door. Someone stood in the doorway, backlit by the sun, looking around. She didn't pay it any mind until the door swung shut and she recognized who it was. Andrew Santos was heading straight for her.

CHAPTER TWENTY-SIX

Andrew gave Nora a small wave as he approached, zeroing in on her like a bullet. She pulled back from her hug with Lynn.

"It was nice seeing you," Nora said, unsure whether she'd already said that. Her gaze darted to Andrew, hovering a few feet behind, holding a coffee cup.

"I hope you're not leaving on my account," Andrew said. Lynn turned to face him. Nora's stomach dropped. "Sorry, I didn't want to interrupt," he said, glancing between the faces now looking at him. "I was just at a café down the street, so when I heard you were nearby I thought I'd swing by on my way home. But no pressure." He lifted a hand, palm outward, an *I come in peace* kind of gesture. Except, in this case, peace was the last thing he was bringing. "I can take off if you're not ready to leave yet." He looked from Nora to the others, then back to Nora.

Lynn, eyeing Andrew with curiosity, asked, "Have we met before?"

"No, I don't think so." Andrew smiled politely and stuck out a hand. "I'm Andrew." He regarded her name tag. "And you work at Weber?"

"That's right. I'm Lynn."

"Nora said she knew someone at Weber."

Lynn chuckled. "I should think she does," she said. Nora faked laughter, though it came out maniacal. Back Lynn went to staring at Andrew. "Are you Andrew Santos?"

"Yes," he said through a surprised laugh.

"That explains it! I worked with Tom at Parsons," Lynn said. "I think I saw one of your sessions at a conference."

Nora's eyes darted between the two of them, willing them to stop learning things about one another.

"Then I'm sorry we didn't get a chance to meet," he said.

"You know how it is at conferences," Lynn said with a wave of her hand. "But I'm glad to be meeting you now. And this is Violet, our publisher at Weber." She stepped aside to make room for Violet, who stood to shake his hand.

"Nice to meet you," Andrew said. He looked past her and caught a glimpse of Julie. "Oh, you work at Parsons with Nora!"

Nora's eyes went straight to the name tag on Julie's shirt, the *Parsons Press* written in clear letters under her name. As Andrew and Julie shook hands, Nora peeked at Lynn and Violet. Lynn must have missed it, still smiling at Andrew, but Violet frowned. Nora tried to think of a distraction, but her mind went blank and her mouth went dry.

"Did you say Nora works at Parsons?" Violet asked. "With Julie?"

"Yeah," Andrew said. A wrinkle formed in Lynn's brow. Looking from Lynn to Violet, Andrew appeared to have a rare moment of losing confidence. "I mean, I don't know exactly how Nora and Julie work together." Now he turned to Nora for guidance. Nora stood frozen, mouth open, unable to string a sentence together.

"Our work doesn't cross paths much," Julie volunteered. "I'm the assistant editor for psychology books, and Nora's the EA for the business line. But we work in the same office, obviously."

"But not anymore," Violet prompted, like she was helping Julie complete a thought.

And Julie, Nora's last hope, watching Violet with polite bewilderment: "What do you mean, 'not anymore?'"

"Because Nora left Parsons a couple of months ago, right? To come work for Weber?" As Violet took in Julie's blank face, she focused her gaze—now cold and unwavering—on Nora. Lynn, too, trained her eyes on Nora.

She could see them putting the pieces together. Nora's mind raced through elaborate lies she might be able to tell. Julie didn't know what she was talking about (except Julie was right there to defend herself). Or she'd been under the impression that it was okay to work for Weber and Parsons simultaneously (except she wasn't that stupid). Worse than Nora's inability to think of a lie was her certainty that they could see it all on her face, the lies she was considering and discarding.

"Not exactly," Nora whispered. She could feel Julie staring, wondering why this simple truth was so difficult for Violet and Lynn to understand. Stronger than that was the feeling of Andrew's presence next to her, also watching, probably realizing why she'd been so eager to encourage him to take his book to Weber last weekend.

"You never left Parsons?" Lynn's voice had a hard edge to it, something Nora had never been on the receiving end of before. She'd heard it once, on a call with an entitled author, and she'd loved every minute of Lynn putting him in his place. Nora hated thinking Lynn could unleash that on her right now.

Nora stepped toward Lynn and said quietly, "They cut my pay." Speaking, she hoped, not to Lynn and Violet, her Weber superiors, but to Lynn, her former Parsons boss, who took her to lunch and lent her books. Lynn, who marveled with her when she heard the pay cut news and asked how Parsons could do such a thing.

This Lynn only stared in disbelief.

Violet, however, pasted on a thin smile. "I don't think we need to talk about all this right now." She glanced briefly at Andrew, then back to Nora. "I'll let you get on your way, and we can discuss this later."

"Okay." Nora couldn't even muster a parting smile. The best she could do was glance at Julie and her dumbfounded expression, at Andrew and his wrinkled brow, and stumble toward the exit.

How kind of them to avoid firing her in front of an author. Even though Nora knew that was all this was—knew a dismissal was coming in private—part of her wanted to latch on to the word *discuss* and hope there really would be a discussion, like the way they'd all overlooked the Irene Nichols incident. This, too, she might be able to come back from.

She felt a hand on her back, knew it was Andrew next to her. He stole ahead and pushed the door open. Nora trudged through it.

The sun was in full force, blinding her with a brightness she couldn't understand. She stood there, blinking back tears and sunlight.

"What happened back there?" Andrew asked.

She wanted to cry just looking at him, seeing the concern in his eyes, knowing he'd hate her once he knew the full truth. "Not here," she mumbled.

"Okay." His hand returned to her back and they walked down

the sidewalk, Andrew slowing his gait to match her stunned steps. They passed a trash can and Andrew threw his coffee cup into it. She knew from the heavy sound it made that it wasn't empty. He couldn't even enjoy his coffee now. That, too, Nora had ruined.

They turned a corner and walked almost to the next one before Nora stopped. "Okay," she said. Here, between a bus stop and a barbershop, was as good a place as any. Andrew stood across from her, waiting. Nora leaned against the wall and took a breath. "When Parsons cut my pay, I took a part-time freelance job at Weber. As an acquisitions editor. I told them I left Parsons, but I didn't. I needed the money."

Andrew took this in. "And they didn't know you still worked at Parsons."

"No."

He nodded. "And I'm guessing from Julie's reaction that no one at Parsons knew about Weber."

Nora watched him, wishing she could read his empty expression. "No."

His eyebrows dipped together. "Are you ever honest with anyone?"

"Lately, no." That was the wrong thing to say. Seeing his surprise, Nora raced to explain it, justify it. "If I told anyone, I'd lose one of my jobs, and I needed both of them to pay rent."

None of this had any effect on him. His serious stare didn't leave her. "What about me? Why didn't you tell me?"

Nora shook her head powerlessly. "I didn't know if I could."

He stared at her a moment before looking somewhere off to the side. "You want to know what I think?"

Nora stayed silent, knowing his words were coming either way. Knowing they would hurt.

"I think you had the Weber card in your back pocket this entire time, waiting for a moment to play it," he said. "*I* thought that when I told you I wasn't signing with Parsons, you might run. I told you I've been worried all this time that you were using me for my book. So when you said that didn't matter, and you offered to introduce me to someone at Weber, I thought it meant that you really were interested in me. I didn't expect the Weber card." She'd never seen him smile like this, so bitterly. "And now it makes sense, why you were so against me wanting a big publisher last weekend. I thought it was about Parsons. And then I thought I was being paranoid, but I guess I wasn't. It was never about you wanting what's best for me. Or being interested in me."

"I *am* interested in you," she pleaded. But he was right. She was never honest. It was a lie to say she was interested without acknowledging the distance she kept putting between them. She didn't think he would believe what she believed, that if she could dig herself out of the awful way she felt about her future, if she didn't have to spend every minute desperately running through mental lists to fight the temptation that preceded every thought, if she weren't so exhausted by the constant process of trying to make her will to live win out over her will to die, she'd be able to show him what she felt for him. Ten times over.

"But not enough," Andrew said.

Nothing had ever been enough to pierce through the fog, she wanted to tell him. Any *not enough* she was had nothing to do with him.

Nora searched him desperately. "I could still get you a call with Weber," she said. "I don't work there anymore, I'm pretty sure, but I meant what I said. Weber is an option for you."

He shook his head, like she still wasn't getting it. "Nora, I have options. I got an agent. That's not the point."

Her mouth fell open. "You got an agent?"

"Yes."

"And you didn't tell me?"

He smiled grimly. "I was worried you'd leave if you knew."

"It was never that black and white," Nora insisted, voice hollow.

"I know."

That made it worse somehow. That he knew she was drawn to him for more than his book, but she still chose the book in the end. Nora looked at the uneven sidewalk at her feet, trying to keep her breaths even.

"I think I should go," he said. She looked up. He smiled, barely. "I think we've said all we need to." He took a step, turned to her again. "I *am* sorry about Weber."

"Me too. Wait," she said, before he could turn his back again. He obeyed, nodding for her to speak. Her gaze scrambled over him as she wished she had the words to fix this. "I admit that your book was part of it, but it was the smallest part. I hope you believe that. I have a complicated enough relationship with just the idea of being alive. I didn't want to drag you into that."

"I do believe it," he said, still with that small, sad smile. "And I would have gone in willingly."

Nora swallowed past the thickness in her throat and watched him walk away. When he turned the corner and disappeared from view, she counted seconds in her head, waiting for enough time to pass that she wouldn't run into him when she started down that same street. She pulled out her phone.

Three unread texts from Andrew, sent a catastrophe ago.

I'm offended that you seem to think I do nothing but sit at home waiting for you to show up. That is only sometimes true.

Kidding! I'm actually at a café not too far from the brewery. What if I drop by on my way back and we get dinner?

I got my coffee and I haven't heard back, so fyi I'm on my way! See you in a few, maybe!

Her eyes stung. She wiped them and reread his words, blinking past the blurriness. A longing for this Andrew, the one who didn't yet know what she'd done, crept from within her. She imagined him texting her from the café, making plans to pick her up for a dinner they would never have. She would miss him every time she saw these texts, these reminders of what she'd thrown away. And what a stupid, sentimental concept, to miss someone who was never even hers.

CHAPTER TWENTY-SEVEN

Nora sat in her cubicle staring at the rectangle on her calendar. *Call to discuss contract*, it read. She'd sent the calendar invitation to Rita and Andrew three days ago, in a time that didn't feel real.

Now she knew there was no point to the charade. Andrew had been willing to go through with it before, to have the call and let Rita down easy. But that was before yesterday—before he uncovered her lies and walked away. He wouldn't want to have a call for appearance's sake. It would be cruel to put either one of them through that.

Her mouse hovered over the Cancel Meeting button. She should, under normal circumstances, provide a reason for the cancellation, but she couldn't bring herself to put it in words. Andrew knew. Rita wouldn't, but she knew where to find her.

Nora pressed the button. It was only a matter of time before Rita would come probing and prodding. She could show up and interrogate Nora, for all she cared. It didn't matter. Nora had been through enough in the last sixteen hours. She'd received an email last night from Violet, formally informing her that her services as a freelancer were no longer needed, effective immediately. She was advised to submit a final invoice for the remaining period of her time worked. After reading the email, Nora had paused *Little Women*, wiped graham cracker dust off her fingers, and threw together a minimalist invoice. Not the ones she'd sent them before, formatted from a template she found online. She had no one to impress anymore. They'd get the bare bones information, words uncapitalized, math unchecked. She sent the attachment, unpaused *Little Women*, and blew her nose for the thousandth time that night.

Julie had tried reaching out to her last night, a kindness Nora would have appreciated if she weren't so far gone. I got your number from Beth, she texted. Are you okay?

To answer honestly would raise alarm. To lie would prove Andrew right yet again. His words still rang in her ears: *Are you ever honest with anyone?*

In the end, Nora turned her phone off and went back to *Little Women*.

Sure enough, the meeting cancellation brought an email from Rita, almost instantly.

Did something happen?

Nora inhaled, exhaled, and typed a vague explanation.

He told me he's decided not to sign with Parsons.

Nora watched her screen, waiting to see whether Rita would cancel the meeting she'd set earlier in the week, the one called *Check in about upcoming projects*. It had been scheduled for four o'clock, an hour after the call with Andrew. Either it was a meeting to debrief about the call with Andrew, in which case Rita would cancel it now, or it was something worse: a meeting to discuss Rita's suspicions about Nora, Weber, and disappearing authors. And if that was the case, Rita wouldn't cancel it. The news about Andrew would just add more fuel to the fire.

She kept waiting, knee bouncing under her desk. When a few minutes passed and the meeting didn't leave her calendar, reality started to sink in. Nora took a shaky breath and waited for four o'clock.

She met Rita in the same small phone room Nora used to have her weekly Weber calls in. She took a seat at the small round table and noticed the way Rita shut the door when she came in the room.

"How have you been?" Rita asked.

Nora faked a smile and mumbled something positive. She couldn't be bothered to ask after Rita.

Rita settled into her chair and tucked her dark hair behind her ear. "What happened with Santos?" she asked. Her tone was gentler than it needed to be, making Nora eye her warily and wonder what she knew. "I thought it was a little strange that he agreed to the meeting on Monday but canceled it today. Did he tell you anything?"

"He said he got an agent," Nora said. "I think he's looking for a publisher that can offer him more than Parsons can."

Rita nodded, not looking entirely surprised. "I guess that's fair." She sat back, sharp eyes on Nora. "I know he's not the first of our authors to go with another publisher lately."

Nora forgot how to make normal eye contact. She focused

on trying to keep her face in the same expression it had been in before, whatever that was, maybe a sort of understanding grimace.

"I know it's not something we can always help," Rita said. "Some of them want their old editor back. Or they want a publisher that can offer things we can't."

Rita kept watching her. The grimace may have been the wrong choice.

"I saw you getting lunch with Lynn," Rita said, "a couple of months ago, at the Italian place on Sutter? I saw you on my way out. I started wondering if you'd try to get a job with Weber."

Nora opened her mouth, excuses on her tongue, but Rita kept going.

"And when I saw Lynn at a conference last month, she told me you were freelancing for her."

Nora swallowed. "She did?"

"Yep. She said it was terrible that our pay was cut, and that it was too bad it was driving away talented people like you. And she said she was glad you'd already bounced back and found some part-time work at Weber." She related all of this so calmly, eyes boring through Nora.

"What did you say?" she croaked. She thought back to yesterday, how betrayed Lynn had seemed. Lynn couldn't have known.

"I said I was glad you found some work too."

Nora waited, sure more was coming. When Rita said nothing, Nora asked, "That's all? You didn't tell her?"

Rita shrugged. "In a weird way, I understood. They cut my pay too. I used to be an EA; I know how tight things get. I thought it was just a way for you to make ends meet."

"It was," Nora insisted.

"And then on Monday, I saw Vincent Cobb post on LinkedIn

about writing a book for Weber. He mentioned being approached to write for Weber at CEF, and that struck me as a little strange. Because Weber doesn't attend CEF." She rested her piercing gaze on Nora. "But you did."

Nora's breath left her. "I didn't think it would matter," she protested weakly. "He only ever published one book with Parsons, years ago. And it didn't even sell."

"I know. But it makes me wonder how many other Parsons authors you've done this with. How many other authors I don't know about. It makes me question everything you do. And now, thinking about how we had Santos in the palm of our hand and he didn't sign with us, I have to wonder whether you played a role in that too."

Nora, piecing this together, clung to her last hope. "I didn't lead him to Weber. He didn't know I worked for Weber until yesterday. He and Lynn both found out everything at the same time yesterday."

This, at least, cut through Rita's cool exterior. She gave Nora a quizzical look. "What were you doing with Andrew and Lynn yesterday?"

Nora could have laughed at Rita's expression, how bizarre it all sounded. How badly she managed to intertwine and screw up so many areas of her life, all at once. "I ran into Lynn at a networking event for women in publishing. And Andrew came by to pick me up for dinner."

A double-take from Rita. "You and Andrew were...?"

"Hanging out," Nora finished. It sounded so insignificant out loud. It made her feel foolish for being so affected by someone she was only ever *hanging out* with. "But I didn't lead him to Weber," she insisted again.

Rita nodded once, taking this in. "Even if he didn't sign with Weber," she said. "He didn't sign with Parsons, either."

Nora tensed. "I can't control what he does."

"But I'd guess you could influence it."

Nora thought of the first time she visited Andrew's apartment, her confession about the pay cuts. Even before that, over dinner at the conference, she'd told him more than an author should know when she talked about her ambivalence toward publishing. Rita wasn't wrong. And Nora needed to stop feigning innocence and take accountability.

She took a breath and met Rita's gaze. "So what does this mean?"

"I think maybe you should step back from editorial," Rita said. "I can't have this happening again, us losing authors like this."

"It won't," Nora said, throat growing tighter. "I promise. Lynn fired me yesterday. I'll never do anything like this again." From the careful way Rita studied her, Nora thought she might almost believe her.

"I have no way of knowing that." Her tone was apologetic but her words were firm.

It was a fair point. She'd already defected once. But it stung to know she could add Rita's name to the growing list of people whose trust Nora had broken.

"What does stepping back from editorial look like?" Nora asked.

"I'm still thinking it through. Part of your work is already administrative—you know, distributing pub schedules, maintaining our meeting agendas. You'd keep on with that. You can pass off your remaining editorial tasks to Kelly. And I know you've been working with Henry Brook on getting those conflict resolution seminars off the ground. I think the rest of your work can shift to that. Candace told me he even stopped his search for an assistant because he said it was going so well with you." She watched Nora with a thoughtful expression. "I think this could be good for you. It's something new. It could even be exciting." Rita gave her a hopeful smile, and Nora could see how badly Rita wanted her to accept this. Not that she had a choice.

"Okay," Nora heard herself saying. She tried to keep her face expressionless as she blinked back tears.

"It would be gradual," Rita said. "Not an overnight change or anything."

"Yeah." Nora studied her fingernails in her lap.

"I shouldn't be asking you this," Rita said, "and you don't have to answer if you don't want to. But...have you been looking for jobs?"

Nora nodded, eyes still on her lap.

"That's good," Rita said. "I think a new challenge would be good for you. You've been through so many changes here. I know from experience how that can take a toll on you."

She was empathizing? It only made it worse, to be treated so kindly during her demotion.

Nora returned to her desk in a detached sort of disbelief. She combed through every interaction she'd had with Rita over the last couple of months. Rita said she saw Lynn at a conference, the one Rita went to the same week Nora was at CEF in Baltimore. It was before the conference that Rita had told her about getting a promotion if she signed Santos. That, then, was genuine.

But what about afterwards? Andrew had emailed both of them the day after the conference, hinting that Nora was convincing him to sign his contract. Rita was quick to reply with excitement, praising Nora for a job well-done. It must have reassured her that Nora's loyalties laid with Parsons.

But as Andrew stalled on the contract, Rita had started asking questions. Nora remembered the conversation they'd had after one of their weekly meetings, the way Rita had casually mentioned Parsons authors leaving for Weber, her unwavering gaze. Rita may not have put all the pieces together until the Vincent Cobb post this week, but Nora had to wonder if the news of Lynn's authors leaving Parsons for Weber was Rita's first inkling of suspicion that Nora might one day try stealing authors for herself.

How blatant Nora's actions must have seemed. Camping out in a phone room for the Weber call every Monday. Sitting in the Parsons office on Parsons time, having calls with Parsons authors to lure them to Weber. Smiling fakely at Rita and assuring her Andrew was coming around.

She sank into her chair in disbelief. The total, blatant stupidity.

She noticed a new email in her inbox. A part of her she couldn't yet silence hoped it was from Andrew. It wasn't.

Npra,

The logo on the binders and padfolios is all wrong. Let's schedule a call to discuss. Make it another weekly check-in.

thx,
H

Nora's eyes narrowed. *Npra. All wrong. Call to discuss.* His goddamn inability to spell out the word *thanks*.

But it was *another weekly check-in* that made her stomach tense. The reality of what her demotion meant came crashing down around her as she read and reread his email, breathing in and out through her nose to try to control her quickening breaths.

She considered the prospect of spending the foreseeable future as Henry Brook's assistant: taking his calls, having multiple weekly check-ins with him, listening to him explain file names to her like she was inept. The thought of this new existence drained her of rage and filled her with nothing. Absolutely, utterly nothing.

Her old team was gone. Beth was gone. Everyone had left and found their place. Nora didn't know where her place was supposed to be, but as she stared at Henry Brook's email, she felt irrevocably that this was not it. This was something Parsons had hammered into her long ago, but never had it been so obvious.

Parsons Press was not a publishing house. It was a sad, lonely vacuum where Nora existed only to please Henry Brook. A task left to her because she was there. Because she couldn't be trusted. And because she accepted it.

The thoughts came back to her, offered as they always were by the creature in her head who slunk forward in her moments of desolation. They went through their usual routine. Again the creature suggested she might prefer a peaceful alternative to the aimless life that awaited her. It held her hand, compelled her to look into the empty blackness where its eyes should be, and asked her why she would want to continue living if it made her so unhappy.

But now a second creature walked in the door, Parsons incarnate.

Sitting at her desk and looking at Henry Brook's email with

such intensity that the words blurred, she felt Parsons was trying to tell her she didn't deserve to be an editorial assistant. It was imploring her to accept this new role she'd unwittingly shaped for herself through her acquiescence and deceit. Her new job was to serve Henry Brook, completing tasks that mattered even less than her usual work.

But the creature made a mistake. It underestimated just how much she hated Henry Brook.

Before her thoughts formed completely, Nora felt herself standing. She was walking to the phone room. Rita was still there, door ajar as Nora had left it, leaning back in her chair and looking at something on her phone.

Nora tapped on the door. "Can I come in?"

"Sure." Rita set her phone on the table, eyeing Nora with curiosity.

Nora shut the door. "I need to quit." She forced the words out before she could sit down, before she could talk herself out of it.

Rita nodded, and Nora noticed she didn't seem surprised. But it wasn't surprising anymore when people left. "Did you get a job offer?"

Nora shook her head. "I just—I can't be here anymore."

"Okay." Rita paused. Speaking in a slow, measured way, she asked, "Do you know when your last day will be?"

Nora wished she'd consulted a calendar. "No."

"You don't have to decide right now. It's not official until you tell HR." Seeing Nora still working this over in her mind, and perhaps knowing Nora had never quit a job before, Rita added, "It's okay if you want to give more than two weeks if you want time to transition. But two weeks is fine too."

Nora tried to balance how much longer she felt she could stay there with how long she would need to figure out her next step. She didn't want to lose this urgency that had her taking action, but she knew she needed more time. "Maybe a month," she said, her voice uncertain.

"Okay. Are you sure there's nothing you want to discuss?"

She took a deep breath. "No." Her thoughts felt too swirly for coherency.

"Okay," Rita said again. She was still watching Nora like she expected an explosion. "Is it okay if I tell Candace?"

"That's fine." Vaguely, she wondered if Candace knew about Weber, too, but Nora couldn't bring herself to care.

Nora walked slowly to her desk, the conversation running through her mind. This was a moment she'd imagined for months. She'd thought it would be a moment of victory, in which Nora would storm up to Rita, job offer in hand, refuse all of Rita's attempts to keep her, and put in her two weeks. This way was sadder, but she reminded herself it was necessary. It was good. It was taking a chance and choosing to live.

Nora thought of texting Beth, but she dismissed it. Beth would ask what she planned to do, and she didn't know yet. She needed time to figure something out.

But she knew one thing she would do. She clicked on the email from Henry Brook and pressed Delete.

CHAPTER TWENTY-EIGHT

Happy 5 years!

The text was followed by three confetti balloon emojis. Nora wanted to make fun of Beth for remembering, but she loved her too much for it. Here in her gray cubicle, one day after semi-quitting, reaching a Friday on perhaps the worst and longest week of her life, those three confetti emojis brought Nora more cheer than she deserved.

Happy five right back at you, she texted back. She even threw in a party popper emoji.

She stared at her phone. The screen dimmed, and she tapped back on it to wake it up. She still hadn't told Beth what happened. What would she say? *By the way, I was fired from my second job and I quit my main job, except not officially, and if I don't figure things out, I'll be homeless soon?*

Nora tried to imagine Beth's response. Beth had advised her from the start that getting out of Parsons was the key to addressing her three. She would, in theory, be proud of Nora for quitting. And Beth had been skeptical that the Weber job would work out, so she'd say it was just as well that it blew up in her face. But a key component of Beth's advice—getting a job elsewhere—was woefully missing from Nora's approach.

Beth would notice it immediately. She'd congratulate her with genuine excitement before delicately maneuvering the conversation to Nora's obvious lack of a plan. And she wouldn't have time to talk it out with Nora because she was moving into her studio apartment today.

The screen dimmed again, and this time she let it. She wasn't ready to tell Beth anything yet, but she didn't know how to be ready.

Nora pulled her parachute book out of her purse. She'd never been so blatant as to read at her desk, but she'd never quit a job before either. New experiences all around.

Two hours later, she finished the parachute book and still didn't know what she was supposed to do with her life. Further, she'd thought there would be a quiz of some sort that would tell her what color her parachute was, but apparently it was all just a metaphor.

On two separate occasions during her rebellious reading sprint, Nora had typed out a text to Andrew before deleting it both times, because editorial assistants didn't text authors to talk about parachutes.

Beth and Andrew weren't here to help her now. Beth was busy with her move today. Andrew was... Nora's mind trailed off. He wasn't hers to consider.

She ignored the ache the thought gave her and swiped to her text from Julie, still unanswered. Julie had showed concern after the networking disaster, sending her first and only text to Nora to ask if she was okay. She'd been so wise at their one outing at the pub before that, talking about her previous teaching career, her transition to publishing.

She could ask Julie to join her for drinks if she hadn't just lost one of her jobs and quit the other. Instead, Nora created a meeting invitation for that afternoon and added Julie's name. Meetings were free. And harder to turn down.

Nora remembered that Eric, too, had been at the pub that night, had taken an interest in Nora's question about what kept them going in life. Wondering if this was what it felt like to be Beth, Nora added Eric to the invitation too. Then, recalling Kelly's eagerness at being invited to drinks that night, she added Kelly as well. She could use a dose of eagerness right about now.

Her mouse hovered over the subject line. What to call a meeting about getting her life in order? Something that wouldn't seem jarring to her unsuspecting guests. She called it *Planning ahead*. Vague as hell, but that never stopped Parsons execs from using similarly unclear phrases in the subject lines of the company-wide emails they sent. She scheduled it for three o'clock, booked it in a meeting room hardly anyone used anymore, and sent the invitation.

To Nora's surprise, Kelly, Julie, and Eric accepted the invitation without so much as a question. She spent her time leading up to the meeting rereading the exercises in the parachute book, hoping for inspiration to strike.

At fifteen minutes to three, Nora took the parachute book to the meeting room, unable to wait any longer. There she flipped through the book again. This time, she plucked out the folded piece of paper she'd saved there. Even after doing several exercises from the book over the last few weeks, it was this paper she kept coming back to. *Books. Input. One-on-one. Nonprofit.* As if it were a code she couldn't crack. A code to herself.

The moment the door squeaked open, Nora shoved the paper into her book and sat up straighter, eyes trained on the door.

"I need a plan," she announced.

Julie darted her eyes around the room like a cornered animal. Perhaps Nora could have given her and Eric, who was coming up behind her, a moment to settle in. But patience had gone out the window when she quit.

"What kind of plan?" Eric asked. His tone suggested he was humoring her, but she'd take it. He and Julie took seats at the table. Nora didn't acknowledge the way Julie's eyes studied her. She'd explain the networking event mess when everyone arrived. She had no use for secrets now.

The door opened. Kelly peeked her head in.

"You put a meeting on my calendar?" she asked Nora. "Is it this?"

"Yep," Nora said. "Come in." Nora waited for Kelly take a seat before she said, "I've gathered you here to help me figure out a plan for what to do with my life. Let's say you're laid off tomorrow. What are your plans?"

"Cry and update my résumé," Julie offered.

Nora looked over at Eric.

"Sleep," he said. Not especially helpful.

"Honestly, I think I would just find another way to be around books," Kelly said. "My friend works at a bookstore, and if I were laid off today, I'd ask her for a job to pay the bills while I keep looking for publishing jobs."

This, Nora could get behind. Finding a way to be around books—one of the four items on her sad sheet of paper—felt right. But what did it say that she and Kelly had a similar instinct to continue working with books, when Nora prided herself on being so wizened, so much more jaded than Kelly after a half-decade of being chewed up by publishing? She should have been past the idea of looking for magic in books by now.

"Why do you need a plan?" Kelly asked.

"I quit my job."

Julie did a double-take while Kelly and Eric stared at Nora, not seeming to want to react until they heard more.

"It was too much," Nora said.

"Care to be more specific?" Eric asked.

"Julie knows." Nora tossed Julie a knowing glance.

Julie's eyebrows shot up. "I don't know the whole story."

"I know. I'm sorry I was ignoring you. It's been a very shitty week."

She gave Nora a half smile. "I figured. I didn't want to bug you."

"Should I ask?" Eric ventured, head turning between the two of them.

Nora looked from Julie to Eric. It was half-out now anyway. She'd rather Julie knew everything instead of any assumptions she'd put together. It all came falling out: Lynn, Weber, Rita. Andrew, she mentioned only in relation to his presence at the networking event and the significance of his contract. The rest of it—the extent of their growing closeness, their sad conversation on the sidewalk outside the brewery, watching him leave and falling apart—she kept to herself. That wasn't for them to know.

"Working for the enemy," Eric said. There was something like admiration in his voice. Nora felt her jaw unclench.

"I'm sorry," Julie said. "I didn't know what was happening."

Julie was apologizing?

"You're not mad? I was stealing authors from Parsons."

"I think anything's fair game after the pay cuts," Eric said.

"I'd agree with that," Kelly said.

Nora turned to her in surprise. "You weren't even here for the pay cuts."

Kelly shrugged. "It's the principle."

Nora almost laughed. A couple of months at Parsons and already Kelly was side-eyeing the decisions their executives made. She loved her for it.

"Now that I know no one wants to call me a traitor," Nora said, "I need to figure out what to do next. I don't know what happens now."

"You can do anything," Julie said.

Nora felt a twinge at the optimism that reminded her of Andrew. "I mean, I don't know what it is I want to do. I have no...career goals. I want to leave publishing, but I don't know for what, and all I have is a publishing résumé."

"And what *I* mean is if you're having trouble getting a traditional job, there are a lot of other ways you can make a living until you figure out what you want to do," Julie said. She started counting the possibilities on her fingers. "You can Uber. You can be a temp. You can wait tables. You can freelance." (Nora twitched.) "A lot of people have career shifts. Most of them figure out what they want to do by falling into different jobs. I always thought I wanted to be an English teacher—until I was an English teacher. Then I took some classes and got a certificate in developmental editing, and I realized that's what I want to do. Career paths are kind of a lie." She looked to Kelly, who shrugged.

"That's news to me. This is my first job."

"All right, you get a pass," Julie said. "Eric?"

"I don't know," he said. "I always wanted to work in project management."

"Really?" Julie asked. "You're telling me that when you were five years old, you wanted to be a journals project manager when you grew up?"

"Okay, fine." Eric rolled his chair closer to the table. "Out of college, I didn't have a plan. I got a job at a temp agency and they sent me around to different companies. It was a lot of admin work—I remember lots of filing, making copies, answering phones. But after a few months at one company, other departments started coming to me when they needed something. And then when a project management job opened up, I took it. And it eventually led me here."

"Ha!" Julie exclaimed. "See? A lot of people have to figure out what they want to do. Even Eric."

"And you don't have kids," Eric added. "You don't have anyone to answer to." Which was a nice way of saying she was alone.

"Also true." Julie settled her gaze on Nora. "What do you have so far?"

"Okay," Nora said. "We know I don't want to work in publishing. And I hate start-ups."

"*All* start-ups?" Eric asked. "But you don't—"

"All start-ups."

"Then you might want to move," he said.

Nora opened her mouth to protest, but Julie jumped in before she could.

"Another possibility," Julie said. "Let's try it a different way. What do you see yourself doing?"

Nora thought about it. She couldn't just say *Nothing*, even though it was true. "I guess…I'd want to do something that matters. Don't you feel like this doesn't really matter? Like we're only publishing the books that'll make us rich, and it doesn't matter what they're about?"

Julie shrugged. "I think what I do matters. I'm helping authors improve their books. And with every book I edit, I'm getting better too."

Nora glanced at Kelly, the other publishing advocate. "I'm sorry, but that's exactly what I want to be doing," she said, gesturing toward Julie. "I know the work I'm doing now is administrative, but I'm still learning a lot. I want to work on more interesting books eventually, but for now I'm getting experience. That matters to me."

Was that what it was like to be passionate about your work? To see the bright side despite the despair?

"Do you get what I'm saying?" Julie asked. "It's kind of exciting."

Watching Julie's hopeful face, her eager eyes and encouraging smile, Nora caught a glimpse of what she must have been like as a teacher. She felt like she was back in school, listening to her algebra teacher patiently explain logarithms to her for the second time. Now, just like then, Nora didn't want to cause disappointment by saying it was hopeless. Not when Julie looked so excited that Nora might finally be getting it.

"I wrote something down," Nora said hesitantly. She flipped through the parachute book, pulled out her well-worn sheet of paper, and slid it across the table.

Julie unfolded it. Eric and Kelly leaned in to read the list. Slowly, Julie looked up, her expression indicating that she was in the process of adjusting her expectations.

"Well, this is something." She used a cheerful voice Nora suspected a teacher might use when a student drew a scribble with pride. "There are a lot of non-publishing directions you could go with books. You could be an English teacher, or a professor. You could work in a bookstore or a library. You could work for a book review site."

"But what if I hate that too?" Nora asked. "Like, let's say I decide to become a librarian. I spend all this time and money getting a master's in library sciences, and then once I actually start working there, I realize I hate it. That's such a waste."

"Who says you have to go all in?" Eric retorted. "Why not volunteer there first to get a feel for it? Or get a part-time job there? Or even just talk to someone who works there?"

All points she'd never even considered. She looked down at her hands in her lap as Eric's questions swirled around her. "What if I don't have anything in mind yet? I don't know where to start."

"This is your start." Julie pushed the paper back to Nora. "Just narrow it down."

Nora nodded. She folded the paper back up, determined to make sense of it. Julie's confidence had Nora thinking her code might not be uncrackable after all.

Even seeing an email from Henry Brook when she returned to her desk couldn't bring her down.

Nora,

Did you get my email? The logo is outdated. We need something more modern if we want to reach a new audience. This one is too 90s. We need to update the logo and order new materials. Put that weekly check-in on my calendar. My Tues afternoons are open.

thx,
H

It would have been futile to point out that he was the one who told her to proceed with the old logo. She suspected his fellow executives had laughed him out of the branding meeting and he'd blamed her to save face. He'd apparently done it to such a great extent that he truly did believe Nora was the mastermind behind this outdated logo scheme.

She might have been frustrated by this email, but not anymore. The quitting and uncertainty were worth it for this. Reading his email made her feel more powerful than she'd felt in a long time. She read it again just for fun. Then she deleted it.

The day was slow, as she expected. It was a late Friday afternoon, and most authors had already started their weekends. Nora spent her time googling temp agencies and considering her options.

But nothing sparked in her as she scrolled down job listings. As sure as she was that she didn't want to work in publishing, she didn't know who she was without it. *Editorial assistant* was so tied up with her identity at this point. She would have to find meaning in something other than a persuasive email or a mention on an acknowledgments page.

Nora stepped toward her cubicle shelf and picked up *Retaining Top Talent* by Bonnie Jackson. She flipped the first couple of pages to the book's acknowledgments section and scanned her eyes to the familiar first paragraph on the second page.

...and Tom, for being such a brilliant editor. Thank you for convincing me to write this book! I'm also grateful to Nora Hughes. Nora, thank you for all your help throughout this process!

Nora's goal for the longest time was to be mentioned in the acknowledgments section of a book—any book. Mentions were common for editors, far less so for editorial assistants. With every manuscript she received, she slowly scrolled by the acknowledgments section, looking for a mention of her name. It was vain of her—why would an author thank the editorial assistant who did nothing more than route contracts and send them boring permissions information?

But sometimes they did. Beth was first to get a mention. She held it up, finger pointed at the two words, just a *Beth Bodine* nestled between two commas in a long list of names, but it was there. Nora had congratulated her and ignored the pangs of envy.

Nora's mention wouldn't come for another five months. Bonnie Jackson had been a first-time author who'd kept coming back to Nora with questions, feeling too awkward to contact Tom. Most authors knew a relationship with their editor was their natural right and dismissed the editorial assistant as a sort of helpful gnat. But Bonnie had seemed to think of herself as the gnat, and Tom too important to be bothered. Instead, she'd relied on Nora.

Nora, just a few months into her job when Bonnie signed her contract, hadn't been sure of the answers to Bonnie's questions herself. She'd admitted this freely once when Bonnie called her to ask for her thoughts on an unusual citation, and Bonnie had seemed to find solace in not being alone in her ignorance.

The day Bonnie's book arrived from the printer, Nora was certain no two people in the world cared more about this book than Bonnie Jackson and Nora Hughes. She'd cracked open the first copy and flipped to the page, where the words she'd seen in a Word document on her computer screen were now immortalized in a book for all to see. It felt like she'd made it. Like she was a real editorial assistant from that moment on.

The mentions lost their magic over time. It went from a career-defining rite of passage to a pleasant surprise she encountered every now and then.

Nora let her eyes linger on the words for a moment longer. She wondered what the Nora Hughes then would think of this Nora Hughes now.

The trouble was, as inspiring as Julie's talk had been, it didn't help much. Yes, she'd shown Nora there were more choices than she thought possible, but having an excess of choices only overwhelmed her. At least when she wanted to kill herself there was just the one choice to contend with.

Nora opened a new tab and navigated to LinkedIn. First, she searched *Helena Rodgers*, a name she'd frequently encountered when she started at Parsons. Helena had held the EA role before Nora, and it took months before Tom stopped beginning his sentences with *What Helena would do is…* It took longer for Nora to stop seeing traces of Helena—ISBNs written in her blocky handwriting in the corner of contracts processed during the two-year period Helena had held the role, her name written in the corner of permissions correspondence in contract files. But that would never go away. Each EA left their fingerprints on the titles published during their time there. Parsons was a palimpsest of editorial assistants and their contributions. Some of them worked their way through the ranks and became editors, but most of them, Nora was certain, got fed up with the low salaries and administrative work and left for other jobs. Most of them found a way out. She just needed to know how.

Helena, it appeared, was now a content manager for a pop culture website. Nora traced her LinkedIn history back to the beginning. English degree (of course), receptionist at a small press in the Mission, Parsons EA, freelance writer for local magazines during her time at Parsons, writer for an online lifestyle magazine for three years, content manager. It sounded kind of awesome.

More than that, it sounded possible—although Nora suspected it was the freelance writing that had helped Helena secure the later writing jobs, and she had none of that going on. But it was a path.

Nora thought back to EAs from other teams who had come and gone. She searched on.

Maggie Young, former EA for the education team. Psychology degree, Parsons, communications coordinator at a nonprofit, grant writer. Nora didn't even know what grant writing entailed. How many other jobs were out there that she hadn't even considered, simply because she didn't know anything about them?

Jacob Webb, who'd made it as far as assistant editor before bowing out. French degree, Parsons, law degree, attorney, advisor at a legal journal. So, he'd gone into law and fallen back into publishing. Some bonds couldn't be broken.

Jessica Nuñez, who Nora recalled had moved to LA and become a literary agent. A check on her page confirmed she was still employed by the same agency she'd left Parsons for.

Denise Becker. Comp lit degree, Parsons temp, Parsons EA, copywriter for a start-up, grad school for creative writing.

Emma Steinberg. Political science degree, Parsons EA, outreach coordinator at an education nonprofit.

Nonprofits seemed to be a common thread. Maybe these EAs were also jaded by the disappointing practicality of publishing, the need to prioritize profit over content. Nora thought of the *nonprofit* scribbled on her folded sheet of paper and felt a sense of solidarity.

Nora typed the names of as many EAs as she could remember. Not many left Parsons to work at other publishing houses, but a few had. Most of them left Parsons to escape publishing. Many now held roles that involved writing in some capacity, which made Nora think back to something Lynn said once at lunch: *What's the old saying? Every editor has a novel she's working on in her drawer? There's probably something to it; I have one.* It was only natural. English majors who loved books so much they wanted to publish them didn't sound too far removed from English majors who loved books so much they wanted to write one.

Nora thought back to her favorite part of her job: writing those persuasive emails to authors to convince them they liked their book cover. Was that because she liked writing, or because it was one of the few tasks that gave her any amount of input? There was that word again.

Back to her four-item list she went, the uncrackable code. She added the word *persuade*. She liked being able to give her opinion—being able to *have* an opinion. And it wasn't just in the cover emails, she realized. *One-on-one* jumped out at her. Even at the conferences she detested, even if she hated the long hours and crowds milling at the booth, she took a quiet pleasure in one-on-one interactions with customers. She enjoyed hearing them tell her what they wanted and using that information to recommend a book she thought they would like. It gave her such satisfaction when they agreed with her choice and decided to buy the book.

She felt like she was on the verge of something, but it hadn't come into focus yet. How were those one-on-one moments with potential book buyers different from all the author interactions she had tired of?

It was the power dynamics. Beth had drawn the connection between authors and clients at lunch: both needed to be impressed. These relationships were high-stakes, partnerships that involved contracts and big plans.

But with customers at conferences, it felt more personal. It was learning about them and helping them find what they were looking for.

Kelly's words came back to her about working in a bookstore. Maybe the fact that she still had Kelly's desire to be around books didn't mean Nora lacked wisdom. Maybe it meant that she and Kelly were more alike than she thought. She'd seen herself in Kelly that first day, hadn't she?

In small letters, she wrote *bookstore* at the bottom of her list. It didn't take long before the uncertainty kicked in. Bookstores weren't nonprofit. And how could she be sure she'd like it? Suppose she tried it and hated it; where would that leave her?

Nora sifted through these thoughts and argued against each one. Even if it didn't meet every item on her list, it met almost all of them, and that was better than anything she'd come across so far. And maybe one day, in the future, she'd find a job that checked every box, and her experience at the bookstore would prepare her for it.

It could absolutely be the wrong career for her. But that was true of anything. If she waited until she was sure, she would rot here forever, paralyzed by indecision, and spend her final croaking breath trying to get one last word in with Henry Brook. She had to try something. She had to start somewhere.

Nora closed out her LinkedIn tabs and planted herself in front of Kelly's cubicle.

"You said you had a friend who works at a bookstore?"

CHAPTER TWENTY-NINE

The bell sounded when Nora walked through the door. Her eyes scanned the store, taking in the shelves neatly lined with books and the display in the corner, an ode to a fantasy series Nora had never read. She spotted a young woman behind the counter with dark, shoulder-length curly hair and walked toward her. As Nora's footsteps drew closer, the woman looked up from the display of literary-themed matchbooks she was arranging.

"Hi, are you Regina?" Nora tried.

She nodded, curls bobbing in loose ringlets so shiny Nora wondered if they were still wet. "I take it you're Nora?"

"Yeah. Thanks for meeting with me."

"Thanks for coming," Regina said. "Just a second."

Nora watched as Regina darted between two of the shelves and exchanged a few words with someone kneeling beside a box of books.

"Come on," Regina said to Nora, stepping toward the entrance.

The bell chimed with their departure, and Nora followed her

to the café three stores down, listening to the steady clicks of Regina's boots as they walked.

Inside, Regina paid for their drinks and they sat at a table by the window. Nora cradled her latte in her hands while Regina poured a packet of Splenda into her coffee.

"Kelly said you worked with her at Parsons."

Nora paused, unsure if a question was coming, then realized that *was* the question. "Yes, I've been an editorial assistant there for five years now."

"What's that like?"

Nora launched into her usual description of working with authors and their manuscripts from proposal to finished book. Usually, for marketing-related interviews, she'd emphasize the small amounts of writing she did: drafting press releases, writing book description copy for proposal meetings, editing back-of-book copy. But she didn't have to paint that distorted view this time. She laid it all bare for Regina to parse through.

Regina's next question dove straight to the weak point of her résumé.

"Do you have any retail experience?"

Nora had expected this. "Not officially, but we attend three to four conferences a year, and I'm responsible for managing all aspects of bookselling at those conferences." She outlined the process of booth setup, helping customers find books they were looking for, answering their questions, and informing them of discounts and offers. Her experience was actually relevant, Nora realized, gaining confidence as she spoke.

Regina was listening and nodding. Nora thought with a feeling of satisfaction that Regina couldn't pull what Shawn at BookTap had done, pointing out a use of *we* and making Nora feel like she had no part in anything that mattered. Selling books at conferences was all her. She thought back to those exhausting twelve-hour shifts with pride.

And, yes, she hated when the booth got too busy. But she reminded herself that she hated Parsons more. This bookstore was sure to have busy moments, crowds and long lines. But it would not have Henry Brook.

"Great," Regina said with an easy smile. "What do you like reading?"

What an amazing question. BookTap never asked that. Parsons didn't ask that. It was only relevant here.

"I really like historical fiction. And I like most general fiction, classic and contemporary. But right now I'm rereading *Kindred*."

And had been for months, she didn't add. But she'd gotten farther in the last few days than she had in weeks. Reading came easier now that she'd quit. It became the pleasant escape it was supposed to be, instead of the roadblock her mind was too fuzzy to break past.

Regina's eyes lit up. "I love Octavia Butler."

Regina described the day-to-day operations of the bookstore and what Nora would be expected to do—acquaint herself with the layout of the store and its books, learn their point-of-sale system, answer questions, take orders, stock shelves.

The list was familiar and new at the same time. She knew intimately the necessity of becoming versed in the books Parsons sold, remembered the way she'd pored over the Parsons catalogs on the plane heading to her first conference. She knew the questions to expect from potential customers, how to make recommendations and take orders. But the context of it was completely different. There were no authors to schmooze. No one would expect her to chase contracts. The people she would be dealing with this time were book-loving customers. The novelty of it thrilled her.

"Do you have any questions for me?" Regina asked.

Nora had several, and not just for appearances. Regina answered each one with care and detail. The days and hours would change from week to week, but she could usually expect to work from four until close on three weekday evenings per week, and all day Saturday. And yes, Regina said with a look of amusement, Nora would be able to fill out one of those index cards with a book recommendation. Nora had thought Parsons had wiped all romantic visions of working with books completely out of her mind, but this one they couldn't touch.

"Would you recommend the job to a friend?" Nora asked. Unlike when she asked this question to Shawn at BookTap, hoping he'd stumble the way Nora had when Kelly asked it, she awaited Regina's response with hope in her throat.

"Absolutely," Regina replied without missing a beat. "There are a lot of fun parts of the job. Meeting authors. Hosting readings and book signings. Being around for exciting book releases."

Her answer wasn't fumbly and reaching like Nora's, nor was it smug and braggy like Shawn's. It felt honest. Nora's hopes somersaulted through her.

Regina asked if Nora could send over a few references. In her months of interviewing, Nora had never reached this stage, and even if she had, she imagined it would have come after a long series of interviews, not a casual conversation in a café while sipping a free chai latte. She told Regina she would send them over, making a mental note to tell Tom and Beth that, for the first time ever, they could expect to fulfill the reference duties she'd asked of them last year. Lynn had also agreed to be a reference in a time that felt painfully far away, but that was over now. Two would have to be enough.

She stepped out of the coffee shop feeling like she might actually be moving forward. Like things were coming together. She'd applied to a few different temp agencies, and she'd expanded her job search to include freelance positions she might be qualified for, from copyediting to copywriting. She hoped that, cobbled together, these positions might be enough to sustain her in the time it took to find a permanent full-time job.

Nora took her time returning to the office. She considered herself a fast walker, but she slowed her pace today, letting crosswalks she might have rushed through turn red without her while she stood on the corner and drank her latte.

She returned to her desk with a few sips left of her latte and a lightness in her step. Now that the interview she'd spent half of last night worrying about was finished, she could turn her mind to what still weighed on her.

She owed Andrew feedback on the next chapters of his manuscript. She'd already read through them and left comments before the ill-fated networking event. But her comments seemed so superficial now. There was so much still unsaid.

Nora opened his manuscript and scrolled to the top. Her mouse hovered over the *by Andrew Santos* on the title page. She double-clicked his first name and added a new comment.

As she typed, the comment box stretched longer and longer with everything she'd never told him, everything she'd kept hidden because it made her sound worse. The promised promotion tied to his name. The urgent search for a distraction. The creature in her head, how she'd used Andrew to run from it instead of confronting it. Her mental list of reasons to live.

She told him she knew none of it excused what she did to him. She wrote that even if his royalty checks dried up, if no one wanted his signature anymore, if he decided to stop writing and set his manuscript on fire, she would still be waiting for the moment he'd let her start paying him back for every kindness he showed her: watching the booth, stealing her a lunch, buying her a parachute book, reading a two-hundred-page happiness report, celebrating her every minor accomplishment with stickers. He gave more than he needed to. More than she deserved.

She wrote how grateful she was that he sparked her quest to become something other than a three. She told him she didn't think she was a three anymore. She felt like she was on her way to that six-point-something benchmark he'd set for her. She thought she might be a five with potential now. But, she wrote, if she were to quantify how happy he made her, it would be a ten. No question.

Nora took a long, shaky breath and saved the file. She attached it to an email to Andrew. In the body, she included no greeting, no sign-off. Just four words:

What I owe you.

She sent the email with no expectations, but it didn't stop her heart from racing every time her inbox alerted her of a new email. But they were never from Andrew. Especially not the one that made her sigh audibly.

Nora,

I'm concerned that you haven't been replying to my

emails. If we want to stay on track for November, we
need to get the new logo figured out ASAP. Please call
me when you get a chance.
Henry

He cc'ed Candace. How cute.

Nora clicked on the email and hit Delete. Then she decided
it was time to escalate things.

Candace was sitting at her cubicle staring at her computer,
brow furrowed in confusion.

"Hi, Candace."

"Hi," she replied, taking a moment to tear herself away from
the screen. "Did you see Henry's email?"

"Yeah, that's what I came to talk to you about. I'm done
helping Henry Brook."

She nodded knowingly. "I've been working on a way to be
done with him myself. I think there's a way we can leverage your
leaving."

"I figured we could use that as an excuse to introduce him to
someone else," Nora said. "Kelly, I guess." But that felt wrong.
She couldn't subject Kelly to Henry Brook's demanding, overex-
plaining mania disguised as innovation.

"Or maybe there's another way," Candace said, a devious
smirk crossing her face. Anything that had Candace smirking was
a very good sign—for everyone except Henry Brook, she hoped.

The following day, Nora sat in a phone room, waiting for
Henry Brook's demise. She checked the time. Ten minutes past
when they were supposed to call him. It was almost better this
way, Candace being late. He deserved to wait. She'd love to hear
how Henry might try to chastise Candace about the importance

of punctuality. She had a feeling Candace's rebuttal would knock him to the ground.

"Sorry," Candace said, setting a folder on the table. "Author call went long."

Nora decided not to ask about the call. She didn't have to feign interest in other projects on her way out. She was much more interested in the fact that Candace had closed the door for this meeting.

"You ready?" Candace asked. When Nora nodded, she started dialing Henry's number on the console. A few rings later, Henry's cheery voice came on the line.

"Hello?"

"Hi, Henry," Candace said. "I'm here with Nora."

"Hi, Candace, hi, Nora." To Henry's credit, he didn't say anything about the many emails Nora had ignored recently. "How are you guys?"

"Good," Nora said cheerfully. "How are you?"

"Great. Just working on getting conflict resolution up and running. Thanks for all your help, Nora."

"Yeah, no—you're welcome." It was petty, but Nora didn't want to tell him it was no problem. Although he wasn't welcome either, come to think of it, so really it was a lie either way.

"Thanks for talking to me today," Candace said in her even, measured voice. "I wanted to touch base on a few things before Nora leaves."

"Sure."

Nora hadn't told Henry she was leaving. Either he thought she was going on vacation, or he was assuming a casual tone to make himself sound like he already knew.

"As you may know, there have been a lot of departures around here. With so many people stretched thin, we don't have as much time to dedicate to tasks as we used to. You can understand how it's been a burden on Nora to do these tasks for you, in addition to everything else she's doing."

"Right."

Nora hated the way he acted like he knew what Candace was talking about.

"Nora and I were going over her list of responsibilities, and in light of everything else she's already been doing, it's not sustainable for us to keep up that level of assistance after she goes. We'll just have one EA on our team when Nora leaves, and between her job and Nora's, we have to make some hard decisions about what she can and can't do."

"Okay."

He sounded less certain now. Good.

"Ordering the binders and padfolios," Candace said. "We'll need you to do that from now on. How does that sound?"

There was a pause. Nora met Candace's eyes. There was a mischievous glint to them.

"I totally could, but that's not something I usually do."

Emboldened by hatred, Nora leaned in toward the speaker-phone. "But don't you have a lot of experience with this?" she asked. "That's the impression I got when you kept telling me about how the ordering process works."

"I do have a lot of experience," he said. Nora detected a hardness in his voice. She reveled in it. "It's just a matter of what I have time to do."

"Yeah, I struggled with not having a lot of time to do things, too," Nora said, going so far as to sound sympathetic, "after everyone on my team was laid off and I had to take over their jobs. I guess I just got the sense that you were better at managing your time than me. Especially after you gave me all that advice about how I just need to manage my time better. Which was *so* helpful, by the way."

"Did he?" Candace asked, eyes dancing. "I don't suppose he recommended that book to you—what was it, *Managing Yourself Wisely*?"

Nora nearly laughed in delighted surprise. "He did!"

"Henry actually sent me that book a few years ago," Candace said, voice full of awe and shit simultaneously. She rolled her eyes as she continued, "I can't thank you enough for that, Henry. But I guess Nora has a point. If there's anyone who can get things done on a busy schedule, it sounds like you're the best man for the job."

Another pause. "I guess so."

"I know you're going full force ahead with the conflict resolution seminars," said Candace, "but I hope you understand that one EA doesn't have the bandwidth to take that on herself."

"I know it seems like a lot now," said Henry, "but that's what it's like when you're launching a franchise."

"Is it?" asked Candace, who'd launched the original conflict resolution seminars in the '90s and had in fact founded Parsons's leadership imprint in the first place. Nora watched Candace run a finger over her thumbnail, painted a pale shade of pink.

"I know it's a big initial investment, but it will bring revenue for your line. You need to have someone on this. I can run it like I've been doing"—now it was Nora's turn to roll her eyes—"but if we want to stay on track, you'll need to put another person on this. You have another editorial assistant, don't you?"

Candace raised her eyebrow, unimpressed. "And, knowing we

can't spare her, how do you want to handle that? We don't have anything in the editorial budget to cover a dedicated person. Could you pull that out of your marketing budget, Henry?"

A long pause. "I suppose I could pay for a temp."

"That would be wonderful." Candace met Nora's eyes with a victorious smile. Their first win.

"I know Nora was doing some executive assistant tasks for you," Candace continued. "Managing your calendar, scheduling your calls—is that right?"

"Yes." He sounded almost defensive. "I'm between assistants right now."

"Our EA won't be able to do that, unfortunately." There was a heavy tone to her voice, like she really did find it unfortunate. But watching Candace stare down the phone and issue a silent challenge, Nora knew better. "Could you manage on your own until you hire a new assistant?"

"It would be tough, especially with the conflict resolution stuff. When you lose an assistant, you don't realize how much you have to do on your own."

"I know what you mean," Candace said fake-sympathetically. "When my assistant left and I was told I couldn't hire another, I remember you telling me I just need to manage my time better. Would you say that's the case for you too?"

"I guess so." Nora loved the reluctance in his agreement.

"Then it sounds like you're going to be really well-equipped to handle this. You seem to know more about time management than anyone I know."

Her tone, so airy and carefree. It was glorious.

"Henry, thank you so much for your understanding. Was there anything you wanted to discuss, Henry?" Candace asked.

She loved the way Candace used his name. Like it was hers now. Like the question that preceded it had only one answer, and he'd better not get it wrong.

"Uh…no."

"Okay. Well, thanks for your flexibility. Best of luck with the seminars."

The pause again. "Thanks."

Nora kept her eyes on Candace as she thanked Henry for his time and wished him a good day. Nora stayed silent. She didn't have to say anything to Henry anymore.

After Candace hung up the call, she pressed the Call button. A dial tone blared through the speaker. "Just checking that he's gone," she said, pressing the Call button again. She gave a conspiratorial chuckle. "That was something."

"That was *amazing*," Nora said, still marveling. She felt energized.

Candace sighed, leaning back in her chair. "He'll probably send me a passive-aggressive email later and I'll end up splitting the cost for a temp with him. But it was fun to lower his expectations, wasn't it?"

And Nora's. She hadn't realized it was a ruse.

But she couldn't be too disappointed. Even if they couldn't quite humble Henry Brook by making him do every menial task, at the very least he knew now that things would never be the same. She was leaving this small part of Parsons better for the next EA—for Kelly and whoever came after. This tiny piece wasn't something they would have to worry about. She made sure of it.

CHAPTER THIRTY

Despite the thrill of watching Candace decimate Henry Brook, another worry pressed on Nora as the week wore on. Lynn was still on her mind. Nora needed to talk to her—to apologize, if that meant anything. Or, at the very least, know where things stood so she could move past it instead of having an empty feeling in the pit of her stomach every time she thought of Lynn. She may as well know now whether she was off Lynn's Christmas card list forever.

Nora waited until half past noon. If Lynn's daily habits were the same at Weber as they were at Parsons, by this time she would be partway through her one-mile walk around the sidewalks surrounding the office building. She'd be more likely to pick up the phone if she were out of the office—and maybe even more likely to forgive Nora, if endorphins had any kind of effect.

Lynn picked up, which seemed like a good sign. "Hello?" She sounded more curious than angry.

"Do you have a few minutes to talk?" Nora asked.

"Yes," Lynn said, sounding slightly out of breath. "You've caught me on my lunch walk."

Nora allowed herself a small moment of self-satisfaction before launching into her speech. "I—I want to start by saying how sorry I am," Nora began. "I didn't want to lie, but when my salary was cut, I needed a way to make up the money. And when you mentioned the job, it just…it seemed like the way."

"You mean it seemed like the easy way," Lynn said. She said it like she was correcting a word Nora misspelled.

"What do you mean?"

"What was stopping you from getting a part-time job after work? You could have worked in a yogurt shop, or at Super Duper, or waitressed anywhere. You think I bought my house only working one job my whole life?"

"No," Nora mumbled. She didn't say what she was thinking—that the house comparison didn't really apply, not when paying rent in an apartment off the highway was so much harder now than it was in Lynn's time. "But I wouldn't call anything that necessitates getting a second job the easy way. Nothing about this was easy. Lying to you wasn't easy," she said, feeling her voice waver, "and I never meant to—"

"Oh, honey, I know."

Nora paused at that, hearing one of the affectionate names Lynn used to call her. She didn't deserve it now. "I just wanted to tell you I quit my job at Parsons. Like, really. I'm lining up some part-time work—honest work," she corrected hastily. "I interviewed with a bookstore, and I've applied to some temp agencies. I don't intend to work for a publisher ever again."

Lynn made a sound that might have been a chuckle. Nora chose to interpret it as a chuckle.

"That's quite a change," Lynn said.

"I thought it was about time." There was a pause, which Nora took as an opening to continue speaking. "I'm done with publishing, and I just wanted to let you know. I'm sorry for dragging you into everything."

"I know you are. I'm glad to hear you're doing better. I hope it stays that way."

It wasn't lunch plans, but it wasn't a blow-off, either. It may have been a polite sign-off, but for Nora, it was a small sliver of hope. Lynn had hopes for Nora. Nora, for her part, would hope that if she got in touch with Lynn sometime in the distant future, just to update her on her life like they used to do at their lunches, Lynn might be receptive to it. She could work with that.

———

Nora spent more time watching her phone than working on the transition document she was supposed to be making. She'd sent Regina her references—Tom and Beth—two days ago and was told she could expect to hear back "in the next day or two."

Now, on day "or two," Nora was too antsy to focus on anything but her phone. She carried it with her to the kitchen, to the bathroom. She kept an eye on it as she sorted through the belongings in her top drawer—cards, Post-its, paper clips, highlighters. An ink pad and a rubber stamp of a stack of books, something Beth had bought to decorate the otherwise blank cards they sent authors to congratulate them on the publication of their book. Nora set the stamp and ink pad in her pile of things to keep. Maybe it would come in handy at the bookstore. If they hired her. She cast a glance at her phone to see if it had anything to say on the matter. It did not.

She arranged paper clips into a pile to deposit in the mailroom.

She stuck a hand in her now-empty top drawer, feeling edges and corners for rogue paper clips, when her phone buzzed.

Nora picked it up in less than a second. She examined the screen. A San Francisco area code. Nora breathed in, breathed out, and answered it.

"Hello?"

"Hi, Nora? This is Regina from Bay Books."

"Hi, Regina." She held her breath and waited. Hoped.

"It was great talking to you the other day. I'd like to offer you the part-time bookseller position if you're interested."

She tried to sound calm when she said, "I am."

"Great!" Regina ran her through expected hours, hourly wages, and ended by saying, "I'll email you with the details."

Nora felt lighter as she hung up. Part of her, the part that saw the negative in everything, reminded her the job was only part-time, that she would need to find other work to sustain her until something full-time came around.

But it was so easy to put things down instead of celebrating victories when they happened. And this—the fact that she'd found something new to be excited about, a way to be around books without having to contend with everything she hated about publishing, getting the job she wasn't even sure she was fully qualified for—was an incredible victory.

She would have a different attitude this time. She wouldn't put all her eggs in this one basket and be left without a plan if it fell apart. She'd put one in, see if it suited her as well as she hoped it could. If it did, she'd add another, and another. And she would never, ever again let a company or a marketing executive named Henry Brook tell her what she was worth.

When her inbox sounded, she hesitated when she saw

Andrew's name. The job offer high was such a good feeling. She didn't want to diminish it by getting swept into guilt and sadness, even if it was her own doing.

But she couldn't help wondering.

Your comments gave me a lot to think about. I haven't made your suggested changes to my manuscript yet. Sometimes when I procrastinate I write other parts of the manuscript. Would you mind giving me your professional editorial opinion on this one?

She opened the file, titled *Acknowledgments*, and scrolled through his thanks to colleagues and former professors. There, in the last paragraph, was an acknowledgment unlike any she'd ever received. It was short but powerful. He'd issued his thanks to "Nora Hughes, a fantastic editor I had the pleasure of working with."

Something prickled behind Nora's eyes. She blinked a few times to keep herself from tearing up as she read the words. She wanted to print them out and attach them to her résumé. When it had felt so difficult to make anyone else see the work she'd been doing, Andrew had put it in print for everyone to see.

She sat there for a moment, staring at the word *editor* and trying to think of possible replies, then walked into a phone room.

"Hello." He didn't say it like it was a question. He seemed to know she'd call.

"Hi," she replied. "I just wanted to say thanks for what you wrote."

"I meant it." There was a pause before he spoke again. "How are things at Parsons?"

"They are...not my problem."

"Why?"

"I quit."

"Nora," he breathed. "When?"

"The day after we last talked."

"Nora, I didn't mean to—"

"It wasn't about you," she said. Andrew had influenced a lot of Nora's decisions in the last few months, but not this one. Resisting the creature, defying Henry Brook, and quitting were all Nora's doing.

"What are you gonna do?" he asked.

"I got a job," she said, surprising herself with the shaky happiness in her voice. "I'm going to work at a bookstore."

"That's amazing." His voice rang with pride. She felt like she was back on his couch, watching him put a sticker over her heart. "So you found your parachute color after all?"

"I don't know yet. It might be. It's only part-time for now, but they said one of the full-timers is leaving after the summer, so I may be able to take that if I like the work. If not, I've applied to temp agencies too. Whatever happens, it's gonna work out." She smiled. Her optimism reminded her of Andrew.

She still had worries under the optimism. Her final Weber paycheck had come through a few days ago, which would help her make next month's rent. She had enough in savings to last two months. Two months of rent, bills, loans, and groceries. She would need a plan—a longer-term plan—by then. She knew her current plan wasn't perfect, or anywhere close to it. This could very well end in failure. It might not be enough to tide her over until she found something full-time that paid enough. She might not find anything that paid enough. She might burn through her savings and have to move back in with her parents in Oregon two months from now. Might, might, might. But she had to try. This was the only thing she felt certain about.

"I'm really glad," he said.

"Me too. And thank you for the acknowledgment. Really."

"Thank you for your comments."

She wanted to ask how he felt when he read her long, apologetic, explanatory comment, but she didn't want to press. She settled for a more general question. "How have you been?"

"Really good, in a lot of ways. I've got some interest from publishers. Major publishers."

"You deserve it." With more hope in her voice than she should have, Nora asked, "What about the other ways?"

"I've been better."

How pitiful that it got her heart pounding to hear he wasn't completely happy. "Me too," she murmured. Even just saying it felt like stepping off a ledge. But she was tired of hiding. Tired of lying.

When they hung up, she still had all the same lightness she did when she got the job offer. More, even—there was a flutter of something else. Acceptance. Hope.

Nora sent her official resignation email to Rita and HR. It was real now. She had a job-ish, which meant she had a plan. She could tell Beth. She started a text.

I just quit!

Beth's first reply was punctuation, followed by a question:

!!!

Did you get the bookstore job?!

Nora's thumb hovered over her phone. Beth didn't know yet that it was part-time, and that it wasn't enough to live on. Even if she wasn't making a living wage, she wanted to make Beth understand it was still a win. How much it meant that Nora Hughes, for so long a three on the happiness scale, had found something to be happy about.

Just part-time for now, but we'll see what opens up. I just couldn't with Henry Brook anymore.

Oh my god he is the worst, Beth was quick to reply. I passed him in the hall once when he was visiting the office and he told me to smile. Congrats! When's your last day?!

A warm, appreciative feeling radiated through Nora at the realization that Beth understood what this meant to her. It wasn't leaving for a full-time job at a start-up like Beth, but it was finding a new way to chase books. A way that might suit her better than publishing ever did. And that was worth the uncertainty of a part-time job.

Her predecessors had shown that there were options available for making ends meet. She regretted not exploring those during her time at Parsons. Why hadn't she freelanced before—not in the secret traitorous way she'd done at Weber, but as an honest-to-goodness writer, copy editor, or developmental editor? Why had she relied on her unfulfilling job to give her the experience she needed for a fulfilling one?

But she told herself that she'd only messed up this time. Next time, for the next job, she would get it right. Or the job after that. There were more chances ahead.

CHAPTER THIRTY-ONE

Nora didn't know much about Isaac. She knew his name, she knew he worked in journals, and she knew his last day at Parsons was today—the same as hers.

She used to imagine having a joint goodbye party with Beth. Wouldn't it be cute, she used to think, if the same two people who started at Parsons together ended up leaving together?

She was right that she wouldn't be leaving alone. Having the same last day meant a joint goodbye party, just with Isaac instead of Beth. Isaac had been with Parsons for longer than Nora—thirteen years, she overheard—and most of the focus was on him. It meant she got to dodge most small talk and stand hidden near Kelly and Julie.

"What does Isaac do on journals?" Nora asked, watching him talking to Eric across the room.

"I don't know," Julie said, "but Eric said they're not replacing him."

Another consequence of the DIC(k), Nora figured. "I guess Eric's job's about to get busier. And yours," Nora added, shifting her eyes onto Kelly. "Except you won't have to deal with Henry Brook."

"Thank god," Kelly said. Nora clinked her plastic cup against Kelly's. Nora wasn't over it yet, the fact that her goodbye party had cups. They made her feel like royalty.

A chorus of voices arose, sounding much too excited about a goodbye party of sparkling cider and potato chips. She looked up to see Beth standing in the doorway, talking to someone. Beth met Nora's eyes and lifted her hand in a wave.

Beth left the conversation and started across the room, only to be pulled into a hug from Isaac, and he really needed to get over himself because Beth wasn't here for him. Nora widened her eyes and nodded her head toward the empty space next to her a few times, willing Beth to hurry up with her pleasantries. Beth suppressed a laugh and shook her head before turning her attention back to Isaac.

When Beth sauntered over to Nora's corner at last, her cup was nearly empty, like she'd been at the party for ages.

"You came!" Nora reached her arms out toward Beth, pulling her into a hug and getting swept in her familiar floral perfume.

"I was there for your first day. I should be there for your last, right?"

Nora nodded, too touched to say anything. She knew how she felt about Beth, but it was reassuring to get confirmation sometimes that this wasn't all in her head, this work friendship she'd always believed could transcend the walls of the office.

"I want to sign your card too."

Nora shared a look with Kelly. "I don't think there is a card," she said, and Kelly shook her head to confirm it. "I think we stopped doing cards."

"I got a card! I didn't leave that long ago."

Nora had to stop herself from getting sentimental. The urge

kept coming and going throughout the day. The urge wanted to tell Beth it felt like *that long ago*, back when Nora was left to navigate her first days at Parsons without her.

The urge did some strange things. It made her want to send long, emotional emails to even the difficult, curmudgeonly authors and tell them that transmitting their lengthy books taught her the most when she was just starting out.

She overcame most of these urges, but she did tell the authors she'd been in contact with that she'd be leaving Parsons because "another opportunity came up," because Nora was fluent in vague business speak. Some replied with a line or two to wish her well. Her favorite author, Dana Garnett, was the only one she was honest with. Nora had told her her long-term plans were still up in the air, but that she had to leave Parsons to figure it out. And Dana Garnett had sent a response so kind and thoughtful that Nora was still going over the last line of that email in her mind, even now.

After telling Nora about a time in her twenties when she too felt lost and uncertain, Dana told Nora she was doing the right thing, assured her she would find the right fit somewhere, and wrote:

You may not know how wonderful, kind, and smart you are, but I know it.

It was so stupidly lovely and touching that it had Nora regretting, for a moment, her decision to leave publishing, to leave authors who could be this genuine. She knew it was the urge and the sentimentality talking, but there was something else. Dana's words tapped into that little part of Nora that wanted to be understood.

It was that same part of her, she was sure, that made her walk up to Rita before the party and tell her she was glad that it was Rita who became her boss after the layoffs. She couldn't bring herself to apologize again and dredge up everything that stood between them: Nora's underhanded scheming, Rita's silent awareness. She hoped, through her guilt and her cowardice, that when Rita pulled her in for a hug, it was because she understood somehow.

She'd also looked up Other Nora on LinkedIn in her desire for connection and understanding. It took a few searches, but she found her: Abby Johnson, marketing coordinator at Friedman Books. She'd hovered over the Connect button for a few moments before decisively pressing it. She went a step further, clicked Add a Note, and tried to think of an introduction that wasn't *Hello you're Black I've been watching you for years*.

She decided on something less creepy: I meant to say hi from the Parsons booth at CEF but didn't get a chance! Would love to connect.

And just a few hours later, Abby had accepted her LinkedIn request, even sent a message back: So glad you reached out! Hope I can see you at the next conference! And, well, Nora wouldn't be at any next conferences. She couldn't tell if Abby responded out of politeness or if there was a genuine interest there, something mirroring Nora's curiosity, but she still felt a sense of accomplishment from crossing that divide. It was virtual and it was after the fact, but she'd done it. It might even open the door for future conversations.

After hugging everyone on her team—even Isaac, even though she couldn't remember the last time she'd ever spoken to him—Nora knelt in her cubicle when the party ended, dumping the contents of her snack drawer into her canvas bag as Beth surveyed the dark, empty office.

"It's weird to be back," Beth said, skating a finger along the spines on the bookshelf.

"Does anything look different?" Nora closed her now-empty snack drawer and moved on to the drawer where she kept the cards she'd amassed over the years. She picked up the stack and opened one with a penguin on it. Tom's scrawled handwriting congratulated her on turning twenty-four. She closed it and tucked the cards into her bag.

"No." Beth sounded closer, a familiar kind of distance away. She must have been standing in her old cube. "Except for my cube being empty, it's like I never left. It's like life goes on without me or something."

"Preposterous." Nora stood, her entire work life now contained in two cloth bags on her shoulders.

Beth joined her in her cubicle. "You ready?"

Nora nodded and they set off. As they stood on the elevator, staring straight ahead, Beth said, "If something happens and you need a place to stay while you're figuring out the part-time stuff...I have a couch."

Nora turned. She ran Beth's words over in her mind once, twice, heart leaping from Beth and her thoughtfulness.

"It's a studio," Nora said.

"And my studio has a couch." Beth turned to glance at Nora, eyebrows raised in a challenge, daring her to even try turning the offer down.

Nora cracked a smile under the pressure. "Okay, I acknowledge your couch and I thank you for it."

"Good," Beth said. "When do you start at the bookstore?"

"They're training me tomorrow."

"You're gonna get a discount on books," Beth said, eyes

lighting up. "That's awesome. So much better than our useless discount on Parsons books."

Nora laughed, thinking about how she already had her eye on a few books she wanted. She'd scoured the bookstore's website and social media in the last two weeks and made note of books she was drawn to, often because they were described so passionately that it stirred all kinds of excitement in her. Excitement to be the one recommending books to others, putting her input to good use. Excitement to read again.

Her parents were encouraging, on the limited information they had. Her father listened to her quitting story with pride and gave Nora suggestions for how to make a memorable exit, all of which lacked tact and in some cases legality. Her mother wanted to go over the numbers and make sure Nora was making enough, but after Nora dodged her questions, her mother said bookstores were magical places and launched into a long-winded recounting of their last trip to Powell's.

It made Nora feel whole, hearing the people she cared most about dwelling on what was most important to her—the bookstore, what it meant, what it could mean—and not everything else: the part-time aspect, the logistics, the numbers. She had an interview with a temp agency the following week, which could be something else new to try. Another basket to put one egg in and see what she liked best.

Beth was first to step off the elevator, leaving Nora to waddle behind her, bags on her shoulders digging sharp corners of books and cracker boxes into her sides. They walked to the center of the lobby, and as Nora began to turn for the BART station, Beth paused.

"I have to go back to work."

"Now?"

"I have to finish some things up. I left at four for your party!" There was a note of incredulity in her voice.

Nora decided against pointing out that they used to leave at four all the time, especially on Fridays. But that was Parsons Nora and Parsons Beth. This Beth had new norms to follow. Nora couldn't wait to find out what Bookstore Nora was like.

She continued to stand there opposite Beth, not sure what to say next. She wanted to say something to cement their friendship, keep it viable even though neither of them was working at Parsons anymore.

"We should get lunch next week," Beth said, effortlessly accomplishing what Nora failed to do. "On me," she added.

Nora breathed a quiet sigh of relief. "That would be perfect."

"Text me."

She pulled Beth into a hug. The cloth bags jostled against her hips, and she thought she felt one graze Beth's arm, but she didn't bother apologizing for it. Nora pulled away and fixed her eyes on Beth.

"I'll see you next week." Maybe she said it too intensely, but she had to feel it as she said it, to make sure it would happen. That it would be real.

Beth nodded. "Good." She waved and started walking toward the doors on the far side of the lobby. Nora turned and headed in the other direction.

At the BART station, she stood on the platform looking at the times for the next East Bay-bound train. She felt a gust of air as a train rushed by on the opposite platform. She heard the announcer call out *Daly City train*.

And then she was on it.

It was a close call. It was difficult to speed-waddle to a waiting train on the other side of the platform. She managed to get in and narrowly kept the doors from closing on one of her bags.

As the train took off, she held onto a pole and stared straight ahead, willing her mind to accept what her gut had forced her to do. She thought about texting Andrew to warn him, but if he wasn't home, the text would be a reminder of her bold shame. Better to be unexpected. Either he would be home, or she would quietly slink away, get on a train, and eat Indian takeout with Allie like she planned.

At the 16th Street stop, her legs were a little more reluctant to get off the train, but she pushed onward. Her bags felt heavier as she stood on the escalator, waiting to make the slow ascent to ground level, thinking of nothing except what a terrible idea this was.

She walked the few blocks to Andrew's apartment and rounded the corner on his square blue apartment building hidden behind trees. At the door, she held her breath and pressed the buzzer for *B*.

She waited for several moments, heart pounding. The door buzzed open.

Nora grabbed the handle quickly, as though Andrew might change his mind. She gripped the straps of her bags in her fists as she walked to his door. She knocked three loud, unmistakable raps.

She didn't have to wait long. Andrew opened the door and gave a slow, knowing smile when he saw Nora.

"I thought it was you." He was almost cocky.

"Am I your only friend?" It was hard to sound sarcastic when she was standing on his doorstep holding the last five years of her life, but she tried anyway.

"You're the only person I know who likes to show up spontaneously," he said.

"I don't do it that often."

He stepped aside and gestured for her to come in. "It's okay. I like spontaneity."

Inside, she set her bags next to the door and took her usual seat on the couch. Andrew sat at his desk, where, she realized from his open laptop, he'd been working when she knocked. He closed his laptop and spun around to face her.

"So," he said.

"Today was my last day at Parsons."

"How does it feel?"

"Weird," she said, "but good."

He nodded. "Good." She just stared at him, wondering if he would say anything, when he said, "With you quitting and me leaving, we're both Parsons-free now."

"You know you'll still be getting Parsons royalties forever," she said.

"And you will never stop reminding me of my royalties."

Her heart leapt at this, the future tense of it all. "Some things are certainties."

Andrew eyed her thoughtfully. "I can't help but think," he said, voice a little too lofty, "that I set the example here."

"Hmm?"

"I had a contract in front of me. A sure thing. And I turned it down for something that wasn't concrete but had potential to be better." He fixed his gaze on Nora. "You did the same thing."

"You calling me a copycat?" she joked.

"I'm saying I'm proud of you."

She looked down at her jeans, wondering if she would always

be surprised by his sincerity. "Thanks. I'm proud of you too." She looked back up at him, saw the way he was still watching her, and felt her heart race.

"How will you celebrate your freedom?" he asked.

"By going home and ordering Indian food—which I should probably do," she said, more to herself than to him. She hadn't come here with a plan, which was getting more and more obvious the longer she stayed.

When she stood, he said, "You could order it here."

She shook her head and crossed the room to her bags. She knelt and straightened the straps, then paused and looked at him. "Will you send me your book? When it's out?"

When she left Parsons, she took the books that were most important to her. There was Bonnie Jackson's—the first book to mention her in the acknowledgments—and Dana Garnett's, her favorite author to work with. Andrew and his book were such a crucial part of her last few months at Parsons, but it didn't exist yet. She wasn't sure what her book thefts made her—a serial killer collecting trophies, or a child clutching stuffed animals.

He didn't speak for a few moments, just gazed at her from somewhere between incredulous and flattered. "Definitely."

She swung the straps of the bags over her shoulder. "And maybe..." It was pressing her luck, but she didn't care. "Maybe when your book is out, we can celebrate." She hoped by then she would have her life a little more figured out, or at the very least, the haze in her head would be gone. Andrew deserved her feelings front and center, not hidden in a fog. She wanted him to meet that side of her, the happy, non-hazy Nora who didn't show up at his doorstep on a whim or hide from his sincerity. Maybe by then she would be herself again, and he would get to meet her.

He seemed to know she meant what she said. "It's a date."

"You know what?" Nora rummaged around in one of her cloth bags, feeling for a card. She pulled one out, one of the Parsons anniversary cards, and pushed aside some papers on his desk to make room. "When will your book come out?" she asked.

"Uh…" He laughed and ran a hand through his hair. "I'm still talking to publishers, but I think the earliest date I heard was next August."

Nora uncapped a pen she found on his desk and wrote *Save the Date: August* on the back of the card in neat blue letters. "So I don't take you by surprise next time," she said, handing him the card. Nora watched him as he read it, the wrinkle in his brow giving way to a soft smile. She suddenly felt self-conscious. "Cute or stupid?" she asked.

"You say it like they're mutually exclusive."

She watched him step into the kitchen and secure the card to his fridge with a magnet. When he returned, he stood facing her in the living room. She didn't know how to bridge the distance still between them. There was more she wanted to say, if she could find the combination of words to say it.

"I just…I want to say I'm sorry. With Parsons and Weber and career stuff in general, I've had a lot of conflicting feelings about everything in my life lately, so it's been hard to make sense of things. It was just easier to put you in a box and call you an author and pretend that's all it was. But that was never all it was."

"I know." His expression was solemn, gaze unwavering. He did look like he knew, maybe even understood. She thought maybe this was something he'd been waiting to hear. At least she could give him that.

"If I were in a headspace for a relationship, that's what I'd want with you," she continued. "I think if I had some time to...I don't know, work on myself, get in a better place mentally...we could be something for real. If that's something you wanted."

He shrugged, pretending to think it through. "I think that could be arranged." He said it casually, but his dimples gave him away. "Come here."

Nora let her bags fall to the floor and stepped into his outstretched arms. She hugged him tightly, burying her face in his shirt and breathing in. She closed her eyes and thought about August.

"August is a year away," she said.

"You picked it."

Nora stepped back far enough to look at him. "Okay, well, when would you finish your manuscript?"

"I heard talk of fall. My agent mentioned November."

Three months to work on herself. It was worth a try.

"All right." Nora picked up the pen again and headed into the kitchen. She crossed out *August* on her save-the-date card and wrote *November* underneath, her writing becoming jagged in the places where she had to curve her hand around the magnet.

"That looks really ugly," Andrew commented.

"Shut up."

"November?" he asked.

"November."

She gave him a parting nod and headed for the door.

"But—"

Nora turned around. "Yes?"

"What if I have a question about something as I'm working on my manuscript?" he asked. "Could I ask you?"

"Of course," she said. "And...if you found yourself needing

a book—you know, to help you as you write," she explained, and he nodded sagely, "you could always come by the bookstore. I'll be working nights."

"Maybe I will," he said. "And if you need help with your headspace…"

Even in this moment of sincerity, she couldn't help but give him a suspicious look. "Please don't buy me a cheesy self-help book."

"I just meant you should talk to someone. It doesn't have to be me. But someone."

"Okay. I will." She had to admit distractions weren't an effective strategy for the long term. Especially when she didn't want to reduce Andrew to a distraction anymore.

"But since you mention it," Andrew said, eyes glinting, "there is this book called *Who Moved My Cheese?* that I think you would just love."

"You are banned from my bookstore."

"Oh, I'm coming to your bookstore. But I might get sick of you before November if I see you too much."

"I just meant that in November, I'll be ready. For everything," Nora said. She picked up her bags again.

"I'm looking forward to it," Andrew murmured.

"Good. Now stop wasting time and finish your manuscript." She walked out the door to the sound of his laughter.

Nora dipped into her snack stash on the walk to the BART station, eating almonds and dried cranberries from her Ziploc bag of trail mix. Once on an Oakland-bound train, she took one of the last seats available and set her bags on the floor, bracing her feet against them to keep them from shifting with the train's movements.

As she pulled out her phone to look up the menu for Mehak Cuisine, Nora saw that the screen still showed the email from the temp agency inviting her to interview. Being reminded of an upcoming interview didn't fill her with dread like it used to. It wasn't meaningless. If it wasn't work she enjoyed, it would bring her one step closer to knowing what she wanted to do.

Things would be different this time. She wouldn't go back to staring listlessly at her ceiling fan. She'd disconnect the damn thing if she had to.

Nora knew it wasn't over. Dark thoughts came to her any time she felt hopeless, and they would keep coming. The creature whispering to her from the corners of her mind would be back.

But that didn't mean she had to listen. She could stop trying to fight it alone. She could talk about it, go to therapy once she had health insurance again.

Julie's words about possibilities came back to her. *It's kind of exciting*, Julie had said, and, well, Nora didn't know if she'd take it that far. Terrifying, more like, to feel so uncertain about her future. But some uncertainties were better than a lot of other certainties. Particularly if those certainties had anything to do with a future at Parsons or working for Henry Brook.

Nora swiped over to the temp agency website and scanned the list of industries they served. Not even she could hate everything. There had to be something here—or *somewhere*—that didn't feel meaningless. She had to believe there was.

It was hope she was feeling, she realized. That was the reason for the lightness inside her. She leaned back, thinking about training at the bookstore tomorrow, the interview next week, Andrew in November and maybe even before then. Uncertainty wasn't overwhelming anymore.

READING GROUP GUIDE

1. After five years in a dead-end job, Nora feels trapped and desperate. Have you ever found yourself in a similar position? How did you get out of it?

2. How would you characterize Andrew? What motivates him?

3. Nora's choice to freelance for Weber is a morally ambiguous one. Put yourself in her shoes—overworked, underpaid, and unable to pay rent. What would you choose to do?

4. Beth and Nora meet at Parsons on their first day and hit it off immediately. What makes them such good friends? Outline their similarities and differences.

5. Despite her attraction to him, why does Nora feel so conflicted about starting a relationship with Andrew?

6. Eric, Julie, and Kelly each take different paths before ending up at Parsons. What does this tell you about dream jobs?

7. Name the qualities Nora looks for in a job. Discuss other roles that would suit her.

8. Nora and Andrew rate themselves on the "Happiness Scale." What would you rate yourself on the scale and why?

9. By the end of the book, what does Nora learn about the ever-elusive "dream job"?

10. What do you think is next for Nora?

A CONVERSATION
WITH THE AUTHOR

When did you decide to write this story?

I got the idea for this book in 2015. By that point I'd been working at a publishing company for three years. At the time, though, the idea had nothing to do with publishing—it was just a flash of a thought about what might happen if a lowly assistant's first introduction to someone she needed to impress was getting their sandwich order wrong. The other details slowly trickled in from there. I set it in publishing because that was the industry I worked in, and I was too lazy to think up another. And because I felt so lost about my career, I'd wished there were more stories about people trying to figure out what they wanted to do with their lives. That lost feeling ended up making its way into the book too.

By unpacking the myth of the "dream job," this story explores happiness as a fluid, ever-changing thing. What did your path look like?

Out of college, I spent a year as a receptionist at a publishing company, waiting for an editorial assistant position to open up. I was sure that once I was an editorial assistant—the dreamiest dream job I could imagine—everything would be perfect. And, briefly, it was. Not long after getting the editorial assistant job, I was talking to one of my bosses about how we'd rate ourselves in happiness, and I rated my happiness an eight out of ten. I said I'd be a nine if I had a dog, and a ten if I had a house. (This is an answer someone gives in the book, and I definitely stole it from my past self!)

A few short weeks later, I went to my first conference, hated it, and realized this wasn't the career for me. But my happiness didn't really take a hit. I loved my coworkers so much that I imagined I'd be content to continue working there until I figured it out. But when layoffs hit the company and took some of my favorite coworkers with them, I was left feeling helpless and uncertain. I don't know what I would have rated my happiness then, but it was a long, slow burn of discontent for the next two years, to the point where I eventually quit my job and moved across the country to sleep on my best friend's couch.

Since then, I've had to stop thinking of happiness as something that can be achieved by obtaining what you want. Now, I see happiness as an ongoing fight. I know now that you can get what you want and still be unhappy, which is an odd, disappointing feeling. But it makes me feel a little less helpless to think of happiness as something you work toward, not something you achieve. (But I am pleased to say I do have a dog now! He does not automatically bump up my happiness permanently, but he is very cute.)

As someone who now has experience on both sides of publishing—as a publishing professional to a published author—how do you reconcile those experiences?

It's funny that this book I wrote, about an editorial assistant who is often annoyed by authors, ended up putting me in that author role on the other side of the looking glass. I try to be an easygoing, unflappable author, because those were my favorite to work with. I've also taken great care to meet each and every deadline, because I would not be able to handle missing a deadline for a book in which the protagonist complains about authors constantly missing deadlines. I understand that missing deadlines is par for the course sometimes, but I just could not do it for this book!

What are your go-to books?

A Tale for the Time Being by Ruth Ozeki is a favorite for the way it covers serious subjects very thoughtfully. I can also never resist humor—I read *Good Omens* by Terry Pratchett and Neil Gaiman for the first time a few years ago, and it's become something I keep returning to. *Heads of the Colored People* by Nafissa Thompson-Spires was an instant favorite for the way it manages to be both poignant and darkly funny.

Andrew jokes that Nora "ruins books" for him, because she knows too much of what goes on behind the scenes in publishing. Did you find that this happened to you when you worked in the industry? Do you still feel that way?

I do! There is, to be a fair, a magic in it, too. It's exciting to see a manuscript go from words in a document to something beautifully laid out and bound. But my experience has led me to accept that publishing is a business with flaws like any other.

Writing a book is a huge undertaking. For you, what was the most difficult part?

The delusion it takes to believe your writing will amount to anything is mind-boggling. Most days I doubted anything would come of it, which enabled me to go months at a time without writing. It became easier when I got further along into writing the story, because by that point it became more about wanting to finish what I started than caring whether it ever actually became a book. But those first 20,000 words or so felt like fruitless fumbling. It took me two years to write that first 20,000 words and much less time to write the remaining 60,000.

Some people need to write a little bit every day, others work best in marathon writing sessions... Can you talk a little bit about your process?

Consistency is crucial for me. It's so easy to put something off, especially when you're not sure where your story is going next or you don't see a point to writing. My writing for this book wasn't consistent until I set a daily word count goal for myself. Even when I didn't know what I was going to write next, I still had to write something to meet my count. Just getting something on the page helped get the ideas flowing from there.

Logging my word count in an Excel sheet and seeing the numbers progress every day is very motivating, but what I've found even more motivating is putting stickers in my planner if I meet my word count (which, in turn, inspired the sticker scene in the book!).

Nora ultimately learns that she has to try on different jobs for size before finding the right one. Do you have any other advice for people struggling to find the right career path?

I'm still learning myself! I'm not even sure there is a "right" job or career path for everyone, just some jobs that are more tolerable than others. I, personally, would like a job that involves living in a remote cabin and speaking to no one, but unfortunately no employer has been willing to offer me this position.

I also think it's important to keep in mind that your job is not your identity. Your job does not define you, and it is not a measure of all the skills or abilities you possess. You can always find fulfillment by pursuing your passions outside of work.

San Francisco plays such a large role in this story. Why did you choose it as the setting for Nora's story?

The Bay Area is a beautiful, unique, eclectic region, and I've missed it deeply since moving to the East Coast. But my main reason for setting my novel there is, truthfully, laziness. I worked in San Francisco at the time, and writing about a city I'm intimately familiar with is easier than researching a city I know less about.

It also presented an opportunity to showcase a different side of publishing. So many big publishing players are based in New York. A publishing house in San Francisco, surrounded by tech start-ups galore, has a fish-out-of-water feel that captured my experience at the time.

Nora's story ends on an ambiguous note, but do you secretly have an idea of where she'll end up?

Not really! I think she'll have to keep trying different careers to find something she likes. It may not be the second, third, or fourth job she tries, but she will keep trying. I think she'll learn how to cope with the creature in her head in a healthier way. And as she works toward finding happiness and finding her path, I like to imagine Andrew is by her side all the while, roll of stickers in hand.

ACKNOWLEDGMENTS

My agent, Katelyn Detweiler, has believed in this odd book every step of the way. I'm so thrilled to be working with you. Thank you as well to Sam Farkas for everything she does on the foreign rights side and to everyone else at Jill Grinberg Literary.

My editors at Sourcebooks, MJ Johnston and Jenna Jankowski, have offered countless brilliant insights that shaped this book into something I'm so proud of. It has been such a joy to work with and learn from you both. Thank you to the rest of the team at Sourcebooks for all their hard work on every aspect of this book.

My time at Jossey-Bass/Wiley was filled with the smartest, kindest people I have ever known. Too many to name, but if I can name a few: Steve Robinson, who hired me (and endured all the nepotism jokes that accompanied two unrelated Robinsons working together). Halley Sutton, who read my first draft and gave me the feedback I needed to turn it into something better. David Brightman, once my impossibly kind boss and now my impossibly kind friend. Lily Miller, for her creative mind, caring heart, and delightful supply of snacks.

I'm grateful to the writing community for all their insights and support. The Lit Squad, in particular, is a brilliant, hilarious, encouraging, and immensely talented group of writers I am so happy to know.

Many thanks are owed to my family (particularly my nieces and nephews, who are an endless source of joy). My mum and dad have always nurtured my love of reading and writing. I'm thankful for all the trips to libraries and bookstores and for all the nights spent reading books aloud or telling stories of our own invention. I love you both.

I'm forever grateful to Kate Reed, who has read every word I've written since we were thirteen. Thank you for the immeasurable impact you've had on my life. It was you I was talking to when I first got the idea to write this book, an idea you immediately encouraged. And, when my job got more and more draining, it was you who suggested I quit and live on your couch until I got my life in order. All some of the best decisions I've ever made.

I met Matthew Hocker while I was still getting my life in order and immediately knew I wanted to spend the rest of my life with him (a bizarre thought to have when I wasn't all that interested in living at the time). Thank you for your endless love and support. I'm so glad I get to spend my life with you.

ABOUT THE AUTHOR

Photo © Rachel E.H. Photography

Shauna Robinson's love of books led her to try a career in publishing before deciding she'd rather write books instead. Originally from San Diego, she now lives in Virginia with her husband and their sleepy greyhound. Shauna is an introvert at heart—she spends most of her time reading, baking, and figuring out the politest way to avoid social interaction. *Must Love Books* is her debut novel.